The Second Act of Sinclair

A NOVEL

E.M. VERNETTI

ELZIE MAE BOOKS LLC

For my daughter, whose resilience has always amazed me. This is a reminder that you deserve a love that meets you fully, without compromise.

For my son, who inspires me to be better, and whose faith fills my soul. Proverbs 3:5-6 always!

For my husband, whose love, patience, and support carries me. Without you, this lifelong dream wouldn't have been possible. I'm grateful for you.

Contents

Author's Note

"It's never too late to be what you might have been." — George Eliot

This novel was crafted with care, intention, and too many cups of coffee. My hope is that the characters in this book and the books to follow in this series remind each of us that love and the courage to start over can come at any stage of life. No matter the choices we've made or the mistakes that haunt us, we all deserve a second chance.

Prologue

The rooftop bar overlooking the river downtown sparkled with lights. Strings of bulbs crisscrossed above the tables, spotlighting every glass. Music vibrated from hidden speakers, low enough for conversation and loud enough to rattle inside her chest.

Jamie gripped the counter, palm damp against the polished wood. Around her, the place teemed with Tampa's elite trading stories over expensive cocktails.

Her phone screen still gleamed, face down on the granite, the image she had just seen online burning behind her eyes, her pulse kicking hard.

Laughter rose from somewhere nearby, making her flinch.

Across the bar, two women scrolled through their phones, glancing up in quick darts before lowering their gaze again. Right beside her, a man's shoulders shook with amusement. Someone else stifled a grin.

They were all looking at her!

She tried to swallow, but her throat locked tight.

Don't panic. Not here. Move!

The room spun as she lurched upright, slamming into a server balancing a tray of cocktails. It jerked from his hands, drinks crashing down in a spray of glass and liquor that drenched a nearby table.

The waiter barked. "Jesus, lady, watch where you're going!"

"Sorry." The word came out thin, almost soundless.

The exit sign burned red ahead of her.

She pushed forward, shouldering through the crowd.

When she reached the door, she shoved it open and stumbled into the stairwell.

She braced against the wall, her arms shaking as she struggled to catch her breath. She tried to count, to pull herself back. Nothing worked.

Behind her, laughter erupted again, spilling through the door as a man stepped toward her, lifting his phone. The flash of his camera lit the concrete walls. She covered her mouth and ran down the stairs without looking back.

Chapter 1

Two months earlier

She hadn't meant to throw the phone so hard. It hit the wall near the doorway with a thwack that echoed through the house. She froze, then crossed the living room in a few swift strides to scoop up the device from where it had landed face down on the hardwood floor.

A crack spider-webbed across the screen.

"Shit," she muttered, tracing it once with her fingertip, already calculating what it would cost to replace. Her shoulders tensed. It was barely past seven, and she already wanted to crawl back into bed.

Out of habit, she had opened Instagram minutes earlier, her feed landing on a picture posted from the deck of her ex-husband's boat, all smiles and perfect angles. John, grinning like a man who'd never known consequences, had one arm wrapped around the waist of a woman twenty years younger. They were both holding neon-colored cocktails, the ones that come with a paper umbrella and a sugar rim, as if adulthood were a beach-themed party.

Jamie had stared at the image longer than she should have, her thumb hovering over the screen, resisting the urge to click through more photos.

She'd asked for the divorce, but he was the one who'd moved on as if he hadn't lost a thing. The life she'd built with him was now scenery for someone else's story.

That was when she'd thrown it.

Footsteps padded down the hallway.

"What was that?" Leo stood in the archway to the living room, his dark hair rumpled, wearing basketball shorts and a hoodie two sizes too big.

She turned to face him, phone still in hand. "Nothing. Just dropped it."

He gave her a glance, as if he didn't believe her, but wasn't interested in arguing. Instead, he moved toward the kitchen and began rifling through the pantry.

"I have to go into the office this morning for a meeting," she said, watching as he poured milk into a bowl of cereal.

"Cool."

She hated that word. He used it to cut off conversations before they could start.

He hadn't always been like this. Before the divorce, Leo had been open and inquisitive. He'd been quick to talk about his day, including the awkward parts. Now he carried everything in silence. He didn't speak of his dad, not even in passing, and she wasn't sure if that was grief, anger, or something else entirely.

She let it go. It was too early, and her head already ached.

"Ava's coming in tonight. I'm making dinner so please don't be late."

"Ok, I won't."

She watched him retreat down the hallway, bowl in hand, his door clicking shut behind him.

Silence settled again.

She glanced toward the wide windows lining the back wall of the living room where the morning light glinted off the bay, boats moving slowly through the channel beyond the backyard.

The house, perched on the edge of Davis Island, had been her home for the last twenty years, and John had agreed to let her stay until Leo graduated high school. After that, it would go on the market, and she'd receive no alimony, and no continued support.

Her lawyer called her crazy for not demanding more, but Jamie had no interest in the money, and even less in the ties or obligations. Plus, she knew her husband would hire the most ruthless attorney money could buy, and she didn't have the stomach to drag it out in court. She needed only time to figure out what came next.

On her way toward the garage, she passed Ava's room and paused in the doorway, the scent of fresh linen and the sight of the pink flamingo on the pillow stirring memories.

Tonight, her daughter was coming in from Gainesville, where she attended the University of Florida. It was spring break, and she had made up her bedroom the day before, putting clean sheets on the bed and fresh towels in the bathroom like she used to when she was younger. She'd even pulled an old stuffed animal down from the top shelf of her closet. She wasn't sure Ava would notice it, but placing it there reminded Jamie of when she had needed her for everything.

In some ways, the divorce made Ava more independent, though sometimes Jamie wondered if that self-reliance had come too soon. She had been old enough to understand John's betrayal and old enough to form opinions, and she'd made them known.

She let out a breath, looked down at her phone's cracked screen, then grabbed her bag and keys, and walked out the door.

***

By the time she slid into her car, the morning had sharpened around her. She crossed the bridge from Davis Island into Tampa, her window down just enough to catch the briny tang of the bay.

The skyline stretched in full view: tall glass buildings stacked against the sky, their clean exteriors masking the churn inside. Parking garages bordered the downtown core, and palm-lined streets gave the illusion of calm.

She stepped into the lobby of one of those buildings and rode the elevator to the twenty-second floor, where a sports management company had carved out its presence high above the city. Floor-to-ceiling windows framed the view of the Hillsborough River winding through downtown and the bay glittering in the distance. At the center of the space, the bullpen buzzed with the low drone of phone calls and occasional laughter, while the private, glass-walled offices lined the perimeter, intimidating reminders of the hierarchy everyone understood without explanation.

She nodded to a few colleagues as she passed, most offering distracted greetings. Her cubicle sat in the center, practical and just wide enough for her laptop and a framed photo of her kids from three years ago, before everything fell apart.

After nearly two decades of attending PTA meetings and managing the household to allow her husband to chase his promotions, she had no intention of ending up here. But once the marriage had unraveled, and once she had agreed to no alimony in a haze of pride, her father picked up the phone and called in a favor. A retired corporate defense attorney with connections in every corner office in Tampa, he still knew how to make things happen.

One week later, she walked into this firm dressed in the only suit she owned, trying not to look like someone whose entire life had just quietly collapsed.

That was almost a year ago. Since then, she'd kept her head down, stayed late, asked smart questions, and done her best to prove she belonged.

***

When the morning meeting began, she had gathered her notes and taken her seat at the far end of the conference table. Around her, conversations blurred into posturing and subtle jabs passed off as banter. Being heard here meant talking over someone else, and if you were going to do that, you'd better have the contracts to back it up. Respect followed results.

David Ackerman entered without a word. He had sharply cut silver hair, and a suit tailored with the precision of a man who expected to be watched.

She had worked under him long enough to understand how little he gave away. His tone was never warm, and his feedback was never personal. He demanded results, and if he didn't get them, he moved on without thinking twice.

He began delivering updates on clients and upcoming events. The applause for a recently closed deal was brief and subdued before he continued moving through the agenda, then reached for a folder and glanced toward Jamie.

"Sinclair," he said, handing her the file. "This is Carson Tate. Wide receiver, Florida State alum, second-round NFL pick. His rookie year was rough, but he turned it around the next season. Then re-tore his ACL during his third, spent his fourth on PUP, and hit free agency at the end of his contract. No team's picked him up since."

She leaned forward and accepted the folder. David's tone had remained neutral, but the implication was clear. This was a test.

She flipped it open and stopped cold at the headshot clipped to the front. He was more than handsome; he was striking with light brown skin, and a square jawline that belonged on the cover of a GQ magazine. But it was his eyes that stopped her. Hazel-green that popped against his complexion.

A voice to her left murmured, "I thought he was done."

Steve Waters, one of the firm's senior agents, sat leaned back in his chair, scrolling through his phone as if the meeting were background noise. He had a reputation for closing big deals and for making it clear that smaller accounts weren't worth his time.

***

Back at her desk, she placed the file beside her laptop, and the bullpen resumed its familiar noise.

Steve passed by, pausing just long enough to glance over her partition. "That kid doesn't stand a chance with two ACL tears." He smirked, the comment sounding like a bet he'd already won. "Good luck."

Without waiting for a reply, he stepped into one of the glass-walled offices. Before he closed the door, she caught a glimpse of framed photos and memorabilia from high-profile clients. Proof of the deals he liked to remind everyone he'd closed.

She released a breath and opened a search engine, typing Carson's name. The results loaded fast.

First, she clicked on a highlight reel from Florida State. Carson was in motion. He broke from the line, outpacing defenders, and pulled in a catch with the confidence of someone who made it all look rehearsed.

Next, she scrolled to clips from his second season in the NFL. He was even faster and played as if he had something to prove.

Interviews from that year showed him standing in front of reporters, sweat still on his brow. He had that post game cool, even with the microphones in his face.

Then she found the video. The title was simple: *The Hit That Changed Everything.*

She clicked it open. He stood at the pre-snap lineup, poised with his eyes locked downfield as the ball snapped. He surged forward, cutting inside to find his gap just as the quarterback released the ball, and in that split second, everything seemed perfect.

Then the defender came.

The collision was brutal, the defender's shoulder driving into his planted leg. His body twisted midair before crashing hard onto the turf, the ball skittering away as the stadium went dead silent. He didn't move.

Seconds passed before his arm shifted, bracing himself with one hand, trying to push himself upright while his injured leg lay motionless beneath him. A trainer sprinted across the field, dropping to his side.

The feed ended, and Jamie sat back, thinking of something she had heard during her first weeks at the agency. Someone muttering that athletes were replaceable, that their pain was part of the business. Watching that clip, she felt the truth was far from that.

She looked again at the photo in the file, tracing his steady eyes. Then she leaned forward, closer to the screen, freezing the frame on the moment he tried to push himself up. He could've stayed down. He hadn't. And for reasons she didn't understand yet, she admired that.

***

That evening, she stood at the kitchen counter slicing zucchini into careful, even coins while Ava stirred garlic and onions in a shallow pan on the stove, the scent rising and curling into the corners of the room.

"You didn't have to cook," she said, casting a glance toward her daughter.

Ava looked up, her ponytail loose, cheeks pink from the heat. "I wanted to. Figured you'd be exhausted."

Leo shuffled in just as Jamie was lighting the candles in the center of the table. He tossed his phone down next to his plate and dropped into the chair beside her without a word. His hoodie bunched around his elbows, and his hair stuck up at odd angles, but she knew better than to comment.

"The rolls are done," Ava said, setting them down as she joined them.

Leo immediately picked his phone back up.

"Seriously?" Ava said, eyeing him across the table. "Can you be present for five minutes?"

He didn't respond. He thumbed something onto the screen, then flipped it over, face down.

"Thank you," she muttered.

For a while, they dined without conversation, but as the plates neared empty, Jamie set her fork down and cleared her throat. "There's something I've been meaning to talk to you both about."

She paused, glancing between them. She hadn't planned to say it tonight, but there would never be a perfect time. "Your father...he's planning to put the house on the market after the school year ends."

Leo froze mid-chew. "Wait...what?"

"It was part of the agreement in the divorce. I could stay here with you until graduation, but after that...it goes up for sale."

"So, we're moving," Leo said flatly.

"Not right away. But yes. Eventually."

He leaned back in his chair, arms crossed. "You divorced him because you couldn't cope. Because you couldn't deal with..."

"Leo!"

"It's true." His voice rose louder. "You're the one who blew everything up. And now we have to pay for it."

Ava's fork hit her plate. "You've got to be kidding me. She didn't blow anything up. Dad did. He had an affair, remember? Or are you pretending that didn't happen?"

"That's not the point."

"It's exactly the point."

"You don't get it. None of this feels normal anymore."

"I didn't want to hurt either of you," Jamie said.

Leo stood. "Too late."

He stormed out, the echo of his footsteps thudding down the hall before his door slammed shut.

She sat frozen, the silence in his wake pressing against her chest. She'd known this moment would come. The blame. The anger. But knowing didn't soften the sting.

For a breath, unwelcome thoughts surfaced: *What if I'd waited? What if I'd fought harder?* But it passed just as quickly, buried beneath everything she already knew.

She swallowed the lump in her throat, trying to find the right words, but only two surfaced. "I'm sorry."

"It's not you. It's him." Ava shook her head, resting her clenched hands on the table. "He doesn't want to be angry at Dad, so he blames you instead." She paused for a breath before she continued. "You know what's messed up? I see guys who act like Dad all the time. Sweet on the surface, until they get bored. I'm not sure I can trust anyone again."

"Ava, you don't mean that."

"I do. I just can't understand how someone says they love you and then do something like that."

The words hit hard. Jamie reached for her daughter's hand. "You're young. You have your whole life ahead of you." She cupped Ava's cheek in her palm. "One day you'll find someone who meets you completely."

They sat together as the light outside faded, and she watched her daughter, the soft curve of her jaw so much like her own at that age. Something in her tone carried experience, and Jamie hated knowing where that had come from.

She'd tried so hard to protect her children from the parts they weren't meant to hear, to keep it from bleeding into their lives, pretending that love could be guarded with good intentions and sacrifice. But it had crept in anyway.

Soon, the house would be sold and they would scatter. Ava to Gainesville, Leo to wherever life would take him next, and her? A woman in her forties with no clear plan. There was no version of it she could picture clearly.

Chapter 2

The following morning, she sat at her desk, Leo's anger and Ava's quiet concern still lodged in her thoughts. Her third cup of coffee cooled beside her mouse pad. Around her, everyone had already settled into the day, phones ringing and keyboards clicking. She barely registered any of it.

Sleep had been shallow and scattered. At some point in the night, she had found herself at the kitchen table with her laptop open, scrolling through Carson's NFL career. She'd skipped past the agency profiles and sports commentary, digging deeper for something real.

An old interview had surfaced from his second year. Grainy locker room footage. He was younger. Less guarded. Then another clip, post-injury, his third season. He sat at the end of a long table beside a few teammates during a press conference. The camera panned wide, catching the subtle bulk of a brace on his leg, evidence of the ACL tear that had derailed everything. His face gave nothing away, eyes fixed forward as a reporter asked about his recovery.

"What's your plan from here?"

He leaned into the mic, his tone relaxed, with no need for dramatics. "Work hard. Rehab. Be ready."

She had clicked on a replay next, late in the fourth quarter of a losing matchup. Most of the stadium seats were emptying. The broadcast team had shifted to commentary about playoff implications. On the field, the offense lined up for what looked like a throwaway series, but Carson ran the route as if the game wasn't already decided. A hard hit dropped him. The kind that would've rattled most players. But he got up, shook it off, and went straight back to the line.

Conversations carried across the bullpen, but her mind was still on that replay. She sat back in her chair, feeling a quiet recognition stir inside her. She knew a bit about setbacks. How life could wear you down and demand more. She'd gone to college, kept going even after Ava was born, determined to make something of herself. Next came law school. Then Leo. Somehow, she had made it through all the late nights and the constant pull of everything she was supposed to be.

After graduation, John had convinced her there was no need to take the bar, not right away. He had promised financial security and told her she could focus on the kids, on the house, that there would be plenty of time for her career when they were older.

Fifteen years later, she was still fighting, trying to carve out a place for herself in a world that had rarely made room for women like her. In Carson, she saw the same fight. He didn't need saving. He needed someone who understood what it meant to start over.

A co-worker leaned over the partition beside her, breaking her thoughts. "Hey, is that your guy?"

She looked up.

He was striking even from a distance. Tall, broad-shouldered, and carrying himself with a quiet charisma. He wore a dark T-shirt, plain and close-fitting, and jeans.

She noticed a shift. Heads turned, conversations slowed, and the receptionist's smile lingered a little longer than usual, as she pointed in Jamie's direction.

He tipped his chin, his eyes scanning the space and started toward her with an easy stride.

She stepped out from behind the cubicle, and he stopped just short of her, flashing a quick smile. "Jamie Sinclair?"

"That's me." She extended a hand, masking her nerves. "You must be Carson."

A grin tugged at the corners of his mouth, his grip warm. He held it long enough to make an impression before clearing his throat. "I'm sorry. I thought you were..."

"A man?" She asked.

It wasn't the first time someone had made that assumption. The name could go either way, and there weren't many women in her line of work. She found it almost amusing now.

"Clearly not a man," he said, his eyes sweeping over her, more curious than intrusive. "Thanks for meeting with me."

"Of course. Follow me. We can chat somewhere more private."

She grabbed the folder with his name on it and a notepad filled with scribbles from the night before. As she passed Steve's office, she caught him looking up from his phone, a smirk tugging at his mouth. He lifted one hand, thumb up, before rolling it down in a mock evaluation and returning to his screen. The gesture crawled under her skin, a small reminder of how easily he could get to her.

***

Inside the conference room, she motioned to the chair across from hers and opened the folder slowly, careful not to seem too eager.

"So," he said, watching her. "You've read the file."

"Yes."

"And?"

She met his gaze. "I think we should talk."

He leaned back slightly, but his eyes didn't leave hers. "Okay. Talk. That's why I'm here."

She loosened her shoulders, attempting to match his calm. "You played at Florida State. One of the most explosive college careers in recent memory. First-team All-American, led the ACC in receiving yards two years straight. You were projected as a first rounder, but after the ACL tear your senior year, you slipped to the late second."

He didn't respond. Just watched her.

She went on, careful to keep composure, though her pulse ticked up. "You signed with Miami. Missed most of your rookie season after surgery but came back in your second year and broke out. Over twelve hundred receiving yards, eleven touchdowns, Pro Bowl selection."

She paused. "But..."

"I got hurt again," he said. No defensiveness.

She glanced down at the file. "Same ACL, third year. And now..."

"Now nobody's calling." His expression didn't shift, but there was something behind his eyes, as if he was still deciding whether she was up to the task.

"You did your homework." He tilted his head. "How'd you end up with me? Your firm trying to stay on Darian Vaughn's good side?"

That made her blink. Darian Vaughn was one of the firm's marquee clients. An MVP and endorsement giant.

He continued, the grit in his voice clear. "So, they hand me off to the new agent. Rookie for the guy with a shaky resume. Nice symmetry."

Something in her flinched, though nothing moved.

"Is that how you see this?" she asked after a beat. "A handoff? A box to check?"

"Tell me I'm wrong," he said, shrugging.

She closed the folder but didn't look away from him.

"Yeah. I am new. And you're right. Nobody was fighting for this assignment. But I watched your tapes and not just the highlights. I saw the snaps when you were gassed and the score was slipping." She didn't blink. "Most guys would've checked out because no one was watching, but you kept getting back up. You stayed in it. Every play."

Silence hung in the air for a beat.

"You don't need me to tell you who you are. You already know. What you need is someone who recognizes what you've kept doing after everything went sideways."

She held his gaze, waiting to see if anything she'd said had landed. "We can take a chance on each other. Or you can walk out of here. Your call."

He studied her for a moment, and something flickered in his eyes. A glimmer of surprise. Maybe even a trace of respect. Then, he gave a brief, yielding nod of his chin. "Fair enough. So, what do you see in my future?"

"I see a story people will want to root for. And a shot to prove something."

"Ok, what do you need from me?"

"Do you have any workout footage?"

"Nothing recent but I'll send it to you."

She made a quick note. "Do you have a trainer?"

"Used to. But after Miami let me go, I cut some things loose."

"What about connections? Anyone still in your corner? Coaches, teammates?"

He leaned back in the chair slightly. "A few. Mostly teammates. A couple of coaches still check in. But no one who could pull strings other than Darian. And even he can't talk a team into signing a guy with two ACL tears and a question mark next to his name."

She tapped her pen lightly. "So, we're starting from scratch."

"That a problem?" he asked.

She looked up. "No. It simply means I know where to begin."

***

After walking him out, she returned to her desk and stared at the blank monitor.

He was attractive; that much was obvious. But that wasn't the only reason her pulse refused to slow. What lingered was the responsibility she'd just stepped into. His career. His future.

She opened the folder again, his stats staring back at her as she traced a finger along the corner of his picture.

"Jamie." David stood outside his office, gesturing her in without waiting for a response.

She grabbed the file and followed him inside.

He didn't sit. He leaned against his desk, arms crossed, and asked, "How'd it go?"

"Good. He's smart, and cautious, but he seemed to be open to the conversation."

He studied her with the same calm detachment he used in contract negotiations. "And what's your impression? Is he worth the time?"

"Yes."

A beat passed. Then: "Did Darian ask you to meet with him?"

He circled behind the desk and sank into his leather chair. "He did."

"So, this isn't about potential. It's a favor."

"He vouched for him. I wasn't going to say no."

The chair creaked slightly as he leaned back, his eyes drifting toward the window. "Do you know why I gave him to you?"

She stayed quiet.

"Because no one else wanted him. He's not a headline anymore. He's a gamble. And you're still green enough to need the win."

There it was. Confirmation of what she'd suspected the moment he'd given her the assignment.

"You get him signed, and we'll talk about bigger clients."

He glanced down at the desk and picked up another folder, already moving on to something else. She took his cue and pivoted toward the door, but as she reached for the handle, his voice stopped her.

"And Jamie, don't get too emotionally invested. This isn't personal. It's business."

She nodded, more reflex than agreement.

***

Later that evening, Jamie stepped into a sleek restaurant in the Channelside District where a twenty-dollar cocktail passed as reasonable. She spotted Julia already seated at a high-top table near the windows, with a glass of red wine in front of her and her phone face down beside it. A second glass sat across from her. Jamie's usual.

They'd always been close. Two decades and two very different lives later, they still returned to each other easily. Julia had that annoying way of reading her, knowing Jamie was in trouble before she even asked. It was shorthand, built living side by side with only a wall between them. They had shared catastrophic breakups at seventeen, cheap vodka poured into water bottles, and secrets they swore would never leave their rooms.

Growing up in a house where silence mattered more than conversations, their father's expectations filled every quiet space. His reputation was one thing, but his physical presence was another. Intimidating one minute, charming the next. It just depended on the day.

Their mother had always waited for him to finish speaking before she offered an opinion. Most of the time, she didn't. When it came to her daughters, though, she found her voice, usually to repeat his.

Jamie had absorbed those lessons early, always navigating between his moods and doing what was expected.

Julia, on the other hand, had pushed back, questioning, challenging. She'd bristled at her mother's submission, swearing she would never be the woman who stayed silent to keep the peace. When she turned eighteen, she had left like the house was on fire.

Now, Jamie sometimes looked at her sister with envy. She wondered what life might have been like if she'd followed Julia's lead instead of their mother's example.

"You're late," Julia said, standing to greet her with a hug. "But you look fantastic, so I forgive you. Did you do something different with your hair?"

She gave a half-smile, brushing a hand over the loose waves that fell past her shoulders. "Just a trim."

"Well, it works. Seriously, sometimes I can't believe we're sisters. You got all the looks."

"Please."

Julia tilted her head toward the bar. "Tell that to the three guys who've already looked over here twice."

The comment hit closer than she'd ever admit. Still, she waved it off with a casual flick of her hand. The stares weren't new or flattering. She had spent years brushing them off, learning not to react, because reacting only gave them power. She had long understood how people saw her before they listened to her, and most never got past the surface.

"And you have all the brains. I'd trade you."

"Yeah, but that doesn't get you out of speeding tickets. Or free drinks. Although being a doctor does help with insurance claims."

Jamie laughed, easing into the seat across from her. "There it is. Always the practical one."

"So, I saw the boat photo," Julia said as she took a sip of her wine. "The audacity of that man." She shook her head. "Posting that smug little 'Sunday Funday' crap like he's in a beer commercial. And with her? She looks twelve."

"Twenty-six."

Julia blinked. "You actually know?"

"Ava looked her up. She's in marketing or something."

"Of course she is. Marketing her way into a house she didn't earn. God, I want to punch him in the face sometimes."

Jamie stayed quiet. She'd stopped counting how many times people had made similar comments about John.

"How are the kids holding up?"

"Not great. Ava's angry. Not just at him. At everything. Every guy she meets now, she assumes he's lying. That he'll cheat, or bail, or both."

"Well, it'll harden her in the right ways. She won't fall for anyone's bullshit. And Leo? How's he taking it?"

"He's quiet. Keeps to himself more." She paused. "He blames me. I was the one who asked for the divorce. In his mind, I broke up the family."

"But you didn't commit adultery, Jamie. John did. You spent far too long protecting the kids from his affairs."

"I don't think that's how Leo sees it or that he even cares who crossed the line."

Julia reached across the table, resting a hand briefly on her wrist. "You did the right thing." She leaned back, the bite returning to her voice. "You're doing all of this, working your ass off, rebuilding, while John plays house on a boat with someone who probably thinks FICA is a trendy clothing brand."

A smirk tugged at Jamie's mouth. "I'm sure she's not that dumb."

"It was a joke, Jamie." The humor faded. "Seriously though, you always carry yourself like you've got it all handled."

Jamie smiled faintly. "That's the trick, right?"

"No," Julia said, raising her glass. "The trick is making that asshole realize he made a terrible mistake and not giving a damn when he finally does."

They clinked their glasses together in agreement, the sentiment warm, but it didn't quite land. She wasn't at the point of indifference yet. Nowhere close. But hearing her sister say it, believing it, made her feel a little closer to solid ground. Something she hadn't felt in a long time.

Julia set her glass down and rested her elbow on the table with a smile, clearly ready to change the subject. "So, how's work going? Any exciting clients lately?"

"Maybe. I had a meeting today with someone new."

"Another cyclist?" She asked, lifting her brows.

"No, this one plays a sport people watch on TV. A football player."

Julia's eyes widened as she leaned forward. "Jamie, that's great news!"

"Well, it isn't all great news." She lifted her wine glass, turning it slowly between her fingers. "He's been in the NFL for a while, but injuries knocked him off track. He's fighting his way back."

"What's his name?"

"Carson Tate."

Julia blinked. Her head tilted. "Wait, seriously?"

"You know him?"

"Not personally, but yeah. He's kind of a big deal. The hospital partnered with a youth outreach program in East Tampa last year. He was there every weekend. Played football with the kids, passed out meals. Quietly, too. No press or social media. He just showed up and did the work."

"That's unusual."

"Not really. Guys like him don't do it for the credit. They do it because they remember what it was like to grow up with less."

She leaned back in her chair, processing that. The grit she'd seen in all those clips made more sense now.

A pause settled between them, amusement flickering in Julia's eyes in a way that said she already knew where this was going. "Jamie…"

"What?"

"You've got that look."

"What look?"

"Oh God, that's the face. Are we developing a tiny, wildly inconvenient crush on our client?"

A low laugh slipped out as Jamie shook her head. "No. It's not like that."

"Are you sure? Because a little something with a younger man might be exactly what the doctor ordered."

"That line is beneath you. And a bit hypocritical, don't you think? You just called John out for the same thing."

"Yeah, yeah." She waved her hand, brushing the comment aside.

"It's strictly professional," Jamie said, paired with an eyeroll that even she knew didn't quite sell the conviction.

"For now." Julia raised her glass again, mischief curling at the corner of her lips. "Can you imagine Dad's reaction if you brought home a man like Carson Tate? He'd absolutely lose it, and I would love every minute of it."

Jamie smiled, amused. "How does your wife keep you in line?"

"She'd tell you I'm hopeless." Julia opened her mouth to say something else, but her eyes flicked over Jamie's shoulder and widened. "Oh my God," she whispered, leaning in like she was about to share a secret. "Speak of the devil!"

She turned her head enough to glance toward the entrance where Carson had stepped into the restaurant, flanked by two friends. He was wearing a dark button-down, sleeves rolled casually to his forearms. The room didn't exactly fall silent, but there was a definite shift.

"You've got to be kidding me." She grabbed a menu and held it up, half a shield, half a joke. "Don't look."

"Too late," Julia said under her breath.

He was already walking toward them.

She lowered the menu slowly, composing herself. When he reached the table, his lips curved into a polite smile. "Hello, Jamie."

"Hi, Carson." She tucked a loose strand of hair behind her ear, smoothing an invisible crease in the tablecloth, her fingers twitching slightly.

He looked at Julia, recognition blooming across his expression. "We've met, right?"

Julia, still working to regain her composure, extended a hand. "Yes, I'm Julia. We met at Healthy Kids Day at the YMCA in East Tampa. My hospital partnered with them last year."

"Right," he said. "I remember now. You were the one in the superhero cape and glittery tights."

She laughed, glancing between them. "Guilty. Jamie is my sister."

"Small world." He turned his attention back to Jamie. "Didn't mean to interrupt. Just wanted to say hello."

She flashed a nervous smile, and he gave them both a nod then returned to his friends.

Julia stared after him for a beat before turning around with a grin already full of trouble. "Just wanted to say hello," she said in a masculine tone, mocking him. Then, in her own voice, "Tell me again how it's strictly professional?"

A balled-up napkin sailed across the table in response.

Julia laughed hysterically, and despite everything, Jamie found herself laughing too.

Chapter 3

She was already at the kitchen island when the sun cracked the horizon, her second cup of coffee cooling beside the trackpad. The overhead pendant light cast a soft light across her workspace: legal pad to the right, laptop angled slightly to avoid the glare from the bay windows behind her.

She had Carson's college highlight reel open in one window, and an audio recording of his post-game interview playing quietly through her earbuds. His voice filtered through as she rewound the play for the third time. On screen, he exploded off the line with that elastic speed receivers either had or didn't. She paused mid-sprint, scrolled back, and watched again.

The way he adjusted midair, twisting to meet the ball, his timing uncanny, as though he didn't need to see it at all, was clean and controlled, a flash of hunger and precision that made her sit forward slightly. She scribbled a timestamp, underlining it twice in quick, decisive strokes.

On the next reel, he was running again. This time, it's a deep post route, cornerback clinging to him like static. He pulled away in the final five yards, just enough to make the grab look effortless.

"Damn," she said under her breath.

"Who's that?"

She startled. Leo stood a few feet away, barefoot and groggy, blinking against the kitchen light, his hair stuck up on one side. He was already moving toward the fridge with muscle memory.

She slid her laptop screen down slightly. "Carson Tate."

He pulled out a carton of orange juice and let the door swing closed behind him. "Why are you watching Carson Tate?"

"Because I represent him."

He paused mid-pour and set the carton down. "Wait. You're his agent?"

She nodded, noticing the corner of his mouth lift before he turned back to the screen.

"No way," he said. "That's...kind of insane."

She tilted her head. "Is it?"

"I mean, yeah. At FSU, he was everything. Dude had hands like magnets. He should've been a top three pick."

"You think so?"

He gave a half-shrug, keeping his eyes on the screen. "He made it look easy. Even when they double-teamed him, he'd find space."

She watched him, surprised by how much he seemed to care. It wasn't often he volunteered anything these days.

"You think he has a chance?"

"If he can stay healthy...I don't know. Anything's possible." He finished pouring his juice, his brows lifting slightly. "Didn't think they were handing you real athletes yet."

"Thanks for the vote of confidence," she said, arching a brow.

He shrugged, not looking at her. "Just didn't expect it. That's all."

He turned toward the hallway, pausing just before disappearing around the corner. "Hope he gets picked up. Would be cool to see him back on the field."

She waited until the sound of his footsteps faded, and reached for her coffee, took a slow sip, and pulled her laptop closer. Carson's frozen image still filled half the monitor, jersey stretched across his chest, hands curled around the ball mid-stride. There was power there, even in stillness. She'd seen a lot of players flame out early, their eyes already dimming by the second or third year. But his weren't like that, not in the video and not in person.

A knock at the front door broke her focus. She frowned, not expecting anyone.

Through the frosted glass, two silhouettes came into view, her stomach sinking before she even opened it.

John stood there in a golf polo and loafers; a subtle indication of impatience already set in the thin line of his mouth. Beside him, a woman in her early forties smiled politely glancing past Jamie toward the foyer.

"Good morning," he said, as if they were still on speaking terms.

"What are you doing here?" She folded her arms, posture stiffening.

"This is Sandra. She's the agent I mentioned. I thought we could walk her through the house this morning."

She blinked. "You didn't mention anything."

"Sorry to drop in unannounced," Sandra said as she held out a hand. "John said it would be okay to take a quick look around to get a sense of the layout. We won't be long."

She ignored the handshake. "I thought we agreed you'd give me notice before bringing someone over."

He raised an eyebrow with a tight smile, and she recognized the expression. He didn't like being challenged, and he especially didn't like being embarrassed. "You've had months, Jamie. We're listing in a few weeks. I assumed you'd be ready."

Behind her, she heard footsteps, likely Leo, probably having overheard the voices. She turned slightly, blocking the entrance with her body. "Now's not a good time. Come back later."

John's jaw flexed, but he didn't push. "Fine. We'll reschedule. Sandra, I'll call you."

Sandra nodded politely and turned toward her car, heels clicking against the walkway, while John lingered on the porch, not moving.

"Jamie..." His voice cut through the space between them, clipped and tense.

She stayed in the doorway, arms crossed. "You need something else?"

"You can't change the inevitable. The house is going on the market."

She lowered her voice. "Do you even care what this is doing to Leo? This is the only home he's ever known."

"You're the one who wanted a divorce," he said, scoffing, hands on his hips. "It was your decision to break up our family, not mine."

She crossed her arms tighter, jaw clenched. "Right. Dragging this out another ten years would've made us all happier." Her eyes held his, refusing to flinch. "Let's not pretend you were some innocent bystander."

He didn't respond immediately. His posture faltered, shoulders drawing in before he recovered and turned, walking down the steps toward his ridiculously expensive car. The sort of thing men buy when going through a mid-life crisis.

Without stopping, he threw a response over his shoulder. "It's just a house. You need to start clearing out all the clutter. No buyer will see past the chaos and make an offer."

She shut the door and stood there a moment, hand on the doorknob, heart ticking a little too fast. Part of her wanted to open it again and yell after him, to say anything that might cut through that smug indifference.

To him, the house was about square footage and market value. None of it mattered. But to her, it was about birthdays and Christmas mornings; back-to-school pictures on the front steps and Sunday's with Leo making pancakes, splashing batter from one end of the kitchen island to the other. It was the backdrop to the years she'd spent being a mother, the one role she'd never questioned, even when everything else had come apart.

***

By midmorning, she was back at the kitchen island, laptop open, sketching out a one-page player profile: Former Pro Bowl Receiver-Comeback in progress.

She pulled quotes from past scouting reports and dropped key stats into a clean spreadsheet. It was groundwork for the packet she'd send when she started calling teams.

Then, she opened a second browser tab and searched for athletic training centers in Tampa. She jotted a name: Precision Elite Training Center. The facility was known for training professional athletes in the off-season.

She dialed the number before she could overthink it. "Hi, yes. This is Jamie Sinclair. I'm calling about scheduling a session for a private workout. I have a client I'd like to get some video on. Yes. Wide receiver. Carson Tate."

She paused while the man on the line checked something.

"Tomorrow morning? Nine o'clock? That works." She added the appointment to her calendar. "And I'll need someone on-site for filming. Do you have a media partner, or should I arrange that separately?"

She hung up five minutes later, having booked both the field time and a videographer. She had yet to run any of it by Carson.

The opportunity was too important to wait. If she gave him room to hesitate, it might not happen at all.

She typed out a quick message: *Hey. Scheduled a workout for tomorrow morning, nine o'clock, at Precision Elite. Just you and a camera. Thought it would help to give teams something recent to see. Let me know if that's okay.*

She read it again before deleting the last line and hitting send.

For a moment, all she could do was stare at the screen before she pushed back from the island, poured herself another cup of coffee, and opened a clean document.

She titled it: CARSON TATE—COMEBACK STRATEGY.

The cursor blinked beneath the heading.

She didn't have a network to lean on, not yet. No group chat of agents, no years of contacts saved in her phone. So, she did what she knew how to do. She researched.

She searched team websites one by one, scanning front office directories, reading job titles until she found the roles that mattered: General Manager, Director of Player Personnel, Pro Scout, Player Evaluator.

She copied names into a column, followed by titles, then email addresses into the next, and notes of where she could find them in the last.

After an hour, she sat back, rolled her shoulders, and opened a second clean page. She drew a small box in the center and labeled it: Workout Footage. From there, she traced arrows outward: Reel Cut, Profile Sheet, Outreach Email, Follow-Up Call. Then beneath that, a list of steps. Linear. Practical.

Step 1: Get usable footage.

Step 2: Build a one-page evaluation profile.

Step 3: Send to selected personnel staff.

Step 4: Follow-up call if no response in 72 hours.

Step 5: Repeat.

She didn't hear Julia come in until she was already leaning against the doorframe, a to-go cup in her hand and sunglasses still on her head.

"Well," Julia said, taking in the flowchart. "I take it you're problem-solving."

"Just organizing my thoughts."

Julia crossed the kitchen and set her drink down, peering over her shoulder. "No, see, most people would make a to-do list. You," she tapped the page lightly, "are constructing a military-grade strategic assault."

"It's just steps."

"Mmm-hmm." A small knowing sound. "Step one, conquer the NFL. Step two, espresso refill."

That pulled the faintest smile from her. "I didn't have the contacts, so I'm building them. I can't pitch him blindly."

Her sister's expression shifted at that. Still amused but no longer teasing. "I know. And he's lucky you're the one doing it."

She stilled and glanced back at the screen. The plan wasn't perfect. It might not work. But it was movement.

Julia nudged her lightly. "Did you have breakfast yet? Or are we in 'I forgot to eat today' territory already?"

She checked the clock and blinked. "Apparently the second."

"Figured." Julia moved toward the fridge. "Sausage and egg wrap okay?"

"That's fine."

Her sister set plates on the counter, the quiet stretching between them for a moment before Jamie spoke again. "John came by this morning. He brought a real estate agent. He said…" She swallowed, her words coming thinner now. "That I'm the one who wanted the divorce and broke our family apart. Like this is some punishment I signed up for."

"That son of a bitch is gaslighting you. You know that right?"

"I just..." She stared down, sliding her fingers into her hair. "Leo is still here. And I didn't ask for anything. I could've kept the house. I could've..."

"No." Julia pulled out a stool and sat beside her. "Look at me." She met her eyes, steady and sure. "You chose peace. You chose your dignity. And Leo is going to be okay. In a year, he'll be off at college, too busy with campus life to care about any of this. And you'll be in a new place. Somewhere that feels like yours."

Her breath wavered. "I just don't know where that is yet."

Julia reached out, resting a hand over hers. "Then we'll figure it out. You don't have to have the whole thing mapped out today. Just...don't let him convince you this was your fault."

Chapter 4

Thursday morning, she pulled into the lot behind Precision Elite Training Center just before nine. The building itself was sleek and modern, tucked back from the road with mirrored glass and a wide awning that shaded the entrance.

Inside, the lobby was all polished concrete floors and oversized digital screens looping highlight reels and training montages. A young woman at the front desk directed her toward the private turf area she'd reserved for the shoot.

Carson was already there. She spotted him from across the facility, standing near the hash marks in black compression shorts and a gray dri-fit shirt that hugged his frame. He was mid-conversation with the videographer, hands gesturing toward a set of cones lined up downfield.

She approached, willing her expression into something neutral. But, when he turned, the smile he gave her cut straight through her poise.

"You beat me here," she said, tucking a strand of hair behind her ear then pulling it forward again.

He gave her a look that made her wonder what he'd just read in her face. "Good morning to you, too. Didn't want to keep the boss waiting."

"You're learning." A small smile tugged at her mouth despite herself.

The videographer, a guy in his mid-twenties with a hoodie pulled over a ball cap, lifted his chin in greeting before retreating to his gear setup.

"You've been here before?" She asked, glancing around.

"Off-season, mostly. A couple times after rehab. They've got good people."

She let her gaze sweep the space. "It's impressive."

"Yeah, it is." He ran a hand along his jaw. "It's been a minute since I've done one of these."

"You'll be fine. Just be yourself."

His mouth curved. "That's the part that gets me in trouble."

"Then behave for the camera." She folded her arms, hiding a smirk that faltered almost as quickly as it came.

He chuckled. "No promises."

The session began with basic movement drills: high-knees, leg swings, quick feet, jab steps. She stayed near the sideline, notepad in hand, observing quietly.

In his old footage, his movements had looked precise and explosive, but in person, she noticed how little he wasted. There were no extra steps, no flare for the camera, just clean breaks and a body that did exactly what he asked of it. Every motion revealed the sheer power in his frame and the easy balance between strength and grace.

"Damn," she muttered under her breath, before reminding herself why she was there. *Work. Strictly work.*

Halfway through, he paused for water, jogging over to where she stood as the videographer approached, tablet in hand. "You've got to see this one," the guy said, motioning them closer.

She stepped forward, and Carson did the same, close enough that she caught the mix of sweat and soap clinging to his skin. The screen came to life, showing the playback in slow motion: Carson cutting hard on the route, muscles coiling and releasing with effortless control.

"What do you think?" Carson asked, his breath brushing her temple.

She blinked, her throat suddenly dry. "Looks good," she managed, though she wasn't entirely certain she was talking about the footage.

He glanced sideways at her, the corner of his mouth lifting as his eyes drifted down to her notepad, noting the blank page. "You sure? You haven't written a thing since we started."

She pressed it to her chest. "You're awfully nosey for someone who's supposed to be running drills."

He laughed at her, his eyes bright with amusement that stayed on her a beat too long.

When the trainer called five minutes to wrap, Carson turned serious again. He ran one last full route: deep post, fast feet, tight cut, perfect catch before jogging off, breathing hard.

"That was solid."

"Felt good," he said, wiping sweat from his brow with a towel. "So, what happens next?"

"We review the footage, pick the strongest clips, and I start making calls. It's time to shift the narrative."

***

Back at the office, she tapped her pen against the table, her gaze steady on the large wall-mounted display at the front of the conference room. Beside her, Carson settled into his seat, arms loosely crossed as the footage played.

The videographer had framed the angle cleanly. He burst off the line, cutting across the turf with a quick, effortless change of direction. The ball was out fast, already in the air as he planted, hips turning, shoulders squaring. His hands met the pass clean and controlled, the catch unfolding in one fluid motion, without a single wasted step.

"Rewind it," he said.

She did, the image freezing mid-stride before he pointed.

"There. That's what I want them to see. The break. Most guys round it off."

She made a quick note on her pad.

"You think it's enough?"

She paused to choose her words carefully. "I think it's a start, but it depends on who's watching. The right eyes. The right timing."

He nodded slowly. "So that's where you come in."

"That's the idea," she said, lifting her thumb to her mouth, pressing her teeth against the nail.

She wasn't sure her name carried weight yet. Not in the rooms that mattered. She could make the calls, send the reels, write the pitches, but whether anyone listened was still a question mark. The men at her firm were seasoned; she was still proving she belonged. Every move felt like a test she hadn't been taught how to prepare for.

He exhaled beside her, and she saw the subtle release in his shoulders, like the tension he'd been carrying all morning was finally starting to loosen. "I'm starving."

"I can have something brought in."

He shook his head immediately. "No. Let's get out of here."

"I have a lot to do this afternoon."

"You can bring your laptop," he said, standing. "I won't be offended."

She hesitated, David's voice echoing in the back of her mind, *don't get too emotionally invested*. But her stomach made a stronger case. She hadn't eaten since a protein bar at sunrise. "Alright, but I'm paying."

He grinned. "Generous and bossy. I'm starting to think you're trying to impress me."

She leaned down to pack her MacBook in her bag, focusing on it instead of him.

On their way out, they passed Steve's office, his door half-open. He lounged in his chair as if he owned the place, both legs kicked up on his desk, scrolling on his phone.

She dipped her head, hoping to slip by without being noticed, but his voice cut through. "Sinclair."

Her muscles coiled before she looked up.

"Got a minute?"

She glanced at Carson. "I'll meet you at the elevator."

He nodded once, slipping his hands into his pockets as he headed down the hall.

"Word of advice," Steve said. "Get yourself a backup plan for when he washes out. Nobody's going to remember the agent who hitched her wagon to a broken player."

Her jaw tightened, but she tried to hold her tone even. "Good thing I'm not here to be remembered. I'm here to get him signed."

He gave a low chuckle, already looking back at his phone. "Sure. Keep telling yourself that."

She turned on her heel and headed down the hall toward Carson, where he waited, one brow raised in silent question. She managed a smile for him as the elevator closed, Steve's words settling somewhere she refused to show.

***

The doors swung open with a soft clang of the overhead bell as Jamie followed Carson into a popular restaurant in Ybor City, the scent of roasted pork and garlic washing over her. She barely had a chance to glance at the hostess stand before she heard a familiar voice.

"Mom?"

Ava sat a few tables away, accompanied by two of her girlfriends, who were mid-laugh with oversized sunglasses perched atop their heads.

She straightened, smoothing a hand over her blazer, her eyes flicking from Ava to Carson and back again. She could already imagine what this looked like—walking into a restaurant with a much younger man, one who should be on a billboard, not across a table from someone's mother.

"That's Ava. My daughter," she said, trying to keep her voice low. "She's home from UF this week."

He blinked, his gaze darting from Jamie to Ava. "You have a daughter in college? How old are you?"

Before she could reply, they were already making their way over, Ava's smile faltering as they approached.

"Hey," Ava said. "Didn't expect to see you here."

One of Ava's friends, tall with dark curls and a fitted sundress, was staring at Carson. "Wait...are you, Carson Tate?"

"That's me."

Ava looked at her friend, then at Carson, one eyebrow arched. "Should I know who that is?"

Her friend gaped at her. "Um, yeah. You don't remember him from FSU? He was, like, insane. Broke all those records before he went to the NFL and made the freaking Pro Bowl. Seriously, Ava?"

Ava looked back and forth between Carson and Jamie, her brows knitting as if fitting pieces of a puzzle together, and Jamie could see the gears turning in her head.

"Carson's a client. This is a business lunch."

He grinned, though there was a trace of something else in his eyes. "I'm not lucky enough to be on a date with your mom."

Jamie shot him a quick look before she turned back to her daughter with a smile that barely masked her discomfort. "He's just kidding."

Ava's lips curved, but her face held an expression that said she wasn't amused by his teasing. "We're heading to the beach. I'll see you at home tonight."

"Ok. Drive safe."

She nodded, pulling her sunglasses over her eyes as she turned to leave. Her friends followed, though the curious glances over their shoulders lingered a little longer.

Jamie watched them go, then exhaled, Carson's comment still echoing in her head, louder than it should have.

The hostess appeared beside them. "Table for two?"

"Yes," she said.

They followed her as she led them to a small table near the window, a few diners turning their heads to look.

Jamie slid into her seat and set her bag down beside her, while he eased into the chair across from her, casually scanning the room.

The hostess placed menus in front of them with a polite smile before she slipped away. Jamie opened hers more to keep her hands busy than to study the food. She already knew what she would order, but it gave her something to focus on other than Carson's presence across the table.

He leaned back slightly, looking at her over the top of his menu. "So, Ava. She seems sharp."

"She is," she said, a small smile tugging at her mouth. "And opinionated."

The scrape of silverware from a nearby table filled the space between them before he asked, "Are you married?"

"No. Divorced."

The corner of his mouth lifted, just slightly. She caught it and wondered if he was glad or if she'd imagined it.

"You seemed a little thrown when she spotted us," he said, his tone casual, as if he were commenting on the weather.

"It caught me off guard. I wasn't expecting to see her here, that's all."

"Or maybe it was how it looked. You and me, walking in together."

"What do you mean?"

He raised an eyebrow. "Come on. She saw us and probably thought this was a date. You panicked a little."

"It's not a date," she said, exhaling as she sat back against her chair.

"I know. I'm just wondering. If it had been, what would've made that so bad?"

Her eyes dropped to the menu, unable to hold his. A slow dip followed, low in her stomach.

"Would it be the age difference? Or something else?"

The answer rose in her mind fast, reckless. She could pass for his mother, the thought of that absurd and humiliating all at once. She swallowed it before she forced herself to look up. "No. It's more complicated than that."

"Well," he said. "You looked like you'd seen a ghost the second she called your name."

She let the silence stretch for a few seconds before responding. "I've worked hard to be taken seriously. I know how things look. People make assumptions."

"People always will," he said, tapping his fingers lightly on the table. "Whether you give them something to talk about or not."

"And what about you?" She asked, studying him for a beat. "You're a professional athlete. People expect you to be with a model or some influencer with a million followers. Aren't you worried what it looks like, being seen with a divorced woman who has a daughter not much younger than you?"

He smiled, slow as if unbothered. "You think I care what people expect? I've been judged since the day I was drafted. For how I played, for where I came from, for how I carry myself. If I worried about what people think, I wouldn't get out of bed in the morning."

She let out a quiet breath, her fingers brushing the corner of the table, but she didn't speak. She wished she could be more like him, at ease and self-assured, untouched by other people's perceptions.

Managing expectations had always been second nature. First her father, then a marriage built on appearances, had taught her how quickly judgment followed women who stepped out of line. Starting over meant walking a narrow path. One wrong assumption or one misplaced choice, and everything she was building could be questioned.

He picked up his menu again, flipping a page like the moment had passed, even though it hadn't. Not really.

She looked back down at her own menu, but the words blurred. Her appetite had faded, replaced by a restlessness she couldn't quite name. He hadn't pushed, but he had opened a door she wasn't ready to walk through. Still, part of her wondered what would happen if she did.

Chapter 5

Jamie sat at the kitchen table, sleeves pushed up, one knee tucked beneath her while her laptop ran video editing software full screen. On her legal pad, she'd scrawled a column of stats in blue ink: *forty-yard dash splits, vertical jump height, bench press reps, three-cone time.*

She pressed play again.

Carson entered the frame, poised at the cone markers, then exploded into motion with sharp cuts, clean breaks, and a final burst of acceleration that ate up the last five yards. He looked fast. More than that, he looked ready.

She clipped out an idle frame where he reset his gloves and added a lower-third caption: Route Tree Drill - 15 Yards Clean Break Timing

The next clip played slow-motion footage of Carson tracking a deep ball over his shoulder, pulling it in with one hand just before hitting the turf. She let that one run longer. Coaches valued body control, and he owned it.

She added a recovery note near the bottom: Medically cleared, 15 months post-ACL - No limitations

When David handed this to her, he offered no real support. "See what you can do," he'd said. He'd considered it a low-risk, expendable assignment without marketing support or anyone cutting tape. Jamie took that as fuel. She wanted her fingerprints on every frame.

She muted the background chatter, letting the sound of Carson's footwork and catches come through clean without music or performance.

After watching the full play through one last time, she exported the file in multiple formats. While it was processing, she opened a new email draft.

The body rewritten five times read:

Hi Coach,

I hope your offseason is going well. I wanted to put Carson Tate back on your radar as you continue building out your receiver depth chart. He's fully recovered from the ACL tear, medically cleared, and has been training consistently here in Tampa. I've attached a short workout tape and brief overview. If there's any interest, I'd be happy to arrange a private workout or call.

Best,

Jamie Sinclair

She attached the reel, a one-page stat summary, and a cleanly designed profile sheet: height, weight, age, college and pro production, previous teams. Everything a scout could skim in sixty seconds.

Next, she queued up coaches and player personnel directors from New Orleans to Seattle, Buffalo, and Chicago. A long shot, but still worth the effort.

By the time she had sent the last message, her coffee had gone cold. She stretched, rolled her neck, and blinked against the sting behind her eyes. For a breath, she let herself believe it was enough.

She closed the laptop and moved to the living room, lowering herself onto the couch until her shoulders met the cushions. Her eyes closed and the tension drained from her neck as she pressed her head into the fabric. For a moment, the house was quiet.

Then her phone rang, an unknown number flashing on the screen. She answered it.

"This is a message from Plant High School," said a flat, automated voice. "Your student, Leo Sinclair, has been marked absent for first and second periods today."

She stared through the bay window, her thoughts already turning.

He'd left for school. She was sure of it. Maybe he'd shown up late or had an appointment she'd forgotten. But two classes? The explanations thinned fast.

She opened Find My iPhone, hoping for the familiar pin to appear on the map, but the screen showed a message instead: *location not available.*

She called, but his voicemail picked up right away.

"Leo, call me the second you get this."

She texted next. No response.

Then, the morning replayed in fragments. He had skipped breakfast and left quietly. There hadn't even been a trace of his usual sarcasm. Now that she thought about it, it seemed like he didn't want to be noticed.

Her hand shook as she grabbed her keys and headed for the door.

He walked out of this house. That much she knew.

So, where the hell did he go?

***

The front office at Plant buzzed as she stepped inside. Phones. Printers. Each sound clipped, quick, like her pulse.

A student at the counter glanced up, offering a polite smile. "Hi, can I help you?" She asked, her voice tentative.

"Hey, yeah. My son, Leo Sinclair, is a student here. I got an attendance call that he missed first and second period. I've tried to reach him but his phone's off."

The girl turned toward the secretary seated behind the desk, who had already caught most of the conversation. She pushed her glasses up the bridge of her nose, focusing on Jamie. "Let me see if he's in class," she said, lifting the phone and dialing an extension.

After a brief exchange, she set the receiver down. "His third period teacher hasn't seen him either."

Jamie folded her arms, nails pressing into her skin. "I saw him leave the house around eight this morning. He's never skipped before."

The secretary leaned forward slightly, her hand still resting near the phone, eyes soft with concern. "Would you like to speak with our school resource officer?"

"Yes. Please." Her voice wavered despite her efforts to control it. She bit down on the inside of her cheek, holding back tears, panic catching in her throat. For a second she thought she might break right there in the middle of the office, but she drew a slow breath and forced it down.

Officer Daniels appeared a few minutes later, and motioned her into a small room, shut the door behind her, and flipped open a notepad.

"You said he left the house around eight?"

"Yes. Same as always."

"Has anything happened lately? Something at home, or with his friends, or a girlfriend? Anything that might've upset him?"

She paused. Until a year ago, everyone had assumed her life was flawless. Explaining otherwise sent a flush of heat to her cheeks. "His father and I divorced recently."

He nodded, jotting notes. "Has he skipped before?"

"Never."

"Give me a few minutes. I'll check the cameras."

***

She stared at the wall posters while he was away—crisis hotlines and student resources—each one landing like a reminder that something terrible might have happened to him. She checked her phone again. Still nothing.

Daniels returned. "I reviewed the footage at the main entrances. There's no sign of him coming in this morning."

She pressed a hand to her mouth, fighting the urge to cry right there in front of him. "What do I do now?"

He placed a palm gently on her shoulder. "Take a deep breath."

She did, air trembling in her lungs, before he continued. "I'm sure he's okay. Kids skip school all the time, even the good ones. Wait a few hours. If he doesn't show up, file a report."

She swallowed hard and murmured a thank you before pushing herself up to leave his office.

***

Inside her car, the reality of Leo's absence hit harder. She started the engine and began to drive, scanning side streets, gas stations, sidewalks, and all the places he used to hang out. Nothing. Not a trace.

The farther she drove, the more her heart pounded. When was the last time they had talked? Really talked. She hadn't tried hard enough. Work had filled her days, exhaustion her nights, and it had been easier to accept the distance than to reach across it. Now guilt twisted in her mind for every time she'd chosen another email or call over sitting down with him.

***

Back at home, the house was still, too still, elevating her panic. She walked straight to Leo's room, the air faintly boyish with the mix of worn sneakers and cheap cologne. The bed was unmade, clothes draped over the chair, a tangle of wires sprawled across the desk, and empty energy drink cans lined the windowsill. The disarray of an ordinary teenager's room. Nothing unusual. She opened drawers, flipped through his closet, searching for anything. A note. A clue. Any sign of where he might have gone.

When her search yielded nothing, she tried to breathe, but her stomach dropped, and her hands began to shake as her mind went back to another time. Leo at eight, red-faced and furious after she took his video games for lying. He slammed the front door so hard the windows rattled. She waited ten minutes before realizing he wasn't sulking in the yard. He was gone. She drove through the neighborhood calling his name, heart pounding, anger dissolving into fear. When she finally found him two blocks from the house, sitting on the curb with his backpack, he said he was going to live with Grandma. She wanted to scold him, to tell him how scared she was. But instead, she pulled him close and let him cry.

That memory pressed now vividly, the same mixture of anger and helplessness curling through her. She thought of every time she pushed too hard or looked away too soon, how easily small moments became fault lines. She wanted to believe that he would walk through the door like he always had, but doubt bore down heavier than hope.

Finally, the latch clicked. She turned toward the foyer, a hopeful spark flaring in her chest. "Leo?" But when she saw Ava step in from the beach, towel wrapped around her waist and flip-flops slapping lightly against the floor, that hope shattered, and she dropped to her knees.

Ava ran to her, crouching beside her, voice trembling as she reached for her arm. "Mom, what's wrong?"

She could barely get the words out. "It's Leo," she managed. "He skipped school. I can't find him."

Ava's eyes widened, her fingers curling around Jamie's sleeve. "Did you check his location?"

She nodded weakly, her hands shaking, still clutching her phone like a lifeline. "I did. He turned it off and he's not answering his phone."

"Did you call the police?"

She shook her head, her mind already spiraling through what-ifs too dark to speak aloud.

Ava dropped her bag with a thud and gripped her mother's arm tighter. "Get up. We're wasting time."

The sharpness in her daughter's tone broke through her daze. She blinked hard, disoriented, before letting Ava pull her to her feet. The floor seemed to shift beneath her, the room still wavering.

Ava was already moving, hair swinging as she turned down the hall toward Leo's room. Jamie followed, slower, pressing a hand to the wall for balance, unsure what Ava expected to find that she hadn't checked herself.

She crossed his bedroom and tapped a key to wake Leo's laptop, the screen coming to life.

"What are you doing?" Jamie asked, hovering near the doorway.

"Trying to see who he's been talking to."

The light from the monitor cast Ava's face in cold blue as her fingers flew over the keyboard.

"You know his password?"

"I set it up when you bought it," she said, eyes fixed on the display. "Same for his socials. You told me to keep an eye on him, remember?"

She stepped closer, a knot of dread coiling in her stomach. Ava opened the Messages app, scrolling through synced conversations. The names blurred until she stopped at one. *Tyler.* She clicked on a link within the thread, and a Venmo page appeared. Rows of transactions filled the screen—hundreds of dollars, each tagged with vague emojis or single letters.

"Who's Tyler?" Ava asked.

"I don't know."

She turned to her mother, eyes wide. "Mom...do you think Leo's doing drugs?"

Jamie shook her head, the denial automatic. "No. There's no way."

"Well, it's something," she said, frowning at the screen. "You don't send that much money for nothing. We need to call the police."

"Not yet."

"Why not?"

"Because I don't want to make it worse. Or humiliate him. We don't know the full story."

***

She checked her phone again and again, the light shifting across the floor, deepening toward evening. Her thoughts looped in circles that led nowhere. Every car that drove by outside made her glance through the window, hope flaring and fading before she could catch her breath.

Then the latch scraped and the hinge groaned, the sound slicing through the stillness, pulling her upright before she even knew she'd moved.

Leo froze in the doorway, his hoodie hanging low, and his eyes blood-shot.

The sight of him knocked the air from her lungs. For a second she had to grab the back of a chair to steady herself. Then the fear curdled. "Where have you been?"

"My phone died."

She took a step closer, her breath shallow. "That's not an answer."

"I'm fine," he muttered, brushing past her toward the hall. "Can I just shower?"

Her fingers twitched, the instinct to grab his arm almost overpowering. "Leo..."

Ava cut in, her tone edged. "We saw your messages. The payments to Tyler."

He froze mid-step. His shoulders stiffened, the air between them thickening. "You went through my stuff?"

"We thought something happened to you."

"You had no right."

Jamie's hands trembled, nails pressing into her palms as she tried to ground herself. "I drove around Tampa thinking I'd find you in a ditch." The sound of her own voice startled her.

Leo looked down, the defiance slipping just slightly, his shoulders sagging. "It's not what you think. I was helping a friend. He needed money."

She studied him, searching for the truth. "That's all?"

He nodded without meeting her eyes.

She wanted to press harder, but something in his expression made her pause. "Alright," she said softly. "Take your shower. But we're not done talking."

He disappeared down the hall before Ava crossed her arms, exhaling hard.

They stood there listening for the sound of running water. It came seconds later.

"He's lying, Mom."

Jamie's answer came out quiet. "I know."

"What are you going to do about it?"

Her gaze drifted toward the hallway, the steam already curling from under the bathroom door. "I don't know yet."

Chapter 6

Cars curved around the block outside the Barrymore Hotel, head-lights weaving beneath strings of soft amber lights as a valet attendant opened her door. Jamie stepped out into the cool evening air, handing him her keys and smoothing the front of her black satin gown.

Julia and her wife, Nicole, were already waiting near the entrance.

"You good?" Julia asked, greeting her with a hug before giving her a once-over.

"Fine." She managed a smile, though her smile faltered as she avoided Julia's eyes, her head still fogged from the sleepless hours she had spent wondering what Leo wasn't telling her. But she'd promised her she'd come to the fundraiser for St Joseph's children's unit; an event her sister had helped organize.

"You look amazing," Nicole said, looping her arm through Jamie's. "Seriously. If I didn't know you were my sister-in-law, I'd hate you."

Jamie laughed, shaking her head as she and Nicole followed Julia through the wide foyer and into the ballroom.

Crystal chandeliers reflected off gold-accented decor, and white linen covered every table. She took a slow breath. Nights like this always made her stomach knot, the scent of perfume thick at her throat, camera flashes popping too close.

Across the ballroom, she recognized a few hospital board members from photos Julia had shown her, along with local media personalities clustered near the step-and-repeat backdrop.

Nicole caught Julia's eye. "I'm going to find the ladies' room before we sit."

"I'll meet you at the table," Julia said, then turned to Jamie. "You want a drink?"

"Yes, please. Preferably a shot of tequila."

Julia laughed. "It's a hospital fundraiser not 'Girls Gone Wild.'"

"Then champagne," she said dryly. "Lots of it."

Julia smiled and disappeared into the crowd while Jamie stayed where she was, trying to find her footing. She turned slightly, then stopped when she saw him.

Carson.

He had just entered the room, tall and composed in a tailored tux.

She froze. He hadn't seen her yet. "What the hell," she said under her breath, barely enough to move the air.

Julia returned a minute later, two glasses of champagne in hand. "What's with the face?" She glanced toward the entrance. "Oh." A smile tugged at her mouth. "Surprise."

"You knew he'd be here?"

"I might have heard he was an honorary guest."

"A warning would've been nice."

"You look stunning. He should be the one surprised."

Julia's words were still settling when Carson's gaze found Jamie's. For a split second, she looked away, tried to pretend she hadn't noticed him, but it was too late.

His eyes lit up, subtle but real, before he excused himself from the conversation and made his way toward her.

She straightened her shoulders, willing the heat from her face as he approached.

"You clean up alright, Sinclair."

"So do you," she said, trying to sound casual.

He looked around, then down at her again. "Didn't expect to see you here."

"I could say the same."

"I was asked to present one of the awards. Youth leadership stuff." He shrugged slightly, but the thread of pride in his voice wasn't lost on her.

Julia still stood beside her, watching the exchange with a look of open curiosity as Jamie turned to reintroduce them, though Carson was already smiling in recognition.

"Good to see you again, Julia."

Julia returned the smile and then leaned in close to Jamie, just out of Carson's earshot. "Breathe. It's not like he hasn't seen you in heels before."

She gave her a warning glance before Julia lifted her glass in a mock toast. "I'll let you two chat," she said, disappearing into the crowd moments later.

He watched her go, then turned back to Jamie with an amused smile. "Your sister always that subtle?"

"That *was* her being subtle."

She felt it, the way her pulse ticked up, and warmth crept into her neck. There was no hiding the effect he had on her, not in that tux, not when his eyes kept finding hers. She crossed her arms loosely, more to occupy her hands than anything else.

The corner of his mouth faded, and his eyes narrowed just a fraction, as if he'd caught the change in her. "You alright?"

She nodded quickly, too quickly. "Fine. It's just warm in here."

A few seconds stretched between them, a brief silence that seemed to amplify the noise as she pretended to sip her champagne, eyes darting around the room.

"Want to get some air?" He asked.

She paused, considering how walking outside alone with him might look and what people would assume. Saying no would've been easier—safer—but she wasn't in the mood to lie to herself. She glanced toward the corner of the ballroom, where Julia had disappeared, then back at Carson.

"Yeah," she said finally, her voice more controlled than she felt. "Fresh air sounds good."

***

The terrace was quiet, set apart from the noise of the gala by a thick pane of glass and a pair of velvet-draped doors. Outside, a soft breeze brushed across the bay and lifted a strand of hair from her shoulder. She folded her arms against the chill, wishing she'd brought a shawl.

He shrugged off his tuxedo coat without a word and handed it to her. She hesitated. "I'm fine."

"You're not," he said. "Just take it."

She did, slipping her arms inside. It was still warm from his body, the sleeves long on her frame, and it carried the subtle scent of his cologne, something clean and woodsy that made her pulse flutter. She adjusted the collar with a small tug and stared out at the lights reflecting across the water, grateful for the brief stillness.

They stood like that for a minute, side by side, not speaking. Below, the distant sound of a boat motor drifted, followed by laughter from a group somewhere down the walkway.

She finally broke the silence. "It's easier to breathe out here."

He glanced at her. "You seemed a little off in there. Everything okay?"

"Yeah," she said, her tone softer now, almost hesitant. "It's just been a week...things at home."

"If you ever want to talk, I listen better than I run a slant these days."

She gave him a sidelong glance, lips curving faintly. "That's a pretty high bar."

"Maybe. But I mean it."

She remembered standing beside John at a gala like this one, believing her life was complete, that she'd mapped it all out: a beautiful home, children who'd grow up secure. But the years had passed in a blur of school meetings and household chores while he built his empire. Somewhere along the way, she lost sight of what she wanted for herself, and that realization sat heavy.

"This isn't where I thought I'd be at forty." The words slipped out before she stopped them.

He turned toward her but didn't interrupt.

"I spent my twenties changing diapers and kissing scraped knees, and my thirties trying to hold a marriage together. And now here I am, fighting to figure out where I belong in a world that kept moving without me."

She wrapped his jacket tighter around herself. "I used to think if you follow the rules, things fall into place. Turns out, the rules were just for show."

He didn't respond immediately, and she appreciated how he didn't rush to fill the conversation with something easy.

When he did finally speak, his tone was calm and affirming. "You're doing more than most people would, Jamie. And you're doing it well. Doesn't matter how long it takes to get here."

She met his eyes. "That's generous."

"It's honest."

She straightened, the movement deliberate, as if to clear the air between them and redirect the moment, grounding them both in something safer.

"I sent your reels out."

Surprise flitted across his expression. "Already?"

"Yep. Yesterday. A handful of teams."

"I thought we were going to talk about it first."

"You were busy training, so I made a judgment call."

"Who'd you send it to?"

"Seattle, Buffalo, New Orleans, Chicago. All have issues with depth at wide receiver. They've got cap space, and their front offices should be open to taking on a guy with your history."

His expression stayed neutral, but she saw the subtle drop of his shoulders.

"We can talk about next steps depending on who shows interest," she said, staring out toward the bay.

She felt him watching her in that calm, perceptive way of his, making her feel more seen than she was ready for.

"How do you keep going?" she asked suddenly, facing him. "After the injuries...being passed over."

He took a breath before he spoke, his voice calm. "My dad worked the docks at the port. Longshoreman. Spent most of his life loading cargo in the heat, and the rain. It didn't matter and he never complained, but a body only holds up so long."

He leaned forward, resting his forearms on the balcony railing. "Football was the only thing I was ever good at," he said. "It gave me a way out. Still does and that's why I keep going. My father was a great man, but I don't want to end up like him. He deserved better than what he got."

His gaze stayed fixed on the water, and she understood he'd lived through something she'd never been forced to face.

Maybe they were both chasing approval, trying to prove themselves in opposite worlds. Jamie's pursuit was shaped by the expectations of her family, by the image of what a woman like her was supposed to be. Compliant. Pleasing. Carson's was survival, fighting for opportunity, for every inch forward.

He turned slightly, adjusting the collar of his shirt beneath his vest. When he looked at her again, the intensity in his gaze had softened. "You're not the only one proving something."

A gust of wind swept across the terrace, and she clutched the lapels of his jacket.

"We should go back in," she said.

He nodded, but he didn't move.

A beat passed. Slowly, he reached out and adjusted the collar of the coat where it had folded awkwardly near her face. His fingers barely grazed her, but it was enough.

She held her breath.

Then, as if on cue, the terrace doors creaked open behind them. Jamie turned toward the sound, the spell broken, and saw a pair of guests step out, laughing about something neither of them had heard.

She looked back at Carson, and he caught her eye, the corner of his mouth lifting as he stepped aside to hold the door.

***

When she turned into the driveway and pulled into the garage, the evening still clung to her, the faint trace of his cologne still on her skin. For a few minutes, she stayed in the car, hands resting on the steering wheel, her mind replaying fragments of the terrace conversation—the look in his eyes and the things she hadn't meant to say.

Finally, she stepped inside, slipping off her heels. Darkness filled the house, broken only by the soft glimmer of a nightlight and the flicker of the digital clock on the oven.

Padding across the hardwood floor, she stopped outside Leo's room and pushed the door open gently. The light from the hallway spilled across his bed, and at first glance, it appeared undisturbed. But when she stepped inside, she saw him, burrowed beneath the covers, his arm flung over the pillow, the rise and fall of his breathing visible in the dim light.

She walked closer, careful not to wake him. He looked so much older than he had even a year ago, his jawline more defined, his features no longer boyish. For one fleeting second, she saw him as he'd been at five years old, curled in the same position, clutching his stuffed dinosaur, back when he needed her for everything.

She reached down and gently brushed the hair from his forehead. He stirred but didn't wake, and she lingered a minute, then turned and slipped out, easing the door shut behind her.

In the stillness, she stepped into her closet and unhooked the clasp of her dress. She paused, staring at herself in the mirror, the reflection catching the soft trace of crow's feet and the fine lines on her forehead. The image blurred as she remembered how Carson's eyes had held hers a beat too long, stirring confusion and longing all at once. She couldn't understand what he saw in her, someone so much older. It left her both rattled and alive, pulling her back to a version of herself she thought she'd outgrown, one who still wanted to be touched, and desired after years of pretending she didn't.

That realization mingled with the memory of John's betrayals, the slow erosion of their marriage until all that remained was duty and distance. The first affair had gutted her. She had found a letter by accident, had sat at the foot of their bed afterward, unable to decide whether to scream or stay quiet for the sake of the children. The second carved something out of her she never quite got back; she stopped asking questions, stopped looking too closely. By the third, she was already numb, moving through the days as if the marriage were a business arrangement, closing parts of herself she wasn't sure she would ever open again.

She pulled her dress over her head and stepped into her bathroom, starting her nightly routine. The water felt cool on her skin as she washed her face.

After brushing her teeth, she changed into a pair of cotton pajamas and climbed into bed, pulling the covers up and letting her face sink into the pillow. Fatigue weighed on her body, yet her thoughts refused to slow.

Just as she reached for her phone to silence it, a notification buzzed across the screen. An email. She opened it without thinking, thumb hovering over the message.

Subject: RE: Carson Tate Workout Film

She sat up straighter, pulse quickening as she scanned it. They had watched the footage, and they were impressed.

Her breath caught. This was what she had been working for, proof that someone was paying attention, that her instincts had been right, but as she read it again, a weight pressed into her chest.

Seattle, across the country.

If this moved forward, Carson would be gone. But she'd done her job. Wasn't that what this was all for?

She let the phone rest on her lap, eyes unfocused. It was irrational, she knew, yet the reaction still bloomed somewhere deep within her.

She opened her contacts and scrolled until she found Carson's name. Her finger hovered over it, a beat stretching out before she tapped the call button.

He picked up on the first ring. "Sinclair? Everything okay?"

"Yes, I'm sorry. I know it's late, but I didn't want to wait until tomorrow to tell you." There was a lump in her throat.

"Tell me what?"

"I heard from Seattle." Her voice softened, almost a reflex, but she swallowed and steadied it before she continued. "They want a private workout."

A brief pause followed, just long enough to make her wonder what he was thinking.

"That's big," he said. "You sound...disappointed."

She cleared her throat, adjusting her tone. "No, it's good news. Really good."

There was another pause, this one longer.

"Let's meet tomorrow so we can work on a reply," she said, needing to fill the awkward air between them. "I'm going to brunch with my mother, but I can meet you right after."

"Okay. Sleep well, Sinclair."

"You too."

Chapter 7

That night, she'd tossed and turned until nearly three a.m., her thoughts looping through the evening at the gala. And though she hadn't slept enough to welcome it, Sunday arrived anyway, sky bright and restless.

She drove along the causeway toward the marina to meet her mother for brunch, waves rolling rough across the bay, just like the uneasy flutter in her stomach. What was she doing, letting her mind drift to Carson like this? The age difference alone should have stopped her, not to mention that she represented him. Besides that, she had just come through a divorce, one that had stripped her of faith in permanence...in men. Trust had become fragile, not something she could give freely anymore.

She turned the rearview mirror toward her and checked her reflection, wincing as she realized her mother would spot the sleepless night.

They met for brunch on the third Sunday of every month, a standing tradition that had started years ago, though lately it slipped her mind more often than not.

She eased into the restaurant parking lot and parked between two cars, letting the engine idle while she pulled a small makeup bag from her purse. She dusted powder over the dark circles and added another layer of lipstick. After a deep breath, she killed the engine and stepped out, her heels clicking softly against the pavement as she walked toward the entrance.

The restaurant was the type her mother always chose, refined, and far enough from the city to feel exclusive. It overlooked the marina, with cream-colored umbrellas dotting the patio and tables covered in fresh linens.

She spotted her immediately, already seated with the poise of someone born knowing how to command a room. Evelyn Maddox's silver-blonde hair was swept into a neat twist, her lipstick a shade of rose that matched the scarf draped over her shoulders. Even from a distance, she looked impeccably put together.

Jamie approached with careful steps, smoothing her blouse and tucking a strand of hair behind her ear, then pulling it forward again.

"Darling," Evelyn said, standing to kiss her cheek. "You're right on time."

She summoned a small smile, sliding into the seat across from her. "You look nice."

"So do you." Her mother's eyes moved over her, as if taking in every detail. "I love the dress. The color suits you. But you seem tired, dear. Are you getting enough sleep?"

"Yes, I'm fine, Mother." She swallowed the comment and reached for the menu.

The server came and went. She ordered a fruit plate and an omelet; Evelyn chose the poached eggs with toast, specifying exactly how she wanted her yolks cooked.

They chatted for a while, talking mostly about Ava and Leo. Evelyn asked about work, but only in passing, never showing much interest. To her, Jamie's career had always been a phase, something to fill the time post-divorce, such as painting or tennis.

"I saw Julia's Instagram pictures from the gala last night," she said, stirring her coffee. "She seemed very...comfortable. Nicole seems like a lovely person."

"She is," Jamie said.

Julia had never introduced their parents to Nicole, never even hinted at trying. She hadn't spoken to them in years, not really.

"Well. I suppose everyone finds their own happiness eventually." The curl of her mouth made it seem less like acceptance and more like disapproval.

Jamie bit back the sharp retort that threatened to rise, reaching for her glass instead.

"You and Julia have always been so different." Evelyn sat a little straighter, fingers curling around the handle of her cup as if bracing for her own words. "She never thought about the consequences of her actions, not once. But you were always the good one, the dependable one. You never questioned what was expected, never made a scene. Exactly the kind of daughter any mother would hope for. But lately..." She paused, stirring her coffee again, as if she hadn't just dropped a match on the table, her tone landing with that same backhanded bite Jamie had come to expect.

"Are we talking about the divorce now, or circling it?"

Evelyn folded her napkin in her lap. "I wonder if maybe you acted too quickly. Stability matters more than the mistakes a man makes. John can give you that, Jamie. He always has."

"So, all the affairs? I should just forget about that?"

Evelyn's eyes narrowed slightly, but she kept speaking, her expression detached, as if what Jamie had asked barely warranted acknowledgment.

"And now look. Ava won't speak to him. Leo is so distant. You live in that big house on borrowed time. Was it worth it?"

She looked at her mother and leaned back, feeling the heat rise behind her collar. "You think I wanted this? That I planned to raise teenagers alone while trying to restart my life at forty?"

"Marriage is a marathon, honey. It's about resilience. Your father wasn't easy, but I stayed. For you girls."

And how did that work out for you? Jamie thought. But it remained lodged in her throat. What was the point? She already knew the answer. Her childhood had been a slow study, her father always away, and when he was home, his voice carried through the house louder than the rest of theirs combined. She remembered how often her mother had smiled through gritted teeth, the air thick with everything no one dared to speak. Evelyn had stayed, yes, but happiness had never seemed like part of the bargain.

"I'm not Julia." She spoke softly, her eyes shifting toward the horizon. "But I'm not you either. I'm still figuring it out. On my own terms."

Evelyn tilted her head. "Well, don't take too long. The world isn't kind to women who hesitate."

***

Oxford Exchange always felt quieter than it should for a place that busy. It was mid-afternoon, sunlight streaming through the windows and across the wooden tables and rows of books.

She paused near a display of hardcovers, running her fingers lightly along the spines without really reading the titles. It had been one of her favorite bookstores for years. Back when Leo was little, she used to let him pick something from one of the children's displays while she wandered the cookbooks and biographies, pretending she had time to read them.

A glossy pink cover displayed on one of the tables caught her eye: *Hotter Than He Left You: A Divorced Woman's Guide to Reclaiming Her Second Wind.* She glanced around once before picking it up.

On the back, a woman in red heels leaned against a convertible, laughing at something off camera.

Newly Single? Wondering if anyone will ever look at you the same way they used to? You are not alone. In this unapologetic roadmap for women over forty, bestselling author, Marla Kent, explains how to rediscover confidence and remember that desire doesn't expire because your marriage did.

"Research?" a voice said behind her.

She yelped and dropped the book, the cover slapping against the floor loud enough to turn two heads. Carson bent to pick it up before she could, turning it face up. His mouth twitched as he read the last few words of the title aloud. "Reclaiming your second wind?" he asked, glancing up at her. "Ambitious."

As he stood, she stepped forward and took it from his hands a little too quickly. "I wasn't actually—I mean, I didn't—It was just there," she said, setting it back on the table. "You want to grab some coffee?"

He didn't answer right away, the corner of his mouth still tipped up, like he was cataloging this version of her for later. "Sure."

***

They ordered, waited shoulder to shoulder while the barista called out names, and then carried their cups toward a small table near the window. She chose the seat with her back to the wall out of habit.

"How was brunch?"

"Eventful," she said, running a finger over the rim of her coffee cup. "Let's just say my mother still knows how to push every last button." She forced a smile, flipped her phone over, and pulled the email back up before sliding it toward him. "Read it."

He picked it up, reading it and she watched the way his brows lifted slightly.

"So, it's real." He leaned back, sliding her phone back across the table before he looked up. "This is big."

"It is."

"Are you coming with me?"

"I don't know yet." She exhaled slowly. "I have a son. Leo. He's seventeen." She paused, stirring her coffee. "The divorce was rough on him, and now John, my ex, is putting the house on the market. It's the only place Leo's ever lived."

Carson said nothing, but the way he leaned in told her she had his full attention.

"Everything familiar is being pulled out from under him." She folded her hands around the coffee cup, her gaze drifting back to the table. "He's withdrawn, angry. He keeps to himself more than he used to. I've been trying to keep him grounded, but sometimes it feels like I'm barely holding it together."

"You aren't failing. You're showing up. That's more than some parents do."

She looked at him, caught off guard by the sincerity in his voice.

"It's Seattle," she said after a beat. "Not a short trip."

He nodded once, but didn't speak right away, his gaze dropping to the table before drifting to the window as if measuring the distance in his mind. She watched a muscle tick in his jaw, the tension in his expression telling her he was thinking about it too.

"You've done this before," she said. "You don't need me there. You're more than capable of handling it on your own."

"I get it. But if you can work it out…I'd like you there." His voice was gentle, not demanding. But there was something in it that pulled at her.

***

By the time the sun sank behind the bay, the house had settled into stillness, the scent of garlic and basil drifting through the kitchen.

The front door opened without warning.

"That you?" She called over her shoulder, already knowing the answer.

"It's us." Julia's voice rang through the hallway. Seconds later, she and Nicole appeared, shedding jackets and kicking off shoes like they belonged there, which, in a way, they always had.

"God, it smells amazing in here." Nicole made a beeline for the stove, eyes widening as she scanned the bubbling sauce and full pot of pasta. "You made enough to feed an army."

"Leo's in his room. But he might emerge if he smells carbs."

Julia opened the fridge and grabbed a half-empty bottle of Sauvignon Blanc. "He still sulking?"

She gave a nod, brushing a stray lock of hair behind her ear as she exhaled. "He'll talk when he's ready."

They moved around the kitchen in a familiar routine. Being around them loosened something in her shoulders she hadn't realized was tight.

Once she had served the food and they'd taken their seats around the table, Julia gestured with her fork. "So, brunch with Mother Dearest. Survive it?"

She gave a dry laugh. "Barely."

"Let me guess," Julia said, raising her voice in imitation. "'Jamie, you shouldn't have left him. Your children need stability, not your foolish independence.'"

"Close."

Julia shook her head. "She stayed with Dad out of duty and fear. You got out. That doesn't make you selfish. It makes you brave."

Jamie fell quiet, her gaze dropping to her glass. The conversation about their parents triggered a familiar ache, and her mind drifted, circling back to Leo's silence and Ava's brittle smiles.

She glanced toward the window before continuing, taking time to find the right words. "Mom was never happy. I know that now." Her shoulders drew in as she ran a thumb along the rim of her glass. "I thought John was different, but sometimes I wonder if I was repeating the cycle."

Julia reached across the table, giving her sister's hand a squeeze. "You're not Mom. And Leo and Ava know love in a way we never did. That counts for something."

Nicole glanced between them, sympathy softening her features. Then she leaned forward, her voice light, almost deliberately casual. "So. How's everything going with your new client?"

Jamie caught the shift instantly, how she was trying to steer them somewhere safer. Some place that didn't ache quite so much.

"Good. We got a response from Seattle. They offered to fly him out for a private workout next Friday."

Nicole raised an eyebrow. "That's huge. Are you going?"

She twisted her napkin between her fingers, trying to find words that wouldn't sound like excuses. "I don't know. It's my week with Leo, and asking John to switch might make things worse."

Julia didn't hesitate. "I'll stay with him."

"You will?"

"Of course. And if he tries any teenage rebellion, I'll hide his laptop."

Nicole laughed. "I'll come too. We'll keep him busy. Make sure he doesn't mope himself into a cave."

Julia leaned forward, resting her forearms on the table, her voice dropping into that low, persuasive tone Jamie had known since childhood. "Go. You need this. And not because it's your job. Something about that man makes you light up, and you don't even know you're doing it."

She tried to deflect, but Nicole caught her glance and smiled knowingly before cutting in. "She's right. You haven't looked this alive in years."

"It's strictly business," she said, almost to herself.

A smirk tugged at Julia's mouth. "Sure, it is. Why don't we have your vagina draw up a contract since she's so professional?"

Jamie choked on a laugh, covering her face with her napkin. "Jesus, Jules."

"Hey, I'm just saying."

Their laughter filled the kitchen, light and loud enough to carry down the hall before Leo appeared, rubbing his eyes like he'd woken up five minutes earlier.

"What's so funny?" he mumbled.

Jamie straightened, trying to pull herself together. "Your aunt's being inappropriate again."

"Hey, I'm coming to hang with you for a few days," Julia said.

He blinked. "Why?"

"Because I might need to go out of town. To Seattle with Carson, but only if you're okay with it."

He huffed, half a laugh, half a groan. "Mom, seriously. You act like I'm five. Go. I'm good."

"You sure?"

"Yeah," he said, smirking. "You hovering around all the time isn't doing either of us any favors."

She wanted to believe he was finally coming to terms with everything, but the knot in her stomach told her otherwise. His answer had come too quickly.

She motioned to the table. "Sit. Let me make you a plate."

He pulled out a chair, scrolling through his phone while she reheated the pasta, trying to convince herself he was fine. That she could go to Seattle and not spend every second worrying. But she didn't dwell on it.

Then, the screen lit up in his hand. He checked it, his eyes going wide for a split second before he pushed his chair back so abruptly it scraped against the floor.

"Whoa," Julia said. "What is it? Your pants on fire?"

"I forgot an assignment," he said quickly. "It's due by midnight." He was already moving toward the hallway.

Jamie called out to him. "I'll bring your plate in to you."

She stood there a second longer, staring at the empty chair, wondering what had really flashed across his screen making him bolt like that.

***

Later that night, after the dishes had been washed, and the house grew still, she sat cross-legged on her bed with her laptop perched on a pillow in front of her. The blue light from the screen lit her face as she opened her email, the message from the Seahawks scout still flagged in her inbox.

She reread it twice before clicking reply. *Thank you for the opportunity. Carson Tate and I will both be in attendance. Looking forward to the workout.*

She hovered over the send button for only a second and then pressed it. Done. Decision made.

She picked up her phone, pulled Carson's name up in her contacts, and tapped out a quick text. *Confirmed with Seattle. We're in.*

His response came a moment later. *We? As in you and me? You're going with me?*

She smiled at the screen and typed back: *Yes.*

Another buzz. *LFG!*

She opened a new tab on her laptop and searched for flights from Tampa to Seattle. The list of options populated in seconds, and she scrolled through them, her mind already calculating logistics.

Leaning back against her pillows, she couldn't help but smile at her phone, at his last message still gleaming there.

Her thoughts drifted to what it would be like traveling with him, staying in the same hotel, seeing him in that space between work and something more. The thought caught her off guard, but she pushed it down, reminding herself this was business. But even she could hear the doubt in that line she tried to hold.

Chapter 8

She spotted Carson as he stepped through the sliding doors of the terminal, the attention he drew from those around him hard to ignore. He wore a simple black hoodie and a baseball cap pulled low, but it didn't make him any less noticeable.

When he saw her, she lifted a hand in a quick wave. His smile came easily as he walked toward her.

"You good?" he asked, falling into step beside her as they made their way toward the TSA checkpoint.

She nodded quickly. "Great."

He gave her a look that said he wasn't convinced, but he let it go.

Dressed in layers, a soft cream sweater under a fitted blazer, Jamie looked the part, even if she didn't feel it.

Her eyes drifted to the passing glances from strangers, a few curious, a few more lingering longer than she liked. She couldn't help wondering what people saw. A professional woman traveling with a younger athlete? His agent or his girlfriend?

Once through security, they stopped at a small newsstand. She grabbed a bottle of water while Carson browsed the snacks.

"So, what changed your mind?" he asked, his tone casual as he set a protein bar on the counter.

She passed a credit card to the cashier with a half-smile. "My sister and her wife, Nicole, are staying at the house with Leo while I'm gone."

"That the woman she was with at the gala?"

Jamie nodded.

"They seemed happy," he said.

"They are. My parents, though…not so much."

His brow lifted slightly, but he said nothing.

"They've never really accepted it." She paused, choosing her words. "Ignoring it is easier for them than trying to understand."

"Damn. That sucks. People should just let others be who they are. Not who they want them to be."

For a beat, she studied him, noting the ease in his voice, the way he said it like it was the simplest thing in the world.

As they walked through the airport, the sound of wheeled luggage and boarding calls filled the silence that stretched. Once seated near their gate, she leaned back in her chair and crossed her legs, trying to settle the flutter in her stomach.

Carson scrolled on his phone, then looked up. "You ever been to Seattle?"

"Once, years ago, when John had a work thing. I came along but barely saw the city."

"Well, you're about to see it different."

She tilted her head. "How so?"

"Because this time, you're going for your own reasons. Not someone else's."

The comment caught her off guard. She opened her mouth to respond, but their row was called for boarding. As they gathered their bags and joined the line, she found herself glancing at him again, wondering if he even realized how easily he could say something that stuck with her.

***

The flight had been smooth. She had dozed off somewhere over Colorado, lulled by the soft drone of the cabin and the exhaustion of the past week catching up to her.

When she woke, her head was resting lightly against Carson's shoulder. At first, she didn't move. The warmth of his body, the rise and fall of his breathing, were dangerously comforting. She pulled away gently, murmuring an apology. He said nothing, just gave her a smile and adjusted in his seat.

It was well past dark when they'd landed in Seattle. Through the terminal windows, the tarmac gleamed under low-hanging clouds, heavy enough to mute the city's outlines.

As they exited the airport, Carson rolled his shoulders and stifled a yawn.

"The hotel's not far," she said, scrolling through her phone. "I booked us an Uber. It should be here any minute."

His eyes lifted. "Are you always this prepared?"

"I've had two children. You're lucky I'm not walking around with a first aid kit."

"That's oddly comforting." His tone was casual, though the glint in his gaze was anything but.

***

The ride through the city was quiet. She watched it roll past in blurred shadows and soft halos of light before the car pulled up to the hotel entrance. It was sleek and understated, with a warm glimmer spilling from the lobby windows onto the wet sidewalk.

Inside, the polished floors gleamed under dim lighting. The front desk clerk smiled politely as she slid their key cards across the counter. "You'll be in rooms 804 and 806."

Jamie returned the smile, though a ripple of unease moved through her. Sharing a hallway with him felt intimate, a reminder that for the next two days, their worlds would be separated by a single wall. She told herself it didn't mean anything, but the thought nagged at her all the same.

She tucked her keycard into her wallet and followed the bellhop to the elevator.

As they rode up, Carson glanced sideways at her. "Not bad, Sinclair."

She arched an eyebrow. "For a rookie."

He shrugged. "Could've been worse."

The teasing warmth in his tone stirred something restless inside her, and when the bellhop shot them a quick, knowing glance, she realized that whatever was passing between them wasn't invisible. That thought unsettled her more than she wanted to admit.

On their floor, they paused in the hallway outside their rooms. The whir of the elevator faded, leaving only the soft sound of rain against the windows at the end of the corridor.

He ran a hand along the back of his neck. "Meet in the lobby in the morning around eight?"

"That works."

They stood for a few seconds longer, neither moving to unlock their doors. She wondered what he was thinking, if he felt the same current pulling at the divide of what was professional and what wasn't.

Finally, she pulled her keycard from her wallet and turned toward her door. "Goodnight, Carson."

***

She wheeled her suitcase into the corner of a clean, contemporary room with soft neutrals and sharp lines, and paused to breathe. The city stretched wide beyond the floor-to-ceiling windows, lights blinking through the mist.

She sat at the foot of the bed, kicked off her shoes, and pulled out her phone to text Leo. *Made it to Seattle. Love you.*

It was already after midnight in Tampa, and although she knew it probably wouldn't come, she watched the screen, waiting for a reply.

With a sigh, she switched to her contacts and scrolled until she found Julia's name. A few rings, then a click.

"Hey, Jamie," Julia said.

"Put it on speaker!" Nicole called out in the background, loud and giddy.

"How much wine have you two had? If you opened a good bottle, I'm sending you a bill."

"Not wine, my dear," Nicole said. "But something equally delightful."

"I don't even want to know what that means." She took a deep breath, pinching the bridge of her nose. "Is Leo okay?"

Julia's voice returned. "Yes. We tucked him in and set the alarm. He's out cold."

"Now tell us about your trip," Nicole said, cutting in. "You're in Seattle with a six-foot-five NFL player whose biceps could ruin lives. Don't pretend you haven't noticed."

"He's my client."

"Uh-huh. Sure," Nicole said. "Just kiss him."

"Wait, wait, wait," Julia said. "Should we make a flow chart? I know how much you like an organized approach." She cleared her throat, adopting a mock-professional tone. "Step one: assess kiss viability. Step two: draft a risk report."

Nicole laughed, chiming in. "Step three: schedule kiss for next Tuesday at 3:15."

"No, she needs approval from HR first," Julia said, jumping back in. "That's step four."

"Oh my God, you two need hobbies."

"Guess what step five is?" Julia asked.

"Seriously, Julia. I'm not going to kiss him."

"Exactly. Cancel due to overthinking."

Jamie sighed. "Goodnight."

"Come on. We're kidding."

She ended the call before Julia could finish, and the room went quiet again as she closed her eyes and let herself exhale.

They'd made it. Tomorrow would be the real test.

***

The Virginia Mason Athletic Center rose in clean lines of glass and steel, its reflection shimmering on Lake Washington. Pine trees framed the property, their branches swaying in a mild breeze. The muffled rush of traffic in the distance blended with the gentle slap of water against the shore.

Inside, a woman in a Seahawks quarter-zip checked them in before leading them to a turf field. Jamie recognized the man waiting for them from LinkedIn, one of the team's pro personnel staff. He was middle-aged and trim, his calm authority needing no announcement.

"Carson," he said as they approached, extending a hand. "Mark De-Witt. Glad you could make it."

Carson shook it firmly. "Appreciate the opportunity."

She stood beside him as Mark reached out again, his grip firm. "You must be Jamie. Good to meet you." He checked his watch before turning back to Carson. "We'll get you started in about ten. You can change in the locker room down the hall."

Once Carson disappeared down the hallway, Mark glanced back toward Jamie. "We liked him his second season with Miami. Fast. Smart on the field."

"Still is."

He smiled slightly but didn't argue. "Let's see what he's got."

She stepped to the edge of the turf as Carson reemerged, now in athletic gear, his sleeves pushed up, revealing the strength in his arms. He jogged a few short stretches, rolled his shoulders, then crouched to retie his cleats.

The drills began simply: sprints and footwork, then route trees. She kept her eyes on him the whole time, noting his speed, the precision of his breakaways. There was no hesitation in his movements, no trace of doubt. He moved like a man who still believed the future hadn't passed him by.

She found herself holding her breath. It was strange how much of herself she'd invested in his career, his second chance. Maybe because it was hers, too.

After forty-five minutes, Carson was sweating but composed, his chest rising and falling in even breaths. He took a long pull from his water bottle as Mark approached from the sidelines. "Still got some burst. Good eye discipline, quick out of your cuts."

Carson wiped his face with a towel and nodded. "Appreciate that."

"Is there any feedback we should keep in mind as we move forward?" Jamie asked, her voice composed.

"Nothing major. We'll take a closer look at the footage, but it's a positive showing."

She let out a quiet breath, warmth stirring inside her. Watching him out there had ignited a spark she hadn't expected—hope, or admiration that felt personal in a way it shouldn't.

Carson extended his hand again. "Thanks for the opportunity."

They watched him walk off toward the facility offices, his steps unhurried, clipboard tucked under his arm.

"You crushed that." Her voice was low as she glanced sideways at him.

"You think so?"

"I know so. And so does he."

***

Later that afternoon, they walked side by side through the lively thrum of Pike Place Market. The cobblestone streets were packed with locals and tourists weaving between flower stalls and fish counters.

Jamie's scarf flapped lightly in the breeze as she followed Carson toward a stall selling steamed pork buns, the scent warm and savory, cutting through the crisp air. He paid for them both before she could protest, handing her one with a smirk. "You can't come to Seattle and not try these."

She accepted it, their fingers brushing, before she removed the paper wrapper and took a bite.

"Better than room service, right?"

"By a mile."

After they ate, they stood near the rail, watching the ferries drift across Elliott Bay.

"So," Carson said, hands resting on the railing. "Not to be rude, but...you don't exactly strike me as someone who grew up dreaming of signing athletes."

She let out a short laugh. "Ouch. Do I give off PTA mom energy or something?"

"Okay, that came out wrong." He chuckled, a self-aware smile tugging at his mouth. "I just meant, you're not what I'm used to. But that's not a bad thing."

She grinned, already knowing what he was thinking. She didn't quite fit the mold. "You can say it. It's not exactly a woman's world."

He nodded slowly. "No, it's not. And look, I've met women who are tougher and smarter than half the guys in this business. More than capable. But if I'm honest, I wouldn't want the job if I were a woman. Some athletes are brutal. Disrespectful. It shouldn't be that way, but it is."

"You're right." She braced herself before continuing. "When I asked John for the divorce, I didn't want to drag it out in court. That meant no alimony, so I had to find something quick, and my dad has connections. So, here I am."

He turned, leaning his back against the rail, and tilted his head. "If you could choose any career, what would it be?"

She drew in a slow breath, aware of how easily she could say more than she should. She usually kept her story tucked away; clients didn't need to know the messy parts, the things that hinted at regret.

But with Carson, it felt different. He asked questions like he wanted to understand her, not just make small talk. Still, saying it out loud would mean admitting how much she'd let life steer her instead of the other way around.

"I thought the dream was to be a lawyer. I graduated from law school, but I never sat for the bar. The plan was to take it once the kids were a little older, but between dance lessons and baseball practice, I just never made the time."

"What's stopping you from taking it now?"

"I don't know. I tell myself it's too late. I'm too old. And the truth is, I'm not sure why I wanted to be an attorney in the first place. Most of the lawyers I've met are either miserable or arrogant or both. Not exactly the kind of person I ever saw myself becoming."

"Yeah, some of them are like that. But not all. You might've ended up one of the good ones."

He turned around to face the bay again, propping his forearms on the railing. "I had a lot of people count me out after I got hurt the second time. Said I was done. But if I had listened to them, I wouldn't be here right now." He paused. "You think it's too late, but it isn't. What if you're exactly where you need to be to start again?"

She gave him a look. "Are you rehearsing for a TED Talk?"

He laughed, shaking his head. "Okay, maybe that's cliche." His expression sobered sightly. "Doesn't make it wrong."

***

As the afternoon faded, the evening wrapped around them, lights warming in the windows, and the air cooling just enough to make Jamie draw her jacket closer. They wandered further into the city. Carson led the way without a set destination, and she didn't ask where they were going.

Eventually, they found themselves at a jazz bar in Belltown, where a four-piece band played in a dimly lit corner. They ordered drinks and settled into a booth, the melody flowing around them.

She leaned back, studying him beneath the soft gold light as he nodded slightly to the flow of the music, his expression half-lost in thought.

"You into jazz?" she asked.

He shrugged, relaxed. "Appreciate it more the older I get."

"You're twenty-six," she said, chuckling.

"I'm old enough to know a good thing when I hear it." There was an awkward beat of silence before he looked her directly in the eyes. "And when I see it."

She lifted her glass to her lips and looked toward the band, pretending to study them as if the rhythm had suddenly become fascinating. If she kept her gaze on him one moment longer, she knew she wouldn't be able to stop whatever was brewing between them.

***

By the time they stepped out of the lounge, the sky had gone fully dark, the city alive with Friday night energy. Carson hailed another Uber, but instead of returning to the hotel, he gave the driver the name of a rooftop club nearby.

Inside, the atmosphere changed once more, louder now, packed and electric.

He ordered cocktails at the bar while she searched for a table, the eyes finding them quickly, people noticing him first, then Jamie as he joined her.

"You okay?" He asked.

"Just thinking."

"About?"

Before she could answer, a tall man in a Seahawks hoodie appeared beside him, grinning wide. "Tate? No way, bro. It's been a minute."

Carson looked up, a brief flash of surprise crossing his face. "What's up, Jordan?"

The two hugged before Jordan glanced at Jamie. "This your girl?"

Carson paused, eyes darting toward her. For a second, she caught something in his expression, a pause that said more than words, then he turned back. "This is Jamie. My agent."

Jordan shook her hand, curiosity flickering in his eyes before he went on. "So, what brings you out here? You talking to the team?"

"Yeah," Carson said. "Came out for a private workout."

Jordan's grin widened. "How'd it go?"

"Good, I think. We'll see what happens."

"Bet you killed it," he said, clapping him on the back. "It'd be crazy if we could run it back. Like FSU all over again."

After Jordan walked away, the music deepened, the bass sliding through Jamie's legs and stealing her balance for a moment.

Carson held out his hand. "Come on. Let's dance."

She hesitated, but only for a breath, before their palms met.

On the dance floor, she felt awkward, her body slow to follow the music. She laughed under her breath when she missed the beat entirely, her heel catching as she tried to turn. The corner of his mouth lifted and something in his expression made her acutely aware of herself. Then he stepped closer and pulled her firmly into his hips.

The shift was immediate, her fingers curling into his shoulders as the world narrowed to the space between them.

His touch slid higher along her back, just a few inches, and their eyes locked.

"Not here," she mouthed, shaking her head.

He paused giving her a slight nod, silent understanding flickering there as he took her hand and wove through the crowd.

***

Outside, the music thumped through the club walls, a dull reminder of everything they'd just left behind. He stepped to the curb and raised a thumb for a taxi.

When the cab pulled up, he opened the door for her, waited until she was inside, then slid in beside her. They didn't touch. Didn't speak. She stared out the window, unsure if the space they shared was shrinking or expanding, unsure which she wanted more.

Minutes later, they entered the hotel. The lobby was empty, quiet, save for the concierge behind the desk and a vacuum running somewhere out of sight.

In the elevator, their reflections hovered in the polished metal doors. She caught his eye briefly and looked away before they stepped off onto their floor.

They walked side by side until they reached their rooms.

Then, she turned toward her door and pulled the keycard from her purse, meaning to end the night there. Before she could slide it into the lock, he reached for her and drew her gently back against him.

Her pulse climbed into her throat. The hallway was quiet, empty. There was no one here to see them.

She closed her eyes, waiting, certain he was about to kiss her. Certain she wanted him to.

Then she felt his hand brush her cheek before he leaned down and pressed a kiss to her forehead.

"Good night, Jamie."

She didn't move; didn't speak.

He turned away, slid his key into the door, and disappeared inside.

Chapter 9

The vibration of her phone jolted her awake. For a disoriented second, she couldn't place where she was, the haze of last night's drinks still clouding her head, until memory clicked and she remembered the hotel in Seattle. She reached for it on the nightstand, a knot already coiling in her chest.

A text flashed on the screen from Julia: *Are you awake?*

She sat up and pressed call, her heart racing as her mind went to the worst places.

"Jamie, hey." Julia's voice came through, thin with fatigue.

"Hey. What's going on?"

"I'm sorry," she said. "I didn't want to just text you, but I figured you'd want to know."

"Know what?"

"Leo skipped again. All day. He didn't even try to come up with an excuse."

"What? I didn't get a notification." She put her on speaker, checking her missed calls as Julia went on.

"Well, John did. He showed up here last night, and walked right in like he still lives here, immediately going off on me and Nicole. Asking what kind of environment we're creating, why we aren't paying closer attention."

She scrolled through a short list of missed calls; all spam before she found the one from the school. "Shit," she muttered. "Here it is. I must have silenced my ringer during the workout." She sighed, pinching the bridge of her nose with her fingertips. "So, he blamed you?"

Julia let out a breath. "He said it's because we don't have rules or structure or whatever. Like Leo wouldn't be spiraling if he were at his house. Nicole told him to leave. It got heated."

"I'm sorry. He had no right."

"I'm not worried about us." She paused. "But Leo? He didn't say a word the whole time. Just sat on the couch, staring at the floor. I tried to talk to him after his dad left, but he barely looked at me."

Jamie swallowed the lump in her throat before she spoke. "I should be there," she said. "I'm failing him."

They hung up a few minutes later, and she sat on the edge of the bed, opening her call log again as if it might change: one call from the school, but no voice mail and she hadn't heard it ring.

Or had she?

She tried to remember the day before in pieces. Pike Place crowded and loud, Carson's hand at her back as they moved past vendors and tourists. The jazz bar later, his knees brushing hers under the table. The night club after that, bass thudding through her limbs, her body warm from the cocktails, laughing as he'd pulled her into him on the dance floor.

When she walked into her room last night, she had gone straight to bed. She hadn't looked for a text from Leo or anyone else. She hadn't even made sure he was home.

Her stomach turned. She pushed off the bed and made it to the bathroom just in time, gripping the edge of the toilet as nausea climbed her throat. She didn't know if it was the mix of wine and vodka or the realization settling in, but she bent forward and retched anyway.

When it passed, she stayed there, palms flat against the cool marble, breathing hard. *What kind of mother misses a call from the school and doesn't even notice? What kind of mother chooses a man over checking on her son?*

She closed her eyes, picturing Leo alone in his room, shutting everyone out. How long had he been pulling away while she told herself he was just being a teenager?

After she pulled herself together, she washed her face and brushed her teeth, then picked up her phone again and tapped out a message: *I love you. I'm flying home today. Please text me when you have a minute.*

She stared at it after it had been sent. No typing bubbles. No read receipt.

A new text appeared, this time from Carson. *Coffee downstairs?*

She drew in a slow breath, then typed back: *Be right there.*

***

She rode the elevator down to the hotel lobby, where she spotted him in the cafe, tucked into a corner booth with a mug in hand and another resting on the table opposite him. He looked up as she approached, eyes soft, the hint of a smile waiting for her.

"Morning," he said.

"Morning. Thanks for the coffee." She slid in across from him, making a conscious effort to center herself, to keep her mind off Leo for just a few minutes.

Outside the tall windows, rain drizzled against the glass. The sky was still gray with early light, and the sidewalk beyond the entrance glistened as if it had been soaked for hours.

"They're saying storms all across the Southeast." He nodded toward the television mounted in the corner. "Might be a mess getting home."

She followed his gaze to the radar map littered with red and orange. "Great."

"Everything okay?"

She paused, dragging her eyes away from the TV, and back to her phone; there was still no reply from Leo.

"I don't know," she said. "Something's going on with my son. I just found out this morning he skipped school yesterday. His dad went over last night and made it worse."

"Is that why you keep checking your phone?"

"That obvious?" She asked, setting it aside.

Carson reached across the table and gently closed his hand around hers. "You don't have to tell me everything, but you can trust me."

She held his gaze before she pulled away and glanced toward the other tables, wary of curious eyes. When she looked back, his expression had changed. The hurt in it made her chest ache, a pang of guilt spreading through her as she realized she'd added another wound to a morning already heavy with regret.

"I'm not sure what this is." Her fingers found the rim of the coffee cup, tracing it with a faint tremor. "Whatever this is between us. I don't know what it means yet."

He leaned back, his features hardening, the warmth from a moment earlier replaced by a wall she could almost see him building. "It doesn't have to mean anything."

***

A town car had arrived at the hotel just before noon. Jamie sat beside Carson as it crept along the wet highway toward Sea-Tac, the only sounds between them the tires rumbling and the rain tapping against the window. She kept her eyes on the city slipping past, one hand resting in her lap, the other clutching her phone. No new messages appeared.

He glanced over once or twice but didn't speak. He'd picked up on her mood, clearly, but wasn't pressing. It should have comforted her, the way he gave her space, but instead it only emphasized how distant she felt from him, and from her own sense of control.

When they reached the airport, he tipped the driver before she could argue and took her suitcase from the trunk. She murmured a thank-you, too distracted to push back.

Inside the terminal, they moved through security with minimal conversation. Once through, they stopped at a coffee shop. She ordered an espresso, hoping the bitterness would cut through the fog in her head, while Carson grabbed a bottle of water and a sandwich from the cooler case. Afterward, they found two open seats near the gate, and she sank into one, phone balanced in her palm, its screen lighting up with every irrelevant alert but not the message she was waiting for.

The nearness between them only made her more aware of how far away he seemed. She thought about apologizing, but the words wouldn't come. They'd sound small now. Too little. Too late.

Her phone buzzed with another notification. *Flight 217 to Tampa—delayed. New departure time: 3:40 p.m.*

She showed Carson the screen, and he studied it briefly. "Figures," he said. "There's a lounge upstairs. I've got access. It's quieter. More privacy."

She hesitated. She knew what he was suggesting. Space to talk, a chance to reclaim whatever they'd lost that morning, but she wasn't ready. Her mind was still looping through Leo's behavior and the tension at home.

"I think I'm just going to stay here," she said, trying to keep her tone light. "In case anything changes."

He dipped his chin, almost resigned, his gaze shifting briefly toward the floor before he picked up his bag. "Suit yourself."

Without another word, he turned and walked away.

She stood in the same spot after he disappeared into the crowd, her pulse thrumming in her ears. Eventually, she moved in the opposite direction until she reached the corner of the terminal. A small bar, tucked between a bookstore and a Hudson News, gave her exactly what she needed. Low lighting and anonymity.

She slid onto a stool near the end and set her carry-on at her feet. The bartender, a woman in her early fifties with close-cropped salt-and-pepper hair and silver stud earrings, was wiping down the counter.

"Start you with wine?" She asked, her voice warm.

"Red. House is fine."

She poured a glass and pushed it toward her. "Tough day?"

"You could say that."

She didn't press, stepping away to refill water glasses and check on a couple further down the bar. Jamie took a sip, then another. The wine wasn't good, but it was enough to distract her.

After a few minutes, the bartender returned. "If that's not doing the job, I can pour you something stronger."

She paused, then nodded. "Sure. Why not."

The woman poured a shot of whiskey, and Jamie downed it faster than she had intended to.

***

The next two hours blurred together, boarding calls and the shuffle of travelers rising and falling around her, unnoticed while the liquor warmed her blood, peeling back the person she pretended to be and leaving behind someone she could almost tolerate.

She found herself talking, skipping over Leo, avoiding work entirely, and circling back again and again to Carson.

"He sees me," she said, her chin propped in her hand. "Not as someone's mom or ex-wife. Just me."

The bartender gave a small smile but didn't interrupt.

"It's ridiculous, right? He's so young."

The woman reached for a glass, rinsed it under the tap, then glanced back, a knowing look in her eyes. "Age shouldn't matter as much as people act like it does."

"You're right but still, my family would never accept him. It wouldn't be fair to him to let this play out like it ever had a chance."

"People judge based on their own fears, or what society tells them is acceptable," the woman said, stacking a few clean glasses on the shelf behind her. "Half of them couldn't recognize happiness if it stared them in the face. You're the one who has to wake up with your choices every day. So, the only question worth asking yourself is what makes you feel whole?"

The words echoed in her head longer than she wanted to admit. Maybe she'd been holding onto the idea of who she used to be, clinging to other people's rules because they felt safer than her own choices. For a moment, she allowed herself to wonder, really wonder, what it would be like to stop caring what anyone thought, to choose Carson openly, to believe she could be happy with him. But the idea hardly landed before her fears rose again.

She took another long sip, then shook her head. "He's barely out of diapers, and I'm already raising two kids. I'm not looking for a third."

The bartender's gaze flicked past her, her eyes lifting in brief recognition at something over her shoulder.

Jamie turned, and her breath caught.

Carson stood behind her, his expression cold. "They're boarding. You're about to miss your plane."

She blinked, her stomach bottoming out. "I—just give me a minute to close my tab."

She turned back, unsure what to do with her hands, her body. The bartender gave her a sympathetic look but stayed quiet; there wasn't much to say.

She rifled through her purse for her wallet and set a hundred-dollar bill on the bar, then managed a small, rueful smile. "Sorry for over sharing."

The woman gave a faint nod, a quiet understanding passing between them as Jamie stood and grabbed her carry-on, suddenly aware of how long she'd been sitting there, how warm her face felt. She hadn't eaten anything since breakfast, and the drinks had settled deep in her limbs, making everything slower, fuzzier.

She moved toward the gate, rolling her bag straight over someone's foot, and bumping a woman hard enough to earn a sharp look. "Sorry," she said, not slowing down.

When she reached the front of the boarding line, the attendant hesitated before scanning her pass. "You okay to fly, ma'am?"

Jamie nodded or thought she did. The scanner beeped, and she started down the jet bridge, her pulse louder than the rumble of rolling suitcases.

Carson had already boarded ahead of her and taken the aisle seat. He didn't say a word as she slid past him to the window. She buckled her belt and folded her hands in her lap, looking out. The sky outside was gray, the rain still falling.

***

The plane landed just after midnight, the lights of Tampa lining the perimeter of the runway. Jamie sat stiffly in her seat, her hands folded over a blanket.

She had spent most of the flight in an uneasy drift, her stomach turning from the mix of wine and whiskey still heavy in her system, her mind replaying every careless word.

Three times she'd slipped past Carson to the lavatory, the cramped space spinning as she braced herself against the wall and tried to breathe through the nausea.

Each time she returned to her seat, he kept his eyes forward, earbuds in, like her misery was something she had earned. He hadn't looked at her once since takeoff. The man who had been easy and open the night before felt far away now.

The terminal was mostly empty, the overhead lights dimmed softly. She rolled her suitcase beside her and glanced at him, hoping for a signal that they could reset things once they were home.

"Long day," she said, trying to keep her voice casual, though it felt forced.

He didn't slow down or meet her gaze. "Yeah. I need a shower...and a diaper change."

She stumbled, her body responding to the weight of his words before her mind could catch up.

They kept walking through the echoing corridor, past the closed coffee counters and empty rental car kiosks. When they reached the garage split, he veered right without pausing.

"I'll text you as soon as I hear from Seattle," she called out.

He raised one hand in something like a wave, then disappeared into the shadows beyond the concrete columns, his footsteps fading until there was nothing left but the low drone of ventilation fans and the distant rumble of an arriving airplane.

She stood there for a minute longer, the air heavy with Florida humidity, clinging to her skin. Then she drew in a slow breath and turned toward the rideshare pickup.

<h1 style="text-align:center">Chapter 10</h1>

The next morning, she didn't wake until nearly eleven.

The house was quiet. She sat up slowly, her limbs heavy, her back aching from sleeping in clothes she hadn't bothered to remove. The blinds were drawn just enough to let in harsh slivers of light that cut across the room. For a minute, she simply stared at the lines, trying to remember what day it was.

She reached for her phone on the nightstand. A text from Julia waited on the screen. *Out to brunch. Didn't want to wake you. Love you.*

The phone landed beside her. An exhale followed before she swung her legs over the side of the bed and sat with her elbows resting on her knees. She pressed her fingers into her temples, working against the throb and the accusation rising in it. She should've gone to Leo's room when she got home, should've kissed his forehead and told him she was glad to be back. Instead, she went straight to bed, too consumed with what had passed between her and Carson.

She moved down the hallway, barefoot on the cool wood floors, and paused outside his door. It was mostly closed, but she could hear his voice. She knocked once.

There was no answer.

She eased it open and found him sitting at his desk, the headset snug over his ears. He spoke into the mic, attention locked on the screen in front of him.

"Who are you talking to?"

His fingers clenched around the mouse as he shifted in his chair. "No one you know," he said without looking up.

"Is it Tyler?"

He sighed, his eyes flicking briefly toward her before darting back to the laptop. "No, Mom. It's someone from the game."

She crossed her arms, scanning the mess of soda cans and crumpled papers on his desk. "Can you take a break for a minute?"

He groaned but pulled the headset from his ears, letting it drop around his neck before he leaned back in his chair, turning slightly.

"I just want to talk," she said.

"About what?"

She moved slowly to sit at the foot of his bed, trying to seem calm even as her teeth found the edge of her thumbnail. "Julia told me what happened. That you skipped school Friday. And that your dad came over."

He rolled his eyes and turned back toward the monitor, his fingers hovering over the keyboard. "So, she told you everything. What is there to talk about?"

"She was worried. And so am I."

"Well, I'm fine."

"You missed an entire day, Leo. You haven't told anyone why."

"I didn't feel like going. That's it."

She drew a slow breath. "Leo..."

He turned to face her fully then, frustration flashing in his eyes. "Can you not stand watch over me? Seriously. You disappear for a couple of days and then come home and act like supermom."

She blinked but tried to control her voice. "That's not fair."

"Neither is this," he muttered, standing abruptly, his chair spinning as he shoved it aside.

"Where are you going?"

"Out."

"We haven't even…"

But he was already walking past her. The front door opened and slammed.

She stood in the middle of his room, staring at the monitor, still aglow with shifting light, his chair still spinning. She pressed her fingertips to her eyes, willing the sting behind them to subside, then turned and walked slowly back down the hall toward the kitchen.

A cup of coffee would help her focus.

After she filled the pot with water, she measured out the grounds in automatic movements, the routine just familiar enough to keep her hands busy.

As the machine brewed, she opened the refrigerator for creamer and froze, struck by the disarray inside. Overstuffed shelves packed with leftovers she didn't remember making, takeout boxes wedged wherever they could fit, expired condiments shoved behind a carton of milk.

John's comment from a few weeks ago came rushing back to her: *It's just a house, Jamie. You need to start clearing out all the clutter. No buyer will see past the chaos and make an offer.*

Dragging the trashcan closer to the refrigerator, she nudged it into place with her foot and reached inside, tossing out anything more than a few days old.

Next, she moved to the pantry, not bothering to check what had expired and what had not. She swept boxes and cans from the shelves into piles without much thought. The trash bag filled quickly, and she started another.

Receipts, pens, tangled cords, keys from the junk drawer all landed on the discard pile, followed by a stack of unsorted mail. She handled each item only long enough to know she didn't want it.

***

In her bedroom closet, she paused before her gaze moved slowly across the collection of designer shoes and handbags. A pair of Christian Louboutin heels sat near the front, red soles flashing when she lifted them from the shelf. She recalled the last time she'd worn them: the winter ball John's firm hosted every December.

She could still see him across the ballroom that night, one hand low on the back of a young associate in a silver dress, leaning in too close as the woman laughed. Jamie had stood there in those heels, smiling for his colleagues, telling herself it was networking, that this was how powerful men behaved, that the room turning toward her when she walked past meant she was winning at something.

The resale value of the bags alone, she realized, was enough to cover a new car. Tens of thousands of dollars hanging from brass hooks, collecting dust. And for what? She had never wanted the labels. She had wanted a husband who came home at night.

If he had been a better man, she thought now, Leo would not be walking around angry, skipping school, testing every boundary.

Her fingers bit into the handles and she dragged them all down one by one, chains clattering, dust shaking loose from the shelves. The thought turned her stomach. So much money tied up in labels and a version of herself she barely recognized.

After she had pulled everything down to the floor, her gaze drifted to the island in the center of the closet, where the rest of it waited. If she was going to do this, she would do it completely.

She lifted the diamond earrings from their velvet slot, let the fine gold of a bracelet slip through her fingers. Then, she picked up her engagement ring, staring at it. She thought of the day he'd proposed, his words full of promises.

Her knees gave before she consciously decided to sit, sinking down into the middle of it all, the heel of one shoe pressing into her thigh, a chain digging into her palm.

Fingers clawed at the hardwood, nails scraping against the floor as heat flooded her chest. She tried to breathe but each inhale stopped halfway as if something were pressing down on her ribs.

The front door creaked open. "We're back." Julia's voice floated in, followed by the sound of footsteps. "What is all of this?" she called out from the kitchen.

Silence answered her.

"Jamie?" Footsteps moved farther into the house. "Where are you?"

A beat. Then closer, "Jamie?"

She turned toward her sister slowly, but she couldn't speak. Her mouth opened, then closed again.

Julia moved to her quickly and took her gently by the arms. "Look at me. You're okay. Just breathe with me."

She tried to follow her sister's voice, tried to match the slow inhale Julia demonstrated, but the rhythm wouldn't come.

"It's okay," Julia murmured. "You're doing great. One breath at a time."

Gradually, the pressure behind her ribs eased, and her muscles loosened, the tension dulling just enough for her to register the comfort of her sister's arms around her.

And then the tears came.

"I don't know how to reach him." Her hands clutched at the fabric of Julia's shirt as another sob caught in her throat. "He's pulling away, and I don't know how to stop it."

"You're not losing him. Just breathe. We'll figure it out together."

Nicole appeared in the doorway of the closet, her gaze sweeping over everything scattered across the floor before landing on Jamie. "I know you hate John, but do you really want to throw all this stuff out?"

Jamie shook her head, tears still clinging to her lashes. "I don't want anything built on lies."

"I wouldn't either, but you should at least consider an estate sale."

"Come on," Julia said, helping her to her feet. "Let's not let Prada be the thing that takes you out."

After they made their way to the kitchen, Jamie lowered herself into a chair at the table, while Julia poured a glass of water and pressed it into her hand.

The front door creaked open again, and Leo returned, his brow furrowed as his gaze landed on the trash bags. "What happened?"

Jamie turned away instinctively, wiping at her face with the back of her hand.

"Spring cleaning. Your mom went full tornado," Julia said.

Nicole stepped forward, brushing her hands on her jeans. "I was thinking of heading out for ice cream. Want to come?"

"No thanks. I'm good."

"Leo. Go." Something in Julia's tone carried an authority that left no room for argument.

"Fine," he muttered. "Whatever."

Nicole grabbed her keys before they walked out, the front door closing with a soft click behind them.

The house settled again. Julia pulled out a chair and sat beside her. "I know you," she said gently. "And I know there's something else bothering you. What happened in Seattle?"

Jamie reached for her glass, turning it slowly between her hands as she searched for words. When she spoke, her voice trembled. "It wasn't anything dramatic. But...there was a moment. A few, actually." She paused, taking a sip of water. "Carson sees me. Not like John ever did."

"So, what's stopping you?"

She let out a breath. "Reality. He's twenty-six, Julia. He deserves someone his age, someone without all this baggage. And I...." She cut herself off, shaking her head. "It's impossible. Even if he wanted it too, I couldn't allow myself to believe in it."

"Can I tell you something?" Julia asked, leaning forward. "You say it's impossible, like love is this perfectly timed, age-appropriate transaction. It's not. It's messy and terrifying. None of the noise around you matters if he makes you feel alive. That's the part that's real."

Jamie threaded her fingers through her hair, tugging it tight as her elbows found the table for support. "It's probably too late anyway. I embarrassed myself. I said things I didn't mean, and I don't know how to come back from that."

"Start with the truth. You're human. You panicked. If he sees you the way you say he does, he'll understand that."

She gave a small, tired smile, wiping half-dried tears from her eyes before Julia lifted her chin, then smirked. "You look like you've been living off caffeine and bad decisions. When was the last time you ate something that didn't come out of a to-go container?"

***

Later that night, after Julia and Nicole had gone home, she sat propped up in bed, her back against a stack of pillows, the soft whir of the ceiling fan the only sound in the room. Her laptop rested on her legs, the screen's blue light painting shadows across the comforter.

She opened her inbox and immediately saw it: Seattle Seahawks - Player Interest Follow-Up.

They wanted to schedule a Zoom meeting to discuss Carson. It wasn't a contract, but it was movement.

She went still, the email blurring for a second as her eyes skimmed the same line twice before the meaning settled. If this led somewhere, if Seattle truly wanted him, he might end up across the country. She should be thrilled. Maybe she was. But the idea of losing him to a distant skyline left a hollow ache she couldn't justify.

Her fingers hovered over the keyboard as she opened her contacts and started to draft a message to Carson, but she didn't type. Not yet. She wasn't sure what tone to strike, what he expected to hear from her, or if he expected to hear anything at all.

With a sigh, she shut the laptop, and the room dimmed. She leaned back into the pillows, letting her eyes adjust to the dark.

A moment passed before her phone buzzed against the nightstand, her mother's name appearing on the screen.

She stared at it for a beat, willing it to disappear, then finally picked up. "Hey, Mom."

"Just checking in. Did you get the reminder about your father's birthday this weekend?"

She rubbed her temple with her free hand. "I did."

"Well, cocktail hour starts at six. Please don't be late."

There was a pause. Then, in that airy tone Evelyn used when she wanted to seem polite while still getting her point across, she asked, "So how was your little work trip?"

"My little work trip? How did you know about that?"

"I spoke to John yesterday. He told me you went to Seattle and left Leo with Julia and that girlfriend of hers."

She sat up straighter, heat crawling into her cheeks. "Her name is Nicole, Mom. And she's Julia's wife, not her girlfriend."

"What's the difference? Why didn't you ask John to look after Leo? He would've made sure he was at school. And why would you go across the country while he's going through such a difficult time?"

She closed her eyes, exhaling through her nose. "It's my job, Mother. I have to work. And I suppose you think John is innocent in all of this."

"He wanted to be a family, Jamie. The least you could've done was let Leo get through school and off to college before creating all this disruption. I worry you're doing irreparable damage."

A clinking noise came through the receiver. Ice against glass, the unmistakable stir of a drink being mixed. She imagined her mother in the kitchen, assembling her nightly vodka tonic.

"And what about me and Julia?"

Evelyn's voice, when it returned, cut deeper with the brittle hardness she often wore after a few sips. "What about you and Julia?"

"Do you think you did any irreparable damage to either one of us?"

"You and your sister had the best of everything because of what I sacrificed. Don't forget that." She spoke as if she were reciting lines she'd delivered too many times before, full of pride and entirely devoid of self-reflection.

Jamie let out a bitter laugh, though there was no humor in it. "You wouldn't let me forget it even if I tried. Look, Mom, it's been a long weekend. I'm exhausted and I don't want to fight with you. I'll see you Saturday."

She hung up without saying goodbye and let the phone fall beside her. Then she lay back against the pillows, staring at the ceiling.

The room felt smaller somehow, the air thicker. Her mother's words lingered in the quiet. *Irreparable damage.*

And then, another voice slipped into the silence.

You think it's too late, but it isn't. What if you're exactly where you need to be to start again?

Start again. How?

Chapter 11

The elevator doors slid shut, and Jamie leaned back against the mirrored wall, adjusting the collar of her blazer. Her reflection looked composed enough, but her eyes told the truth her posture tried to hide, heavy with exhaustion that came from more than sleep loss.

The elevator chimed, and she stepped onto the floor, moving quickly through the bullpen. She caught a nod here, a glance there, followed by the subtle drop of conversation as she walked by. Nothing felt overt, just muted enough to make her wonder if she was imagining it or...*had someone seen her and Carson in Seattle? Had a photo surfaced somewhere she hadn't thought to check?* She remembered the way his hand had found her waist in that nightclub, how easily her body had leaned into his. Anyone could've seen them. What if someone had?

As she neared her cubicle, Steve stepped out of his office, his gaze locking on hers with a knowing glint. The smirk that followed made her pulse hitch. "Hey rookie, heard about Seattle," he said, his tone barbed.

Before she could ask what he meant, a voice called from across the bullpen. "Jamie." David stood in his doorway, thumb hooked in his pocket. "You got a minute?"

She glanced back toward Steve, catching an expression that made her stomach flip.

Her mind jumped straight to an HR email with her name in the subject line, David sliding a termination package across his desk, Steve watching her pack up her desk with that same smirk.

She forced a nod, grabbed a notepad, and walked across the floor, her legs suddenly heavier than they should've been.

After he closed the door behind them, he moved to the far side of his desk, thumbing the corner of a folder.

"Mark from the Seahawks wants to schedule a Zoom with you and Carson," he said, glancing up at her. "He called this morning and asked to get something on the books later this week. They're interested, but they want a face-to-face before making anything official."

Relief loosened her shoulders, followed quickly by a flush of heat creeping up her neck at having assumed the worst.

"Okay. Yeah. He emailed me too."

He finally sat down and shook his mouse, bringing his laptop to life. "Also, set up a meeting with VibeWell. They're a branding firm here in Tampa." After he clicked on something, he jotted a name and number on a post it note and handed it to her. "Let's start shaping his brand, get ahead of it before the media or anyone else starts circling."

She managed a smile. "Got it."

"And Jamie—," David said, barely looking up from his computer screen. "Good work."

***

The VibeWell office occupied a converted warehouse near Tampa's Channelside District, with exposed brick and matte black metalwork that looked curated for an Instagram story.

Jamie took it in as she and Carson stepped through the glass doors. The air inside smelled of white tea and sandalwood, a scent that reminded her of the Ritz. Everything about the place screamed modern...*young*.

She forced herself to breathe.

"You okay?" Carson's voice was light, almost teasing.

"I'm fine." Smoothing her skirt, she let her gaze travel the room. "It's...trendy. I think I'm too old to use the word 'vibe' seriously."

He chuckled. "Everybody's got a vibe. Even you."

Her stomach fluttered, wondering what he meant by that. Was it an offhand compliment, or an insult?

The receptionist, a young brunette with oversized glasses, looked up twice as Carson finished signing in, her grin widening the moment her eyes landed on him. "Mr. Tate? Follow me."

Jamie's skin prickled with an awareness she couldn't quite identify as she fell into step behind them. She hated that she noticed every gaze cast his way, and how her presence seemed like an afterthought.

She led them into a glass-walled conference room with sleek chairs and a long blonde-wood table where a young woman, late twenties, probably, stood waiting, already smiling. She had shiny hair that swung when she turned, and the easy confidence of someone used to getting her way.

"Carson," she said, extending a hand. "I'm Kendall. I've been looking forward to this."

Her handshake lingered a second too long, and her gaze didn't waver.

Jamie interrupted, introducing herself. "Jamie Sinclair. I'm Carson's agent."

"Of course. Nice to meet you," she said, flashing her a smile that lacked warmth.

Her tablet sat ready, queued with a sleek, animated presentation. She launched into her pitch, adjusting the angle of the screen with a practiced flick. "As you know, we're a branding firm. But not just any branding firm. What sets VibeWell apart is how we highlight the entire journey. Setbacks, comebacks, and everything in between. Our audience responds to that honesty. It's not only about image. It's about connection."

She paused, glancing briefly at Carson before continuing. "I lead athlete partnerships, so I work with talent from the start, developing their narrative and making sure it lands the right way."

Carson leaned forward slightly, his forearms on the table, watching her with a look of quiet attention.

"Our work is especially valuable during career pivots, free agency, rehab comebacks, or shifting from the field to the media world."

She swiped to a slide with looping b-roll of athletes training and community footage. "We're a full-service strategy team, curating partnerships and producing short-form content for our clients. We also negotiate social-first campaigns and align with nonprofit causes they care about. If you want to launch your own personal podcast, we can help. Everything's built to scale."

She was magnetic in a way that made Jamie's skin crawl, hitting all the right buzzwords and touching his arm as she emphasized a point.

Worse, Jamie caught how Carson's eyes held Kendall's, and the curve of his mouth. Maybe she was imagining it. She told herself not to read into it. He was charming by nature. He wasn't doing anything wrong. Still, when he smiled at her, she felt a twist low in her stomach.

"We've seen huge success with campaigns that lean into that comeback narrative," Kendall said, swiping to a slide with more looping footage. "But what we're finding now is that Gen Z and millennials crave something even more unfiltered. The messier truth. That authentic vibe really resonates."

She smiled at him, then tossed her hair. "Not everyone from, say, the 'email generation' gets it, but you clearly do."

Jamie froze. Kendall's comment was smooth. Casual. A throwaway that landed like a punch.

When Carson chuckled softly, missing the subtext entirely, her jaw tensed, the urge to retaliate, to call it out for what it was, curling low and hot inside her. But she forced a smile instead. "We'll want to review the licensing language closely. Carson's story isn't merely a brand angle. It's personal."

He shot Jamie a look—curious, possibly even amused—and that only made it worse.

"Of course. We'll loop in legal once the initial terms are approved," Kendall said, waving a hand, her confidence never slipping.

And then she went right back to Carson.

***

By the time the meeting wrapped, Jamie had stopped trying to count how many times Kendall had touched Carson's arm. Each one chipped away at her focus and left her spine rigid.

She stood to her feet handing him a folder and her card, her gaze never drifting far from his. "Text me if you have any questions. Even off the clock."

Carson pocketed the card without comment, and the receptionist returned to walk them out, still smiling brightly.

Jamie didn't say a word. Her pulse pressed against her throat, her thoughts racing all the way to the parking garage.

"You okay?" He asked, his voice low as he caught up beside her.

"Fine." Her response was fast. She didn't look at him.

He slowed his pace when they reached her car. "You didn't say much after the pitch."

"It was solid." She opened the door, clipping her words short. "I'll follow up with her legal team."

"That's all?"

She finally looked up at him. He held himself still, his eyes searching hers, intent.

She wished she had the nerve to call Kendall out, to say what they both knew. That the woman had spent half the meeting flirting under the guise of strategy.

"You need to keep your relationship with her professional," she said. "The optics matter."

He chuckled. "Is that your motherly advice?" He asked, holding her gaze, unblinking. "Because I wouldn't want to burden you with another child to manage."

That stopped her. She wanted to tell him that he was being unfair, and that this had nothing to do with anything that had happened between them. But instead, she glared at him a moment and shut the door.

As she pulled away, she glanced in the rearview mirror and caught a final glimpse of him. He hadn't moved and his eyes held something that looked like hurt. She didn't understand why; she wasn't anything to him. She couldn't be.

***

When she pulled into the driveway, she turned off the engine but didn't move, her hands still resting on the steering wheel as the quiet settled around her. After a moment, she exhaled and stepped out of the car, closing the door softly behind her before heading inside.

She toed off her heels and crossed to the kitchen, every movement mechanical.

The wine bottle on the island had already been opened the night before, and she poured a glass before leaning against the counter, watching the clock on the stove tick forward minute by minute.

She couldn't stop replaying the meeting. Kendall's voice, the way Carson smiled at her. It was all too much. It shouldn't matter. She didn't have a claim on him. But something about Kendall looking at him and ignoring her burrowed in deep.

She was young, beautiful, easy in her body in a way Jamie had never been in hers. She probably had no kids, no stretch marks. Exactly the type of woman who made sense next to Carson. Not her.

He had his whole life ahead of him. And her? She came with history. An ex-husband. A teenage son who barely spoke to her and parents who hadn't stopped being disappointed since the divorce.

Besides, she couldn't compete with women like Kendall. She didn't want to. She'd already played this game before, watching John chase youth, and ignore the life they'd built in favor of someone with tighter skin and fewer opinions.

The front door opened a few seconds later, and she heard Leo's footsteps before she saw him. He moved quickly, barely glancing in her direction—a flash of his hoodie as he passed through the entryway and headed straight down the hall. His door clicked shut, followed by the distinct sound of a lock turning.

Her jaw clenched. She padded toward his room in her bare feet, pausing outside before knocking once. "Leo, we need to talk."

She waited, listening for movement on the other side of the door.

"I'm not upset," she said, her voice softer now. "I just want to know what's going on with you."

She counted to ten, then sighed.

After she stepped away, she returned to the kitchen, pulling a box of mac and cheese from the pantry. Then hot dogs and a bag of shredded cheese from the fridge. Comfort food she used to make when Leo was small.

By the time she was done, the smell filled the house. She plated a serving for him, covered it with foil, and left it on the counter before she returned to his door and knocked. "I made mac and cheese. The way you like it."

"I'm not hungry." His voice wasn't angry. It was hollow.

She leaned against the wall, her shoulder brushing the doorframe. "Okay."

After a beat, she slid down to sit on the floor, knees tucked to her chest.

"You used to hang out in the kitchen with me while it cooked." She paused. "You were five, or six. You'd climb up on the counter and ask a million questions about everything. I remember you asked me if hot dogs had feelings once. I couldn't answer without laughing."

There was nothing from the other side, but she kept talking.

"You were so curious. About everything. You trusted me with all your questions, even the weird ones. And now I can barely get a word out of you."

She swiped at her eye with the sleeve of her sweater. "You're going through something. And I don't need you to be okay. I just want to know how to show up for you."

Another beat of silence. Then, from the other side of the door, a low, strained: "I don't know."

Her breath caught. "That's okay. You don't have to. But you don't have to figure it out alone, either."

She stayed there a little longer, listening to the stillness before she stood and pressed her hand gently to the door. "I'm here. Whenever you're ready."

Chapter 12

Carson arrived early, stepping into the glass-walled conference room in a fitted button-down and dark jeans.

"Hey," she said, standing from her chair at the far end of the table.

He inclined his head, not quite meeting her eyes. "We starting soon?"

"Five minutes," she said, checking the time on her watch.

He took a seat, arms crossed, while she connected her laptop to the projector. The image cast across the screen was grainy at first, and her hands shook as she adjusted the window size.

When the waiting room pinged, she sat up straighter. "Ready?"

He didn't move, just dipped his chin once.

She clicked join and two faces appeared. Mark, wearing a Seahawks polo, and beside him, a younger man in the same shirt.

"Carson, Ms. Sinclair, good to see you again," Mark said. "This is Kyle Brennan, assistant director of pro personnel."

Jamie nodded, offering a brief acknowledgement while Carson leaned forward, gaze fixed on the screen.

"Appreciate you both making time. We wanted to follow up after the workout and talk next steps." He lifted his reading glasses, resting them atop his head as he continued. "We were really encouraged by what we saw in Seattle. You've kept yourself in great shape."

"Thanks," Carson said.

"We've got a crowded receiver room heading into camp. But we're looking for guys who can contribute on offense and special teams. Versatility's key." His tone was brisk and practiced, as if he'd delivered that line a hundred times before.

"What kind of reps would he be competing for?"

Mark and Kyle exchanged a glance.

"Not a projected starter," Mark said. "Depth right now, but he'd have a chance to compete for a spot. Likely special teams early." He leaned back in his chair, crossing his arms before he went on. "As I mentioned, your workout confirmed what we hoped. But with the injury history, some hesitation is natural. We're one of the few teams still looking to add depth before camp, and there's a window here." He paused. Then: "How's the knee?"

"Good."

"Glad to hear it. Before we can move forward, we'll need the medicals. Updated records from your orthopedist and a recent MRI."

Carson nodded. "No problem. I'll get it sent over."

Kyle shifted slightly, glancing at something out of frame, clearing his throat first, the tone turning more transactional. "Here's what we're thinking. We'd like to bring you in for our offseason program with phase two and the veteran minicamp. If that goes well, we'd roll it into OTAs and potentially training camp."

Jamie recognized the role he played here. The numbers guy who seemed to see players as data points instead of people.

"One-year vet minimum," he said. "Standard split if you go on IR: 1 .185 million. No guarantees. But if you make the final fifty-three, there's a seventy-five-k bonus. Plus escalators if you hit certain snap thresholds."

She leaned back in her seat, thinking about that. *Escalators.* Incentives triggered by offensive snaps, a reward system built on risk. The more he played, the more he earned. Simple. Brutal. Fair, if you didn't think about how quickly a body could break. But would it be enough if he got hurt again?

She wanted to argue for more, but she knew better than to push too soon.

"Thanks for laying that out," she said. "We'll review and circle back."

Mark's expression warmed as he leaned forward. "You've still got juice, man. Come in ready. That room's tight but not locked."

The call ended, the window collapsing into a grid of empty boxes before disappearing, and the room settled again, with only the soft whir of the air conditioner filling the space between them.

Carson leaned forward, pressing his palms to his face, dragging them down slowly. "That's it?"

He pushed back from the table so abruptly that the chair legs scraped against the floor, pacing once, twice, before Jamie thought of something to say. "I'm going to send a counter." She pulled her laptop closer. "Push the roster bonus higher."

"They think I'm a risk."

She looked up. He stood still, arms crossed, his stare fixed on her. "What do you think?" he asked.

She opened her mouth, but nothing came. She knew what she wanted to say: *I think you can do better. Keep fighting.* But reason pressed back harder. No one else was calling. A wide receiver's window closed fast, and she couldn't risk giving him hope that wasn't real.

His jaw clenched, his eyes breaking away for a beat before finding hers again. "You not answering says everything."

She blinked. "Carson, I..."

He shook his head once and stepped away before she could finish. The door opened, then closed with a soft click. The air conditioner kicked on again, stirring the stillness.

She stared at the empty space, the question still hanging there, thin as smoke.

After a long moment, she drafted a new message, attached Carson's reel, and sent it to a Buccaneers scouting assistant she'd met through David at last year's charity gala, someone she trusted for a quiet look.

She kept the note brief, professional, but her pulse quickened as she hit send. Logic told her it probably wouldn't matter, that teams made up their minds weeks ago. But part of her refused to believe this was the best he could get. If there was even a small chance of something better, she had to try.

***

Saturday evening came quickly, and the house on Bayshore Boulevard looked as it always did, its white columns bathed in uplighting, hedges trimmed to perfection, everything in its place. Even from the driveway, a familiar weight settled in her chest.

Over the bay, dark clouds were gathering.

She drew a breath and stepped through the front doors, where chandeliers threw golden light across polished marble floors. Near the staircase, a string quartet played softly, their music weaving beneath the murmur of conversation and the clink of glasses. Leo walked at her side, while Ava had gone in ahead of them and was already greeting her grandparents.

Richard Maddox, Jamie's father, tall and silver-haired, wore a tailored navy suit without a single wrinkle. His smile was controlled, the same expression he'd carried into every courtroom.

Her mother, beside him, was radiant in a golden-colored gown, her hair in waves, a pearl necklace at her throat. She held a glass of champagne in one hand, the other fluttering as she greeted guests.

Jamie made her way to them, planting a quick kiss on her father's cheek. "Happy birthday, Dad."

"Jamie," he said, his voice smooth yet distant. "Thanks for coming."

His expression softened as he turned to Leo. "There's my grandson." He pulled him into a brief hug. "You keeping your mom out of trouble?"

Evelyn laughed lightly, setting her glass aside to kiss Leo's cheek. "You've grown again," she said. "And so handsome, too."

Before Jamie could step back, movement caught her eye. John walked in wearing a charcoal suit that fit him better than she remembered, the jacket tailored to his broad shoulders, his dark tie sleek against a crisp white shirt.

She hadn't noticed until now how he'd lost a little weight, how the sharp lines of his face and his trim physique showed a man who'd quietly gotten back into shape after the divorce. For a fleeting second, she thought he looked almost like he did on their wedding night. Infuriatingly handsome. She swallowed hard, forcing the notion away.

"Who invited him?" She asked under her breath.

"I did," Evelyn said. "He's still a part of this family."

Jamie turned to her, incredulous. "Where's his girlfriend? Did you invite her too?"

"They broke up. He didn't tell you?" Her mother's eyes widened, feigning surprise. "You know, Jamie...you'll always be the only woman he loves."

Before John reached them, Ava stepped closer, her tone dry. "He sure has a funny way of showing it." Then, without waiting for a response, she slipped into the crowd.

Jamie wished she could walk away too, but she exhaled slowly, steeling herself as he approached.

Richard greeted him warmly, clapping him on the back. Evelyn followed, wrapping her arms around him with genuine affection, her laughter light and delighted, warmer than any greeting they'd given Jamie.

"Hey, slugger," he said, pulling Leo into a hug.

He reached for her next, but she pulled away, meeting his eyes without a word.

"Ava still won't talk to me?" he asked, looking past them toward his daughter.

Evelyn offered a silvery laugh, linking her arm through his. "You know how young girls are these days. So full of opinions. She'll come around. Just give her time."

The words scraped against Jamie's nerves. If this weren't her father's birthday party, she would've told her mother exactly how wrong she was. How John's affair had hurt their children more than anyone. But instead, she swallowed her thoughts, pivoted on her heel, and walked to the bar.

She ordered a shot of whiskey, craving the warmth and something tangible to hold.

"Jamie?" A voice chimed behind her, familiar in the way of childhood birthday parties and forced greetings.

She turned to find Virginia Eaton, one of her mother's oldest friends, standing with a flute of sparkling rosé and a predatory smile. "You look wonderful, darling," she said, leaning in for an air kiss, her perfume something floral and suffocating. "How's your career going...what do you call it again? Athlete manager?"

"Sports agent."

"Ah yes," she said with a wave of her hand. "That's such an unusual path for a woman, isn't it? But good for you. Reinventing yourself at this stage takes courage."

"I don't think of it as reinvention. But it beats spending my days gossiping over lunch and pretending tennis counts as exercise," Jamie said, fingers curling into her palms.

Virginia blinked once before her smile reassembled. "Well, I suppose we all find fulfillment in our own ways."

"Exactly," Jamie said, turning back to the bar.

After a pause long enough to sting, Virginia drifted off in search of someone easier to impress.

Across the room, her father stood with John, caught in easy conversation, laughing over something, before he clapped him on the shoulder.

It was surreal, how quickly her family had folded him back in, as if nothing had happened. As if he hadn't broken the foundation of everything she'd tried to hold together.

"Hey," a voice said beside her.

She turned to see Ava, arms crossed. "You good?"

"Peachy."

"You don't have to pretend with me."

"I know." She paused, taking another long sip of the whiskey. "It's like I'm watching someone else's life. Like I slipped out of the frame, and nobody noticed."

Ava followed her eyes to the other side of the room where Richard was laughing at something John said. "They're acting as if he's the golden boy."

"He always was." She finished the rest of her whiskey, then gestured to the bartender for another.

"You know, you don't have to stay."

"I do. It's your grandfather's birthday."

"That doesn't mean you have to sit through it like a hostage."

Jamie let out a humorless laugh, holding the fresh shot of whiskey between her fingers. "I'm not sure they'd notice either way."

"I would," Ava said, bumping her shoulder. "And you should take it easy on those."

She lowered the glass to the bar and placed her right hand over her heart. "My last one. I swear."

Ava gave her a look but nodded.

As the string quartet changed songs, the conversation dipped, and a server stepped through the open archway to announce dinner.

Jamie stared at the shot for a moment, wanting it then, pushing it away before she followed the others.

The dining room shimmered under candlelight, each flame catching crystal. Everything was immaculate, from the aligned silverware to the folded napkins that resembled sculpture more than cloth.

She sat between Ava and Leo, across from John. Richard took his place at the head of the table, while Evelyn stood beside him, raising her champagne flute.

"If I could have everyone's attention," she said, beaming. "Tonight, we celebrate Richard's seventieth birthday. A man of uncommon brilliance, strength, and vision. The best partner I could've ever asked for."

Jamie lifted her glass with the rest, something sour rising in her throat. Her mother's praise rang empty. She remembered the nights Evelyn had come home from charity galas and firm banquets with red eyes, slipping off her heels in the dark.

She had been ten the first time she saw her mother cry in the kitchen, a stiff drink trembling in her hand after one of her father's affairs became too obvious to ignore. Yet here she was, toasting him like nothing had ever fractured between them. Perhaps that was what strength looked like in this family. Perfect smiles over buried wounds.

"To Richard," she said, raising her glass higher. "And to having everyone together again."

She sat beside her husband, her expression self-satisfied as the clinking of glasses faded. For a beat, no one spoke, and thunder rolled outside, closer now.

"We're not all here," Jamie said, glaring at Evelyn, eyes stinging.

Her mother blinked, smile wavering, but before she could respond, Richard cut in. "Let's not get into that." His tone made it clear; the topic was closed.

Then, as if the moment hadn't happened at all, he turned toward John. "How's business these days?"

John leaned back, relaxed. "Good. Very good, actually. We just finalized a new acquisition last week. A fintech startup out of Miami."

Richard nodded. "Always a step ahead. You've got a sharp eye for growth."

Jamie looked down at her plate, then slowly lifted her head. "Are you going to ask how my job's progressing? You know, since I'm your daughter."

A few heads turned before he glanced at her. His mouth didn't move, but a muscle in his jaw clenched. "Alright," he said. "How's work?"

She smoothed her napkin across her lap. "Busy. One of my clients just got an offer from Seattle. Carson Tate. You might have heard of him. Florida State alum. He set records there."

His eyes flickered with something mysterious. There a second and gone the next. But she caught it, unsure if she'd imagined it before a flash of lightning cut across the windows, followed by a crack of thunder that shook the chandelier.

The room stilled for a moment then conversation resumed, forks clattering louder than before. She lowered her eyes.

After a few minutes, she folded her napkin with care and turned to Ava. "Can you get Leo home for me?"

Leo frowned. "Where are you going?"

"Somewhere I don't have to prove I belong."

She stood, drawing a slow breath and glancing at her parents. "Enjoy your evening. You already have everything you want at this table."

Her father didn't speak. His eyes lifted to meet hers, but his face remained still.

"Don't," Evelyn said, her voice low. "Let's not make this into something it doesn't have to be."

Jamie glared at her, the words she wanted to say on the tip of her tongue. That pretending doesn't resolve anything. That silence only keeps the cracks from showing. But she swallowed them, pushed her chair in, and walked out.

***

The drive had blurred into brake lights stretching along the highway and rain streaking sideways across her windshield, the painted lines wavering in and out of focus. She'd thought about going to Julia's, even a bar to drink it away. But she kept driving in circles until she ended up here, outside a doorway that felt both strange and familiar.

Her hand hovered near the door when lightning flared in the distance, a low roll of thunder snapping her back to herself. "What am I doing here?"

She'd told herself she needed to stop drifting through the city like a ghost, but now that she was here, it seemed reckless. She didn't even know what she planned to say.

A soft click broke the silence, followed by the slow turn of a latch. The door eased open, and Carson stepped onto the stoop. He was barefoot, the waistband of his sweatpants resting low on his hips, his chest bare. The sight of him, so close she could almost feel the heat of his skin, sent a quick pulse through her.

"Sinclair?" His voice, caught between surprise and concern, barely carried over the rain.

She swallowed hard. "I'm sorry. I shouldn't have come."

She turned and stepped back toward her car, but he stopped her. "You're here now. Just say what you came to say."

Her nails dug into her palm, a small bite of pain holding her together while she searched for the words. "You didn't give me a chance to answer your question."

He gave her a puzzled expression, brows drawing close before she continued. "After the meeting, when you asked me what I think."

He held her gaze, every muscle taut with restraint. She couldn't tell if it was anger or something else entirely before she pushed on. "I think about you constantly. I'm proud of everything you've done, and I believe in everything you're still going to do. And I've been so afraid of the way people see me, of what it would mean to admit how much I care for you. But I can't keep pretending it doesn't matter. Because it does. You do. More than I ever expected."

His jaw flexed, gaze flicking past her, enough to make something drop low in her stomach. He was pulling away. She knew it.

"Oh my God," she said, shaking her head. "I'm a fool. I thought...never mind. Clearly, I've made a mistake." She turned, moving toward her car again, humiliation burning in her chest.

Before she reached the end of the walkway, his hand caught hers pulling her back against him, his breath brushing her ear when he spoke. "You finished convincing yourself I don't want you?" His fingers dug in slightly, keeping her still. "You have no idea."

He exhaled softly, as if something inside him had just given way. "I've been trying not to make things worse for you. But you showing up here..." He shook his head as if he were fighting with himself over what to say. "It's all I've wanted."

A flash of lightning split the sky, followed by a rolling crack of thunder that vibrated through the air. The rain came harder now, a furious rush that soaked through her clothes in seconds.

He leaned down slowly, his eyes never leaving hers, and kissed her, softly at first, then deeper. The downpour streamed between them, cold against her skin, the taste of it mixing with the heat of his mouth.

Suddenly, her world tilted as he scooped her up, his arms strong.

Inside, the scent of the rain gave way to his. Soap. Cedarwood. Something that belonged only to him. And she let herself sink into it.

When he finally pulled back, his voice was a low rasp. "Are you sure?"

A breath caught in her throat, a rush of warmth blooming so fast it left her lightheaded. "Yes."

He carried her toward the bedroom. At the threshold, he set her down gently, his fingers brushing her shoulder, finding the zipper of her dress and tugging it loose. It pooled on the floor, and he stepped back, his eyes intent and tender in a way that felt almost unbearable. He was taking her in, all of her, his expression telling her more than words ever could.

He reached for her, his mouth trailing down her neck to her breast, a rough sound escaping him as he kissed her there.

She didn't pull away. Her hands stayed on him, moved on him, tracing the length of his back, the curve of his hips.

He lifted her again and she felt the strength beneath her palms as he pressed her against the wall, their bodies meeting with a quiet gasp.

Then, he stopped, his eyes lifting to hers, and for a moment neither of them moved, the look on his face stealing the breath from her lungs.

She knew this would undo her. She did it anyway.

Chapter 13

Pancakes sizzled on the griddle, the scent of vanilla and cinnamon filling the house. She whispered a tune to herself as she flipped one over, smiling at the thought of surprising Leo. Then came the quick patter of small feet, and he burst into the kitchen. Messy hair. Wide grin. And younger. Much younger.

For a second, everything was simple again, his laughter echoing through the house until an abrupt noise split the air, jarring and out of place.

Her eyes flew open. The ceiling was too low. The blinds were different. A deep, even breath reached her ears. The slow exhale of someone sleeping beside her. She turned and saw Carson. The sight of his bare chest and his face softened in sleep sent a wave of clarity through her.

Another loud bang startled her, and he stirred next to her, but she sat up first, blinking toward the door.

A third knock followed. "Carson, are you awake?" Came a strange voice.

He muttered, half-asleep, "Damn. It's too early for this."

He swung his legs out of bed and reached for a pair of sweats.

"Who is that?" she whispered.

"Pamela."

"Who's Pamela?"

"My mother."

"What? She's here? Now?" Jamie asked, heart jumping.

A hint of a grin tugged at his mouth. "You want me to introduce you?"

"Carson, this isn't funny."

He chuckled softly and shook his head. "Relax. She won't stay long."

She clutched the sheet to her chest as he left the room.

Through the door, she heard the soft click of the lock, then Carson's voice. "Morning, Ma."

"Morning? It's almost eleven. You look tired."

"I was up late."

Mortified, she slipped out of bed and snatched her dress from the floor, the fabric wrinkled and still soaked from the night before.

In the small mirror across the bedroom, her reflection stopped her cold. Her hair had dried in stiff, flattened ridges where she'd slept on it, the ends kinked into stiff little zigzags and the roots puffed up in random tufts, giving her the startled look of a cartoon character who'd just run into a wall. She pressed her fingers to her neck and felt her pulse hammering beneath her skin. There was no way she could walk out like this.

Her eyes darted around the room, looking for something—anything—she could put on. She moved to his closet and stepped inside, where his clothes hung in neat rows. After pulling a sweatshirt from the top shelf, she dragged it over her head, the sleeves hanging past her hands. Her gaze snagged on a baseball cap tucked beside a stack of folded jeans. She grabbed it, shoved her hair back as best she could, and pulled the cap low, tugging the brim down and twisting it slightly until the worst of the damage was hidden.

"You didn't answer my text," Pamela said.

"I was sleeping."

His mother's voice carried down the hall, bright, already halfway into a lecture. "I made steak and roasted potatoes. Brussels sprouts too. And banana bread, since you clearly don't feed yourself properly." .

"I eat fine."

"Sure you do. Protein shakes and boiled eggs. That's not food."

Jamie caught the sound of bags rustling while Pamela kept talking, asking if he'd decided to accept Seattle's offer and whether he'd followed up with the physical therapist like he promised. She mentioned a new sermon series at church, the grocery store being out of his favorite ice-cream again, and how the city needed to fix the potholes on her street before someone broke an axle.

"I won't stay long," she said eventually. "I just wanted to see your face."

"You saw me two days ago."

"And?"

Jamie couldn't help smiling. His mother reminded her of herself, strong-willed and worried, trying to hold together more than anyone realized.

The front door opened. "I'm making dinner Thursday night. You should invite that agent of yours over so we can properly thank her for all she's done. What's her name again?"

"Jamie."

Jamie flinched at the mention of it. Pamela had no idea she was down the hall, barefoot and stiff in her son's clothes. The thought of the look on her face if she stepped into his room and found her there made her stomach dip. What the hell had she been thinking?

"Eat the Brussels sprouts first. They don't keep."

"I got it."

The front door closed, and Jamie waited until she heard the lock turn before walking out of the bedroom.

He looked her over, taking in the sight of his sweatshirt hanging loose on her frame, hem brushing her thighs. A slow smile tugged at his mouth. "I think I like that hoodie a lot more now."

"Carson..."

"Stop," he said, before she could say more. "I know what you're thinking, but this wasn't a mistake."

She swallowed, the words barely clearing her throat. "It's impossible."

Silence stretched between them as she closed her eyes. When she opened them again, his expression had shifted, hurt etched into every line of his face.

"I have no idea what to do with this. You..." She dragged her hands over her face, exhaling. "You're my client. I have a daughter who's not much younger than you, and my ex-husband would have a field day."

"I'm not asking you to blow up your life. But don't pretend like this didn't happen. Don't act like it didn't matter."

She glanced down, then back up at him. "It mattered more than I wanted it to. That's the problem."

He didn't move at first. He just looked at her, really looked at her, as though he was deciding what she needed more than what he wanted. Then he stepped forward and gently wrapped his arms around her.

***

She couldn't go home; not when she didn't know what waited for her there. Ava had already texted and called a million times, asking where she was, and her mother had phoned twice. The thought of facing either of them made her stomach knot.

She'd driven straight to her sister's, and when Julia opened the door, the concern was immediate. "What in the world are you wearing?"

"It isn't mine."

"Clearly," she said, raising a brow. "Come in. I'll find something that fits. There's fresh coffee if you want some."

She moved to the counter, grabbed a mug from the drying rack, and poured herself a cup.

When Julia returned to the kitchen with a t-shirt and leggings her gaze shifted to the baseball cap. "You planning to rob a bank later, or is that a new look?"

Her hand went for the brim, but Jamie caught it midair. "Don't."

She let out a breath then peeled it off.

For half a second, it looked like Julia tried to bite her tongue. Then she burst out laughing. "Oh my God. You look like Effie Trinket on a bad hair day."

"Shut up."

"I'm serious. All you need is a pastel suit."

She dragged a hand through the mess and winced before Julia disappeared again, returning this time with a brush and a hair tie. "Sit. We'll triage."

Jamie sunk onto the couch, clutching the clothes in her lap.

"Ava's been calling since last night. She said she was worried when you didn't come home."

"I turned my phone off. I just needed some space."

"I get it," Julia said, stepping behind her with the brush and working it carefully through the snarls before twisting it into a messy bun. "But maybe check in before Ava starts texting me at two in the morning next time."

She gave the bun a final tug, then set the brush on the end table. "There. No more Effie Trinket."

Circling around the couch, she dropped down beside her and nudged her knee. "Presentable. Mostly. Now, are you going to tell me what happened or do I have to pry it out of you?"

"John showed up last night. Mom and Dad wouldn't stop fawning over him." She paused, picking at a loose strand at her temple. "I lost it."

Julia's lips pressed together in a thin line as if to say she'd already guessed as much, but she didn't interrupt.

"They act like he's their son and I'm the ex-daughter-in-law they wish would fade out of the picture. I guess I should be grateful they even invited me."

"They've always treated him like that. You're not crazy for seeing it," Julia said. "They still want the version of you who smiled next to John at holiday dinners and didn't ask for more."

"That version doesn't exist anymore."

"Good. She was boring. Now tell me where you were all night."

Her thumb drifted to her mouth, teeth bearing down on the edge of her nail.

"Jamie?"

"It wasn't planned," she said. "We just..." She stopped, shaking her head.

"Oh, thank God," Julia said, turning toward her fully and tucking her knees beneath her hips like a schoolgirl settling in for a secret. "I was so close to signing you up for one of those vibrator subscriptions."

"Seriously? Do those even exist?"

Julia blinked at her. "Of course. It's called Buzz of the Month."

"You're kidding."

"I'm not." Julia's mouth twitched. "I'd already picked out your first delivery."

Jamie narrowed her eyes. "That's aggressive."

Julia lifted a brow, completely unrepentant. "What's aggressive is how long you went without sex." She leaned forward, closer. "So...how was it? I mean, seriously. Was it like...ruin-you-for-other-men good?"

"You're impossible."

"I'm your sister. I get to ask."

She groaned, pressing her face into her hands. "God. What am I doing? This is crazy."

"Why are you spiraling?"

"Because this is reckless. I don't want to screw up his career or be a reason he gets judged."

"I think the only person doing the judging right now is you."

Jamie huffed out a tired laugh. "Don't psychoanalyze me before I finish my coffee."

"Please," Julia said, rolling her eyes. "There isn't a shrink in the world who could untangle the twisted corners of your mind."

A throw pillow sailed across the couch in response. "You're such an ass."

They laughed, the sound still hanging in the air when Julia's face shifted, amusement giving way to something more serious. "Was that a car door?"

"What are you talking about?"

"Someone's here," Julia said walking toward the kitchen window. "Shit. It's Ava."

Jamie's stomach dropped. She glanced down at herself, still in Carson's hoodie. Without thinking, she slipped it off and hurried into the clothes Julia had given her before shoving it beneath the couch cushion.

"She's probably furious, Jamie."

"I know. I'll talk to her."

Julia gave her a small nod, moving toward the door. "Brace yourself."

She opened it before Ava could knock. Dressed in jeans and a sweat-shirt, with her hair pulled into a high pony, she looked like she'd left the house in a hurry.

Her glare fixed on Jamie. "Where have you been?" she asked, stepping inside without waiting for an invitation. Her voice cracked halfway through the sentence. "I called you, like, ten times."

"My phone died," Jamie said, standing from the couch.

She folded her arms, still glaring. "Oh my God. What are you, twelve? You sound like Leo."

"Ava, take a breath. She's alive," Julia said, closing the door behind her.

But she ignored her aunt, her eyes staying on Jamie. "Do you have any idea how worried we were? I almost called the police."

"You're right to be upset," Jamie said, her voice thin. "I should've come home. I scared you. I'm sorry."

"Then where were you?"

The room went still while Ava waited.

"Were you with him? The football guy?"

She opened her mouth, searching for something, anything, that wouldn't shatter the moment. But Julia stepped in before she could speak. "She was with me."

Ava blinked, thrown off her momentum. "You told me you didn't know where she was."

"Well, I lied," she said with a small, crooked grin. "That's what siblings do. Haven't you ever lied for Leo?"

Her arms stayed crossed, but her expression began to soften. "I mean...yeah. But...I don't understand why you wouldn't just tell me."

Then, a realization seemed to flicker across her face. "You're mad at me for staying, aren't you?" she asked. "I should've left with you."

Jamie's breath caught. "Ava, no..."

Julia stepped in again. "Remember sophomore year? When you got caught sneaking out? You picked up your friends and drove across town to meet those boys." Her tone didn't waver. "On the way back, you got pulled over. You were sure we were all disappointed in you, and you didn't come out of your room for two days." She tipped her head slightly. "Multiply that feeling by a hundred. Your mom just needed to get away."

Jamie shot Julia a quick glance, a silent warning, but Julia met her eyes with one of her own. One that seemed to say, *just trust me.*

"I'm not disappointed in you, Mom. I'm proud of you." Ava stepped forward, wrapping her arms around her, and Jamie froze.

A quiet, shaky breath slipped against Ava's hair, relief loosening every muscle as she sank into the embrace. Over her shoulder, Julia caught Jamie's eye and offered an exaggerated thumbs-up before Ava pulled back, eyes shining.

After she left, Jamie returned to the couch and reached beneath the cushion, pulling the hoodie back into her lap.

"Well," Julia said from the kitchen. "That went better than the time she threatened to legally emancipate herself over a C in Algebra." She picked up two muffins, tossing one to Jamie. "Next time you go off the grid, give me a heads-up so I can at least get our alibi straight before she shows up ready to ground both of us."

Chapter 14

Late Thursday afternoon, Jamie pulled up to a small home on Hanna Avenue. The houses in the neighborhood were modest, the vibe warm and welcoming. A man sat on his front steps talking to the woman next door perched on her swing. Down the street, a group of kids tossed a football between parked cars, their laughter carrying through the humid air.

It stood out as the sort of place where everyone knew each other's names, where a front terrace seemed to invite community instead of anonymity. She took it all in, struck by how different it was from any neighborhood she had ever lived in.

Her hands rested on the steering wheel before she shut the engine off. She inhaled slowly, counted to four, and reminded herself she was only here to meet Carson's family. That was all this was.

He was already on the porch, one hip against the rail, in jeans and a T-shirt. He straightened when she got out, and the easy warmth in his eyes sent a small rush through her that she tried to hide.

From next door, the man on the steps called out with a grin. "She's way too fine for you, Carson!"

Laughter broke out between the houses before he shot back. "Careful old man. Your wife's gonna make you sleep on the couch again."

His smirk gave away the joke, and laughter rippled between them once more before she crossed the short walkway and climbed the steps.

"Hey." He dipped closer than necessary, with a crooked smile. "You look nice."

"Behave, your mother's right inside," she said under her breath, a warning threaded with a beam she couldn't help.

"She can't fire me." His fingers brushed the small of her back, and he led her across the threshold into the house.

She froze for a beat, feeling exposed, like every thought in her head, every charged memory of Carson's mouth on her skin, might somehow show on her face. Pamela would see right through her.

"You okay?" He asked.

She nodded, though something clenched low in her belly. "I just don't want to say the wrong thing."

"She doesn't bite," he said, chuckling.

She followed him into the kitchen, where his mother stood in front of the stove, apron tied at her waist, a wooden spoon in one hand and a skillet sizzling under the vent fan.

"Ma, this is Jamie."

Pamela gave her a once-over, assessing. She had strong features, with high cheekbones and deep-set eyes that seemed to catch everything.

"I'm so glad you could come," she said wiping her hands on her apron before extending one in greeting. "Carson's told us you've been working hard for him."

Jamie smiled and reached out, her palm slightly damp, the nerves impossible to hide. "It's nice to meet you, Mrs. Tate."

"Call me Pam," she said without missing a beat. "Dinner's almost ready." She turned back to the stove, picking up a knife. A pile of scallions waited on the counter, and she began slicing them like she'd done it a thousand times.

Carson and Jamie stepped into a living room that showed life. A crocheted blanket stretched across the couch and romance novels lined a bookshelf. On a wall in front of the staircase, family photos formed a staggered arrangement.

"Ma, do you need help with anything?"

"Set the table. And don't you put the forks upside down again."

He glanced at Jamie and whispered in a stage voice. "She runs an inspection line."

"I heard that," Pam said from the kitchen.

Jamie's laugh escaped before she could hold it.

She followed Carson to the dining room, where he handed her a stack of plates. She set them down one by one around the table as he came behind her with the silverware, close enough that she could sense the heat of his body at her back.

Suddenly, a girl, not much younger than Leo, appeared from the hallway wearing a T-shirt from a high school theater production and jeans. "So, you're Sinclair," she said, regarding her with disbelief, as if trying to match the woman in front of her with whatever picture she'd imagined from Carson's stories. "You don't look like a sports agent."

"Don't start," Carson groaned. "Jamie, this is my little sister, Mia."

Mia raised an eyebrow, her tone flat but her mouth curving slightly. "That was supposed to be a compliment." She shook Jamie's hand and turned to her brother. "You buying the ice tonight or am I using my savings again?"

"For what?" he asked.

"Sweet tea. Mom forgot to fill the ice tray, as usual. Also, salad mix. And..." She looked toward the kitchen, her voice carrying. "What else, Ma?"

Pam called back. "Cornbread batter and the good hot sauce, not that watered-down stuff." She stepped into the doorway, drying her hands. "Would you mind running to the store?"

"Jamie and I can go," he said, already reaching for his keys.

"No, she stays here. Take your sister." Her tone left no room for argument. "And you're not buying candy, Mia. Get the list."

Mia plucked a scrap of paper from the counter and waved. "Come on, superstar."

"You sure you'll be okay?" Carson asked.

"I'm fine. Go, before your mother adds more."

He grinned at that and grazed her waist with his hand in a gesture so brief it could have passed for nothing. Then they were out the door, voices fading down the porch steps, the house settling around her.

She moved back to the wall of photos. The arrangement told a story in dates and shoulders. Carson in a South Tampa Titans jersey, then high school. Next to that, Florida State and then Miami. Different uniforms, the same determined gaze. But it was a wedding photo that threw her off. A small boy, two or three, stood in front of Pam. Beside them was a man, short and stout, smiling proudly. Carson looked nothing like him.

Pam came back carrying two glasses of water, her eyes following Jamie's to the frames. "That was the day Marcus and I got married." She handed a glass to Jamie before she continued. "Carson was three years old."

Jamie turned, slightly unsure if she should say anything.

"I had Carson when I was twenty-three," Pam said. "His blood father's family...well, I'll just put it this way...they didn't approve. And that's putting it nicely. They were wealthy. When he chose me, they cut him off. And after a while, that was too much for him." She gave a small shrug, as if trying to make something heavy sound lighter than it was.

"Marcus came along a few years later. He loved Carson like his own. Gave him his name."

Jamie nodded slowly. "He must've been a good man."

"The best." She let out a quiet breath, smiling. "He taught my son to be one too. To treat people with respect. More than he ever received himself."

"What happened to him?"

"He got hurt down at the docks. Machinery failure. He couldn't work after that, and he never walked the same again." She exhaled, gaze going distant. "After a while, his health declined. He believed he was a burden. That he'd failed me, failed the kids. Maybe that's what really broke him in the end."

The truth of it landed hard. Carson had grown up watching what happened when a man's dignity was taken from him. She finally understood the relentless drive she saw in him, how he pushed through pain as if quitting would undo everything he had built. It was survival.

The warmth drained from Pam's face completely, replaced by something hard. "If he'd gotten the settlement he deserved, he wouldn't have felt like that. But his company's insurance carrier hired some big-shot attorney who fought us every step of the way." Her jaw flexed. "I'll never forget that man's name. Richard Maddox."

She went still, her pulse kicking as everything around her seemed to narrow. *Did she hear her right?*

"Richard Maddox?" She asked, her voice shaking.

"Yes. Do you know him?"

She shook her head, forcing her expression to stay even, hoping Pam wouldn't see the realization taking hold. How intertwined their lives really were. How Carson's pain and her own family's privilege were all bound together in ways she could never have imagined.

But Pam noticed, her brows drawing close, concern softening her features. "Is everything okay, dear? You look like you've seen a ghost."

"I just remembered," Jamie said, scrambling for composure. "I forgot to finalize a contract. I really need to get back to the office."

She gathered her purse and thanked Pam for the invitation, promising they'd talk soon.

Outside, the afternoon light had dimmed; the air was thicker now with the scent of rain on the way. As she stepped down from the porch, the man next door was still on his steps, arms resting on his knees.

He called out with a teasing grin. "Why you in such a hurry?"

"Deadlines," she said, forcing a smile, waving before sliding behind the wheel. He chuckled, but she barely noticed him, her mind already spinning back to the name she'd heard inside the house.

***

The wipers squeaked across her windshield as she turned onto Florida Avenue, the air in the car too warm, her thoughts too loud. She replayed every word Pam had said, and every image that came with it. The photo on the wall, Marcus's smile, the bitterness in her voice when she mentioned his name.

Richard Maddox. Her father. Heat crept up her neck as the traffic lights blurred red and green ahead.

She tried to summon some distance, to remember if he had ever talked about the case. Perhaps at a dinner party, or one of those nights when he bragged about the firm's big wins. Nothing specific came back, only the tone, the smug pride.

And then she remembered the night of his birthday. The expression that had crossed his face when she'd said Carson's name. She had brushed it off, thought he simply didn't care about her work. But now she knew better.

Suddenly, the dashboard lit with a call: *City of Tampa Police Department.*

Her heart lurched before she tapped the screen to answer. "Hello?"

"Ms. Sinclair?" A measured voice. "This is Officer Ramirez with Tampa Police. Is Leo Sinclair your son?"

She gripped the steering wheel hard, knuckles going white. "Yes. Is he okay?"

"He's safe," the officer said. "We picked him up at a house party after a neighbor called in a noise complaint. He was drinking. No one was hurt but we need a parent to come pick him up. He's at the district station on North Armenia. Do you know where that is?"

"Yes." The word scraped out. "Can you put him on the phone?"

A rustle, then Leo's voice, smaller than usual. "Mom?"

She closed her eyes, holding back everything she wanted to say. "I'm on my way. Don't argue with anyone. Do you hear me?"

"Yeah."

"I'll be there in ten minutes."

***

By the time she pulled into the lot beside the station, her nerves had congealed into something cold and dense. She parked, took a breath, and got out.

Inside, the fluorescent lights buzzed overhead as she gave her name to the officer at the front desk. The woman behind the glass offered a tired nod and gestured toward a long corridor. "He's with his father."

Jamie blinked. "John's here?"

"Arrived about ten minutes ago."

Of course, he had.

The hallway felt too narrow as she walked it, her shoes echoing off the tile. At the end, a plain room with metal chairs and a table came into view. Through the glass, she saw John standing near the far wall, arms folded across his chest. Leo sat slumped in a chair, his hoodie pulled low over his face. He didn't look up.

A uniformed officer opened the door, then stepped aside before John acknowledged her. "Took you long enough."

"I came as soon as I got the call."

Leo didn't move, and Jamie crossed the room, kneeling next to him. "Hey."

His eyes flicked toward her, glassy and red-rimmed. "I'm fine."

"You're not."

John cut in. "He was over in East Tampa, at a party. The cops found half a dozen kids with open bottles. He admitted to drinking when they questioned him."

"Why were you at a party like that?" she asked.

He shrugged, his voice dull. "I don't know. Everyone was going."

She looked over at John, who was watching her with a pointed expression. "I'll take him home."

"No," he said, his tone flat. "He's coming with me."

She blinked. "What?"

He glanced toward Leo, then stepped into the hallway, nodding for her to follow. Out of earshot, his voice dropped, smooth and controlled, the tone of a man rehearsing righteousness. "You're never around anymore. Always flying off to God knows where with that hotshot. Carson, isn't it? You make it awfully hard for anyone to believe your family still matters."

Jamie's pulse thudded in her ears. "I left him once, John. And he wasn't alone. Julia and Nicole were there."

The corner of his mouth lifted slowly, deliberately, like he was indulging her. "Come on. They don't have kids. They don't know the first thing about raising a teenager who's falling apart. You don't either, not really. You've been too busy chasing validation."

"This isn't about me," she said, throat tight.

"Oh, but it always is." His eyes gleamed as if he enjoyed saying it. "You want to pretend it's all Leo acting out. This family's been off the rails since the divorce because you wanted freedom. Now you're flying across the country for a guy you barely know."

She stiffened. "You're guilting me for working? You travel constantly."

"This isn't work. Don't insult me. If he were just a client, you wouldn't be making him more important than your son."

"What exactly are you implying?"

He tilted his head, eyes narrowing with smug amusement. "I'm not implying anything. I'm telling you what everyone else already sees." He stepped closer, lowering his voice. "You can lie to me all you want, Jamie. But you should think about what you're doing. What message it sends. To Leo. To Ava. Hell, to Carson. You've made yourself the story again."

She didn't respond. Her body had gone rigid.

"Everything alright here?"

An officer approached. He looked familiar. Mike Andrews had known their family for years, coached Leo's Little League team when he was seven.

"Hey, Mike."

He glanced between them. "I could hear the two of you talking from the front desk, so I wanted to make sure everything was okay."

"Of course. We're fine. Just worried parents, you know how it is," John said, his voice smooth and affable, the sudden ease of it making her stomach twist.

Andrews raised a brow but didn't push. "Leo was with a kid named Tyler tonight. Tyler Reed. You heard of him?"

She nodded slowly, the name all too familiar.

"Kid's been on our radar a while now. Not the type of crowd you want Leo running with. If he were my son, I'd keep him far away."

"Thank you for telling me," she said.

He gave a small nod. "You two take care, alright?"

Then he disappeared down the hall, John's mask slipping as soon as he was gone. "You know this Tyler kid he's talking about, and you didn't tell me?"

"I don't know him, John. Ava found him in Leo's text messages when we were trying to figure out where he was."

"What do you mean?"

"He skipped school. I couldn't find him."

"So, he skipped school twice?"

She peered down at the ground, chewing her thumbnail.

"Jesus, Jamie." He sighed, as if exhausted by her. "I'm taking him with me. At least until you find a new place. We got an offer on the house today. A good one."

"You're really bringing that up right now?"

"It's relevant. You wanted the divorce. This is what it looks like."

When she and John stepped back into the room, Leo didn't lift his eyes. She kneeled beside him, placing a hand on his knee, aiming for calm. "Hey...you're going to stay with your dad for a little while."

He rose from his chair without a word, slow and heavy-limbed, then walked out of the room like he had no say in the matter at all.

John paused in the doorway as she stepped aside, carrying the smugness of a man offering mercy he didn't possess. "You still have a chance to fix this. If you want to."

Her jaw locked as she stared past him, unwilling to speak. The audacity of him. *You still have a chance to fix this,* like he hadn't been the one to break it in the first place. But she said nothing. Not in front of Leo. He'd been through enough.

Chapter 15

Streetlights cut through the windows as she unlocked the door and stepped inside. She dropped her keys on the island and stood still, listening. It was completely silent. No video game noise. No sound of a ballgame drifting from the television. Just stillness that told her what she already knew. Leo wasn't here, and he wasn't coming home.

Her phone buzzed on the counter, lighting the kitchen for a heartbeat. Carson: *Are you okay? Why did you leave?*

She stared at the message, thumb hovering over it, but her hand wouldn't move. What could she possibly say? How could she tell him any of it? She couldn't even face it herself.

She turned the phone screen down and pushed it away from her. Whatever she said would have to wait. The truth was too raw. Too tangled to touch.

Moving out of the kitchen and into the hallway, her foot caught on something and she stumbled.

"Shit."

She flipped the light switch, her eyes landing on the donation piles stacked against the wall. She'd meant to finish sorting them, to take them to the local church, but hadn't found the time.

John's voice rose in her mind, uninvited. *Someone made an offer on the house.*

The words had been circling ever since, pushing her toward the one thing she had avoided. She needed to start packing.

She walked into the garage, pulled down a few flattened cardboard boxes from the attic, and carried them back inside. Then she opened the kitchen drawer and removed a black marker, setting it on the counter beside an unopened bottle of wine.

Running a thumb over the label, she thought: *When had drinking alone stopped feeling strange?* She couldn't remember.

The thought came and went before she reached for the corkscrew. The pop echoed through the house, and she poured a glass, took a long drink, and set it down beside the boxes waiting to be filled.

***

By the time she'd finished organizing and boxing the things she planned to give away she had finished the bottle of wine and opened another.

She moved slower now, sorting through drawers, pulling out keepsakes she hadn't touched in years: a folded card in Leo's uneven handwriting, a seashell Ava had painted pink at Clearwater Beach. At the bottom of an old trunk, she found photo albums she'd forgotten about.

She set one on the counter and flipped it open. There she was, more than a decade earlier, smiling at a man she didn't recognize anymore. Leo on his shoulders, Ava with a mouth full of birthday cake. She traced one of the photos with her finger before she shut the album and stacked it on top of the others, telling herself to keep moving.

As she labeled another box, the marker trembled, dragging a crooked line across the cardboard before slipping from her hand. It hit the floor and rolled beneath the counter. When she bent to pick it up, her elbow caught the edge of the wine glass, the spill spreading from one end of the island to the other, red against the white quartz.

Something in her buckled. She moved before she could stop herself, reaching for the glass and hurling it through the kitchen. It shattered against the cabinets, fragments scattering on the hardwood. The bottle followed, striking low and bursting, wine spreading in every direction. She watched it run beneath the refrigerator, a dark spill that would be impossible to scrub clean.

Her knees gave out, and she slid down to the floor. For a few seconds she could only breathe in short, uneven bursts. Then the tears came, and she didn't fight them.

***

Hours later, when she woke, her cheek was pressed against the hardwood. The air was cold, and her head throbbed. Morning light spread across the kitchen, creeping toward the cabinets where the bottle had shattered. Red stains darkened the lower panels, glass glittering beneath them.

She pushed herself upright slowly. For a moment, she stared at it all, trying to piece together how it had happened, the smell of it hanging thick in the air.

Her phone still sat face down on the island where she'd left it. She reached for it. Another text from Carson waited on the screen, but she didn't open it.

In the bathroom, she brushed her teeth and swallowed two pills for the headache, then turned on the shower. The water was too hot, but she stood under it anyway, letting it beat against her skin until the steam blurred the mirror. When she stepped out, she wrapped a towel around herself and walked into her closet, where her eyes caught on the suitcase she hadn't touched since Seattle.

Then the idea landed. She would get away. Just for a few days. Maybe longer.

She pulled it out, crossed to the dresser, and began to pack, not knowing where she was going yet, only that she couldn't stay here in a house—in a city—that reminded her of everything she was losing.

***

She refused to look back when she left.

Four lanes opened ahead and her car moved north on I-75, steady in the middle lane. Only the tires broke the cabin's quiet, a low, unwavering noise that filled the space.

Signs began to mark distance: Brooksville, then Ocala. She read them without reaction, her eyes fixed on the horizon where the road met the sky. The highway looked endless, its surface shifting from silver to pale gray as the sun climbed.

Somewhere before Gainesville, she thought about stopping. She could text Ava, ask if she wanted breakfast, pretend this drive was something normal. The idea held long enough to picture them at a table near a window, her daughter's expression uncertain. Confusion first. Then disappointment.

She pressed her foot lightly on the gas and stayed in her lane as the exit sign came and went, Gainesville drifting by to her right, unseen behind trees.

An hour later, the *Welcome to Georgia* sign passed in her peripheral vision, white letters on blue and a giant peach. She clocked the miles and knew they weren't putting enough space between her and what she couldn't face.

Small towns slipped by in quick succession. Valdosta, Tifton, the names barely registering before another appeared. She told herself to stop at the next exit, then told herself again before the fuel light turned on, giving her no choice.

At a station with two pumps and a faded canopy, she filled the tank, bought a coffee that tasted of the paper cup, and returned to her vehicle.

Back on the highway, it cooled beside her, untouched. Atlanta's buildings rose, glass faces catching sunlight, cranes pointing at the next thing to be made. The pace shifted mile by mile, held by merges and exits that braided together in ways only locals understood.

Traffic slowed and opened again as she stayed north. The lanes narrowed through a stretch of construction, orange barrels marking the edges. Once past, the road widened.

She thought about turning west toward Birmingham or east to the Carolinas, but she kept straight until the city fell away behind her, the skyline giving way to trees and open sky again.

As she neared Marietta, a green sign caught her eye: *Zell Miller Mountain Parkway*. Below it, a smaller brown one read: *Apple Orchards & Scenic Overlook*.

She hesitated, fingers loose on the wheel, then turned the blinker on and took the exit. The noise of traffic faded until only the engine remained, and her breathing slowed for the first time all day.

The land lifted in quiet, wooded folds as she stayed on the new highway curving gently toward the foothills. Far ahead, the Blue Ridge Mountains rolled into view in long, rounded swells, blue at the base and fading lighter as they rose. They filled the windshield, slowly, until the horizon disappeared behind them. She hadn't been driving toward anything, and yet she found herself here, staring at something that felt chosen instead of accidental.

Fences appeared and fell away, while hand-painted boards promised apples and hot pies. The shoulders narrowed, patched in places, the asphalt a record of small repairs.

As she eased around a long bend, she saw hazard lights ahead, blinking on the right. A silver sedan sat angled off the shoulder, nose dipped into a shallow ditch. A dog with the sharp-eared look of a wolf, looped near the trunk in anxious circles, its solid white coat catching what little light remained.

She pulled well behind the car and set her own flashers. When she opened her door, it trotted toward her, tail wagging, stopping just out of reach, its blue eyes fixed on hers.

A male dog, she realized. And a very protective one.

"Hey," she said, keeping her voice even. She lowered her hand and let him choose. He stepped forward and pressed his nose to her fingers, then turned and looked at the sedan as if to ask her to follow.

The driver's door was open. Inside, a woman sat upright with both hands on the wheel, a shallow cut traced along her forehead. Her gaze moved slowly from the windshield to Jamie and back again.

"Are you okay? Can you hear me?" Jamie asked.

"Yes," she said after a breath. "I drove off the road. I didn't mean..." She stopped there and looked down at the dash as if it might explain something.

Jamie reached inside. "I'm going to help you get out. Take it easy."

The seat belt was slack. "I'm Jamie," she said, pressing the release and guiding the strap clear so it wouldn't catch. "What's your name?"

The woman shifted her weight, turned her legs toward the open door, and set her feet on the ground. "Mae."

Jamie offered an arm, and she took it, standing, a little unsteady but upright. The dog circled and sat at her side.

They stepped back from the car. The ditch was shallow, and a few shards of plastic glittered near the front tire where a reflector had cracked.

"He's gonna kill me," Mae said.

"Who?"

"Hy husband."

"My bet is that he'll be glad you're ok."

"Thanks for stopping." She touched the line on her forehead and checked her fingers. "I guess my head's a little off."

"Let's get you to a hospital. Do you know where the nearest one is?"

Mae looked up the highway and gestured vaguely toward the hills. "North, about ten miles."

Jamie nodded and walked her to the passenger side of her car. "Can you sit? Slowly."

Mae eased into the seat, pulling the belt across her lap while the dog stood with his paws on the door frame, waiting for permission.

"What's his name?"

"Jasper."

Jamie opened the back door and patted the seat. "Come on, Jasper. Back here."

He climbed in, turned once, and settled with his nose pushed between the front seats, watching.

After she slid behind the wheel, she pressed the navigation icon on the dash, the map opening, then freezing on a blank field. No service. She tried again and got the same spinning symbol before Mae let out a chuckle that sounded more like recognition than humor.

"You're not in the city anymore."

Jamie looked over. "That obvious?"

"Take this a mile or two," she said, pointing ahead. "When you see the grocery store on the left, turn right at the light. Stay on that road until you hit a four-way. Go straight. The hospital sits back a bit." She held her hand flat and moved it to the right. "You'll see a water tower near it."

After Jamie repeated the steps out loud to set them in her head, she checked the mirror and pulled onto the highway, bringing the car up to speed.

"Were you heading into town?" she asked.

"The feed store. And another stop for a pie. I reckon I was thinking about it instead of the road. That's on me." She paused. "Thank you for stopping."

"Of course."

The grocery store appeared on the left, a long building with a metal roof and stacks of wood under a covered walk. Jamie turned right at the light and followed the two-lane road that climbed and fell in easy grades.

They reached the four-way as a pickup rolled up from the left and waved them on. Far ahead, a pale tower rose over a cluster of trees.

"That's it."

She pulled in and drove up the lane lined with crepe myrtles not yet in bloom. The hospital was modest: a single story spread wide, with ambulances parked near a bay to one side. She stopped under the covered drop-off and turned to Mae. "I'll walk you in."

Inside, cool air met them, smelling of disinfectant and coffee. A clerk at the desk looked up. Jamie gave Mae's name, but everyone there already knew who she was.

Mae explained she'd run off the road, that she had a small cut, and was a bit dazed, but fine other than that. The clerk told her they'd be the judge of that and asked her to sign a few forms before a nurse appeared, calling her back.

"You can go," Mae said, clipboard still in hand. "You've done enough. Someone here will call my husband."

"I'll wait outside and keep an eye on Jasper until he gets here."

Mae looked up. "Oh dear, I forgot about Jasper," she said, then smiled. "Thank you."

Jamie stepped through the sliding doors and returned to the car. The dog had shifted to the driver's side, nose near the window, ears pricked. She opened the back door to check him and gave him a quick scratch behind one ear before he settled again, eyes on the entrance.

After she moved to a parking spot, she watched the automatic doors open and close, counting the small procession of arrivals.

She opened her browser and tried the map again. Service returned in a thin bar. The screen loaded slowly, finally filling in with roads and names. She marked the hospital location and typed: *hotels near me*. A short list appeared, most of them small motels spread along the main road. It was dusk, and she knew she needed to find a place to stay for the night. She could figure out the rest once she'd slept.

An older man pulled into the parking lot, his truck idling a few spaces away. Jasper barked from the back seat, eager, and she figured he must be Mae's husband.

She got out, opened the door, and the dog leapt down, racing toward him. He crouched to catch his collar, then looked up at her.

"Are you Mae's husband?" Jamie asked.

"That's right. You're the one who helped her?"

She nodded. "She's alright, but she has a little cut on her head," she said, extending a hand. "I'm Jamie."

"Elzie. It's nice to meet you. Thank you for stopping to help her. I swear that woman's gonna be the death of me. I've been telling her for weeks she needs to go back to the eye doctor. Stubborn as a mule."

She smiled. "I should get going. I need to find a hotel before it gets too late."

He raised an eyebrow. "You're not from around here?"

"No," she said. "Just passing through."

"Well," he said, shaking his head. "I'm not about to let the woman who saved my wife stay in one of those roadside motels. We've got a spare room at the house. It's not much, but it's clean. You're welcome to it if you don't mind Jasper."

She hesitated, looking past him toward the line of trees at the edge of the lot. The idea of staying with strangers should have given her pause, but there was something easy in the way he spoke to her, the same kindness Mae had shown. It felt foreign, nothing like the strained courtesy she had grown up with, or the distance people kept in the city.

"Not at all," she said finally. "I love dogs."

Chapter 16

The sound of water rushing over rocks somewhere below the cabin woke her.

For a moment she lay still and listened, struck by the difference. At home, mornings carried the sound of boats moving through the channel and seagulls crying outside her bedroom window. Here, they carried the river.

The night before, she had fallen asleep to cicadas loud enough to drown it out. She hadn't heard it then. Now it filled the quiet.

Above her, beams stretched the length of the ceiling, their edges softened by age. Honey-colored pine paneled the walls and the air smelled of old timber, a chill slipping up through the floorboards.

The quilt she had tucked under her chin looked hand-stitched, the seams uneven, its pattern built from scraps someone once cared enough to save.

Jasper sat near the foot of the bed, his bright blue eyes studying her without judgement.

"Making sure I didn't run off?"

He lifted a paw and touched the bed, letting out a soft whine.

"You take your job seriously."

After she reached toward the nightstand for her phone, the screen lit up, but the service bar stayed empty. Anyone who might've tried to reach her while she drove north would be worried by now, and draw their own conclusions.

A slight weight settled against her ribs. She set the phone down, and Jasper jumped up beside her, tail wagging.

"I'm coming," she told him, swinging her legs over the side of the bed.

The floor was cool beneath her bare feet. Muscles along her back and shoulders protested when she stood, the ache from too many hours in the car finally announcing itself now that she had slept hard enough to let it.

She opened her suitcase, removed a pair of jeans and stepped into them, then pulled a sweatshirt over her head.

Jasper padded ahead of her into the hallway, nails clicking on the wood as she followed the smell of coffee and something cooking in butter.

Elzie stood at the stove in a flannel shirt and worn jeans, turning eggs in a cast-iron pan. A stack of toast waited on a plate near his elbow. He glanced over when she stepped into the kitchen, then down at Jasper, who had trotted straight to a worn spot on the floor by the back door.

"Well, look at that," he said. "You've got a new best friend. If he could talk, I bet he'd ask if you're staying another night."

Heat rose under her skin. "Sorry I slept so late."

"You're fine. There's fresh coffee. The mugs are there." He nodded toward a row of mismatched cups hanging on hooks above the counter.

The kitchen was small, cabinets painted a soft blue, counters clean but cluttered with the sort of things people actually used. The window over the sink faced a stand of trees, their branches thick with new leaves against a pale sky.

She walked to the coffeepot, found an empty mug with a faded orange stripe, and filled it halfway. The first sip was hot enough to sting her tongue, and for a second, she focused only on that sensation, the way the warmth slid down her throat.

Footsteps shuffled in the hallway behind her.

Mae entered wearing pajamas and a robe, her hair dragged back into a loose knot. The bruise along her temple was darker today, edging toward purple, and she moved with care, but her smile came easily when she saw Jamie.

"Morning. You find everything okay?"

"Yes. Thank you again for letting me stay."

"Least we could do. You didn't leave us on the side of the road. That deserves a bed and a shower."

Elzie slid scrambled eggs and toast onto three plates and set them on the table. "Sit down before this gets cold."

Jamie took the chair closest to the wall, and Mae lowered herself into the one across from her with a small exhale, reaching for the jelly.

"I'm going over to drag your car out of that ditch," Elzie said, picking up his fork. "Tow it home before somebody decides it's abandoned and calls it in."

"Good. When you get back, I need to run to the pharmacy and the feed store. Jasper's food is low, and the doc gave me a prescription for ointment."

Elzie shook his head. "You, my dear, are not getting behind the wheel again until a doctor says you can and you've got a new set of glasses." His tone was firm, but he reached over and touched his fingers lightly to her wrist. "You're not invincible."

She made a face. "I never said I was."

He leaned in and pressed a quick kiss to her hairline before returning to his eggs.

It became clear to Jamie how easy they were with one another. Just two people who had moved around each other in the same kitchen for years, used to the small routine of fussing and accepting it.

"I can take you," she said. "To the pharmacy. The feed store. Wherever you need."

Mae looked up. "Are you sure?"

"I don't have anywhere I need to be this morning." That was true in more ways than she wanted to unpack at the table. "I'd like to help."

"Well, if you're offering, I won't turn it down."

Elzie nodded once in approval. "That works. Roads down to town are straightforward."

They ate, taking their time. The eggs were soft, and the toast buttered to the crusts. It had been a while since breakfast had felt like something other than grabbing a granola bar on her way out the door or eating alone while scrolling through emails.

When the plates were mostly empty, Jamie stood and carried hers to the sink.

"Just leave it," Mae said. "You're on driving duty. That's enough."

She rinsed the plate anyway and set it in the basin. After she stepped back into the guest room to grab her purse, she picked up her phone again. The screen woke to the same blank signal bar.

She tried sending a quick text to Ava: *I'm okay. Will explain when I get somewhere I can call home.*

The message hung for a second, then failed, as an alert flashed: low battery. She plugged it up, leaving it on the nightstand before meeting Mae on the front porch.

***

The drive down was narrow, the mountain dropping away on one side, and trees banding the other while sunlight filtered through bare branches, flashing across the windshield.

Jamie kept her speed modest, taking in the stretch of road and the houses scattered along the hillside. It was beautiful in a way that felt almost unfair.

She glanced at the mailboxes and driveways, the quiet signs of ordinary life, and found herself wondering how people made a living here.

"What do people do here?" she asked. "For work, I mean."

Mae didn't hesitate. "There's plenty of work around here. The poultry plant down the road employs a lot of folks. The apple orchards are seasonal, but they provide a living for some. Others commute or run shops downtown."

Jamie nodded, realizing none of it intersected with contracts or negotiations. Her career lived in cities, in glass towers and conference rooms, moving from one deal to the next without much pause. Whatever held this place together didn't need someone like her.

Mae gave a huff, following Jamie's gaze. "A lot of those places don't belong to people who live here anymore. They're short-term rentals." She waved a hand. "That's a conversation for another day."

As they came into town, they passed a wooden sign set back from the road:

WELCOME TO FRIENDSHIP, Established 1894...*A Good Place to Call Home*

Main Street opened up in front of them, paved in worn cobblestone. Older storefronts lined both sides, their brick and clapboard faces painted in black and warm creams.

Wide windows caught the morning light, displays neat and intentional rather than showy, while streetlamps ran the length of the block, each one hung with baskets of flowers spilling over in bright reds and purples.

Halfway down, the pharmacy sat among them, its brick facade freshly cleaned and its door propped open.

Inside, the woman behind the counter brightened when she saw Mae. "Well, you surviving? We heard about that wreck."

"I'm fine. Bruised pride and a sore head. Nothing more."

Her voice was calm, reassuring, and Jamie recognized the instinct. Minimizing trouble so other people wouldn't worry more than necessary.

"This is Jamie. She's the one who found me and took me to the hospital."

The pharmacist gave her a grateful nod and a quick thanks before they collected the prescription and headed back to the car.

Next came the feed store. The entry bell clanged when they walked in, the smell of grain and leather hitting as a man in a ball cap greeted them. Mae paid for a bag of dog food before he loaded it into the trunk, scratching Jasper's head through the rear passenger window.

That's when it dawned on her. Everyone knew each other here.

By early afternoon, Mae tapped the dashboard. "One more stop. Hazel's," she said. "I can't go home without something from her bakery. Elzie would stage a protest."

Hazel's place occupied the end of a block, gigantic windows showing rows of pastries and a counter crowded with jars.

When they opened the door, a bell chimed overhead, and the air felt warmer, smelling of butter and cinnamon.

"There she is." A woman in an apron and red bandana emerged from the back. "You driving into ditches just to see if the emergency room staff still remembers your name?"

Mae waved the comment off with her hand. "I hit a slick spot. It wasn't that dramatic."

"You could've called me," Hazel said, wiping her hands on a towel. "I'd have helped you."

"But I would've never met Jamie."

She stepped back so Hazel could see her, her eyes landing on Jamie, assessing under an amiable smile. "Well now," she said. "You're not from here."

"No. I was just...passing through."

"Mm." Hazel narrowed her eyes, gaze taking her in from head to toe. "Looks like life chased you up the mountain. Careful. You won't want to leave once this place gets hold of you."

The words landed with a little jolt, but Jamie managed a small smile. "I'm not planning to stay long."

"People say that." A grin unfurled across her face. "Then they have my pie and forget all about where they were headed."

She turned toward one of the glass cases in the window. "What are we taking home? Apple? Pecan? Both?"

"Apple," Mae said. "You know Elzie."

"I do." She reached in and lifted out a pie with a crisp golden crust. "This one's for him. Still warm."

Jamie watched her fold the box and tie it with a piece of twine while she and Mae talked over each other about the weather, and a man from church who kept trying to woo Hazel with homemade peach preserves. Although she pretended to be allergic to peaches.

"You coming to the bonfire tonight?" Hazel asked, glancing at Jamie as she slid the box across the counter.

"Bonfire?"

"At the orchard," Mae said. "Every year we burn the old pruning's, clean up the rows, and say a little thank you for making it through the winter."

Hazel gave Jamie a look that carried more understanding than pressure. "You should come. Nobody'll ask you to share more than you're willing."

She rang up the pie and scribbled something on a receipt. "Tell Elzie I added a fee for stress and inconvenience."

Mae chuckled as she waved goodbye, and she and Jamie stepped outside.

***

Back in the car, Jamie settled the pie carefully on the rear seat, the scent filling the space as they drove toward the cabin.

"Thank you," Mae said after a stretch of road. "For driving. For...everything."

"You don't have to thank me."

When they pulled into the driveway, Elzie stepped off the porch to meet them, wiping his hands on a rag. He took the feed from the trunk and whistled low, his eyes on the back seat. "Trying to sweet talk me with Hazel's pie now?"

"If it gets you to stop fussing, I'll bring home two next time."

Jamie walked inside, pulled her phone off the charger, then returned to the front porch, lifting it high above her head, attempting to catch even one bar.

"If you're trying to get service," Elzie said, pointing toward the trees behind the cabin, "best shot's down by the river. Something about the way it all lines up there."

"Thank you."

The path down to the water was narrow, roots knotted under the thin layer of leaves. Jasper trotted ahead, glancing back every few steps as if checking that she was still with him. The rush of water grew louder as they descended.

At the bank, she lifted her phone again. One bar appeared in the corner.

"Come on," she said, pressing Julia's name.

The line rang twice.

"Jamie?" Julia's voice came through. "Finally. I've been trying to reach you all morning. Are you okay?"

"I am. Service up here is awful."

"Up here? Where is up here, Jamie? And what happened in your kitchen. It looks like a crime scene."

"I had a bad night," she said. "I'm in Georgia now. A town called Friendship."

Julia was silent for two beats. "You drove to Georgia. By yourself."

"Yes."

"Why?"

"I just needed to get away for a few days."

"Okay," she said, drawing out the word. "Are you at a hotel?"

"I'm staying with a nice couple I met yesterday." She paused. "Mae ran her car off the road, and I took her to the hospital. Her husband insisted I stay in their guest room instead of a motel. They're...good people. It's not as crazy as it sounds."

"It sounds pretty crazy," Julia said, but there was a thread of relief in her tone. "Have you talked to the kids?"

"I've tried. The calls keep dropping. Will..."

The line went dead.

She pulled the phone away from her ear. No bars. No connection. The call log showed Julia's name and a duration that was far too short.

"Damn."

The river rushed past, churning around rocks. Standing there, phone useless in her hand, she felt her shoulders relax the slightest bit. No one was watching her here. There was only the river, the trees, and Jasper pressed close enough that she could feel his warmth through her jeans.

"You landed pretty well didn't you, boy? Hard to beat a place like this."

He sat beside her, ears tipped forward, eyes on her face.

"I should go back. I just don't know how to do it without making everything worse."

He blinked at her, then nudged her hand with his nose before she slid the phone into her pocket and reached down to touch his head. "Come on," she said. "Let's go see if they need help in the kitchen."

He turned toward the path, tail wagging, and she followed him back up the hill to the cabin, the sound of the river trailing behind her.

Chapter 17

Cool air rushed in as the truck door swung open. In the distance, the orchard stretched in neat lines, branches dark against the night sky.

Elzie called to a group of men stacking wood and Mae touched Jamie's elbow, guiding her toward several women gathered near a long table beside the barn.

"This is Jamie," Mae said.

They looked up with easy smiles, shifting to make room before she introduced them all one by one.

Once the two of them settled in, they slipped back into the conversation they'd been having before, as if it had never paused. Talk that circled around family, church, the crops, school events. No one mentioned jobs or positions, and the omission struck Jamie. Here, who you were mattered more than what you did, and their warmth eased her nerves.

A rustle of footsteps turned their attention as Hazel approached, two young boys trailing behind her, carrying a pie in each hand. She nudged them forward, raising her voice. "Mercy, look what the Lord delivered straight out of the orchard," she said. "Two pie-toting disciples who better not drop a crumb or I'll lay hands on 'em myself."

The boys set the pies down carefully before darting off. Hazel shook her head, smiling.

"Did you hear about Bobby Ray?" One of the women asked, the talk moving again, this time a story that unfolded in fragments between them.

"A tractor rolled on him last month. Pinned him under for near an hour before someone came along. Broke his hip, crushed his leg. They're already pushing him to settle."

"You know who owns that farm now, don't you?" Mae asked. "One of those big outfits from Atlanta with land spread all over this part of Georgia. They have lawyers stacked high."

Several of the women exchanged looks, their mouths set tight as they shook their heads in quiet disgust.

"And none of them cares if he can work again. The man's only in his forties. He has kids still in school."

Jamie lowered her eyes to the table, the conversation pressing hard inside her. She wondered what they would think if they knew her father had been general counsel to large corporations. The kind of attorney who made sure the company had every defense lined up when workers got hurt, hardworking men just like Bobby Ray.

The weight lingered in the air until Hazel gave a quick clap of her hands, as though sweeping off dust. "Alright now, we're getting ourselves too heavy. Y'all up for a little bit of fun?"

She reached under the table and produced a mason jar.

Mae blinked. "Is that moonshine?"

"Shhh." Hazel leaned in, lowering her voice in mock scandal. "It would be a sin to let the Lord's harvest rot. This batch won't kill you, but it'll burn a hole clean through your choir robe."

Jamie felt her eyebrows lift before she could stop them. She hadn't taken these women for the drinking type.

Hazel's gaze slid toward her, grinning like she'd caught the thought midair. "Don't worry, we save it for Saturdays. Jesus can forgive us tomorrow."

The circle broke into laughter, the sound warm before Hazel pressed the jar into Jamie's hand. She hesitated, then tipped it carefully, the liquid fiery and slightly sweet as it hit her tongue. The burn ran down her throat, heat spreading in its wake. She coughed, and the women roared with delight.

"That's the look we were waiting on," Hazel said, slapping the table.

Jamie laughed with them, the edge of tension easing from her shoulders. She passed the jar along, grateful for the moment of levity.

Across the field, the men finished stacking the wood. A cheer rose when a torch met the pile, flames racing upward. Sparks floated into the night sky, and the guitar picked up a quicker rhythm as the children moved closer, their faces bright in the shifting light.

The women stood up from the long table, drifting toward it. Then, Hazel put two fingers between her lips and let out a loud whistle as an older man eased his tractor closer, a wagon hitched behind.

"Come on now, Bill, give us a turn," Hazel called, tugging at the sideboard like a girl half her age.

Another woman clapped and chimed in. "Just one ride, you know we won't tip it over."

He waved them off, shaking his head. "This here's for the kids, not for a pack of grown women fixing to end up in the emergency room and give me the blame."

Hazel planted her hands firmly on her hips. "Don't you go telling me what's proper. We raised those children. We deserve a little fun too."

The others whooped and hollered their agreement, their laughter carrying over the music until even the old man cracked a grin. With a grunt, he shifted on the tractor seat. "Alright then, but don't blame me when you break a hip."

The women cheered and climbed aboard, their hands gripping the wooden rails as the engine rumbled back to life. Somewhere in the scramble, the mason jar slipped and disappeared into the hay. They shrieked and dug through the straw, half-hysterical, until someone held it aloft again like a trophy. Their laughter rose even louder, spilling across the field as the tractor lurched forward.

One of the women struck up a country tune, while the rest chimed in one by one until the whole lot sang horribly off-key.

Jamie didn't know the song, but when Hazel elbowed her, she found herself singing anyway, mumbling through the verses, catching only the last word of each line. No one seemed to notice. Or care. A laugh broke out of her before she could stop it.

"Lord have mercy," the old man said, shaking his head. "Y'all are gonna scare the cows. Pipe down!"

It only made them sing louder.

***

The drive away from the orchard was quiet, the windows down, the scent of smoke trailing them along the dark road.

When they reached the cabin, Jamie veered off the porch and followed the narrow path to the riverbank, phone lifted as she searched for a signal.

Behind her, a soft scuff of movement made her glance back. Jasper trotted toward her, tail wagging, his white fur catching the moonlight. He fell into step beside her, nose twitching at the scents drifting from the woods.

She reached down and brushed her fingers over his head. "You following me again?" She whispered, grateful for the company.

Stepping closer to the river's edge, she tilted her phone toward the sky. A single bar appeared. Then it lit up and vibrated in her hand once, twice, then rapid-fire, a flood of messages filling her screen.

A message from David chilled her more than the night air: *Read your emails.*

Before she could open her inbox, motion flickered at the edge of her vision. Jasper darted toward the woods, slipping between the trees with a low, eager bark. She called his name, but her eyes were already dropping back to her phone.

The emails loaded slowly, the weak signal dragging the moment out until her pulse thudded in her throat.

Finally, the newest one appeared at the top.

From: Tampa Bay Buccaneers College & Pro Scouting

Subject: Interest in Carson Tate

Her breath caught. For a second, the river and the woods seemed to narrow to the light of her screen.

Somewhere behind her, Jasper barked, but she barely heard it. Her fingers shook as she tapped David's name and pressed the phone to her ear.

He answered immediately. "Jamie. Finally. I've been trying to reach you all day." His voice was clipped, urgency threading through every word. "You cannot sit on this. Do you understand me? You need to get on this now."

She opened her mouth to respond, but the call dropped.

The silence that followed didn't feel right.

"Jasper?" Her voice carried only a few feet in the dark.

She thumbed the flashlight on her phone, its narrow beam cutting through the trees as she started forward. "Jasper, come here, buddy."

The woods answered with a low growl, not a dog's, deeper and rougher, rising from somewhere just beyond the edge.

Her heart lurched, and she spun toward the sound as a yelp cracked the air.

"Jasper!"

She ran, pushing through the underbrush, branches whipping at her arms. Her phone cast a small pool of light ahead of her, bouncing wildly with each step.

Another whine reached her.

She found him near a fallen log, his body crouched low, the fur on one leg bloody. He trembled when she touched him, a soft whimper escaping as he tried to lift his head.

"Oh God...Jasper..."

She slid her arms beneath him, lifting him carefully. He was heavier than she expected, his weight pressing into her chest as she staggered back through the trees to the cabin.

The porch lights came into view just as her voice cracked. "Elzie! Mae!"

They burst through the door at the sound of her call. Elzie took one look at Jasper and swore under his breath while Mae grabbed towels and the truck keys.

Within seconds they were rushing toward it, Jasper bundled against Elzie's chest as they hurried him inside.

The engine roared, and they tore down the dirt road, taillights bouncing into the darkness.

She stood beneath the porch light, her phone still clenched in her hand, her heart pounding before she stepped inside the cabin. Under the dim kitchen light, she looked down at herself. Her hands were slick and wet, blood pooling in the lines of her palms and dripping from her fingertips. It had soaked through the front of the sweatshirt, smeared across her chest and stomach, streaked down the sleeves, and spotted the collar near her throat.

She moved to the sink and yanked it over her head, wincing when it brushed her face. After she dropped it into the basin and turned on the faucet, pink rivulets swirled toward the drain. She pumped soap over the fabric, scrubbing hard, then dragged her hands under the stream, rubbing at her skin until it flushed red.

The image would not leave her. Jasper's leg. The sound of his yelp.

She shut off the water and stood there a moment, breathing through her mouth. Then she began opening cabinets, looking for something—anything—strong enough to dull the picture replaying behind her eyes.

When her fingers closed around a half-empty bottle at the back of the shelf, she exhaled.

Just a little, she told herself. Just enough to stop the shaking.

***

Headlights swept across the cabin walls a couple of hours later, bright streaks cutting through the gaps in the blinds. Jamie blinked at the sudden glare, the bottle empty beside her on the table. The engine cut off, and the slam of doors broke the silence.

Elzie and Mae stepped inside with Jasper bundled in Elzie's arms, his leg bandaged, fur trimmed around the wound.

"He's gonna be alright," Mae said, her voice worn. "The vet thinks he got into it with a black bear."

Elzie shook his head. "He was likely protecting you. Fool dog thinks he's ten feet tall."

Jamie's knees softened, the relief hitting her hard enough to crack something loose inside. She covered her mouth, but the sob forced its way through anyway.

Mae's gaze flicked to the empty bottle before Elzie gave her a look that seemed to say, *you take this one.*

"I'll take care of Jasper," he said, disappearing down the hall.

Mae brushed a hand along Jamie's arm. "Come on, honey. Let's sit a minute."

They stepped out onto the back deck. Crickets pulsed in the dark, and the moon hung low above the tree line.

Mae spoke first, easing into one of the wooden rocking chairs. "This ain't the first time Jasper's been banged up protecting someone. And it won't be the last."

She smoothed her palms over her jeans, her voice softening. "We found him years ago. We had a flat, and while Elzie was trying to wrestle the spare out, this scruffy, skinny thing came wandering up the road. Sat right at my feet and looked up like he'd been waiting for a ride home."

A small smile tugged at her mouth. "We tried to find his owner. Asked around, called every number we could. Nothing. So, we named him Jasper and as far as we can tell, whatever life he had before...he let it go the minute he climbed into our truck."

She thought about the way he stayed close to her. The way he watched her, head tilted, as if he understood more than a dog should. Maybe he did. He'd wandered into their lives lost and unsure. And she wasn't all that different.

"Tell me...what's wrong? What are you running from?"

Jamie stared at her hands. "Everything. I don't even know where to start."

Mae leaned in closer. "Start right where you are, honey. I'm listening."

"My son, Leo. He's pulling away and I have no clue how to reach him." She paused, taking a breath. "My career is slipping through my fingers no matter how hard I try to hold it together. And..." Her voice wavered. "I care about someone I shouldn't. And if he knew the truth about me. About my family. He would hate me." She swallowed the lump in her throat. "I just—I don't know how to carry all of this."

Mae didn't respond right away. She waited a moment and then leaned back in her chair. "I lost someone dear to me. A long time ago." A beat passed. "I thought the ache would swallow me whole."

She paused, breathing in the night air. "This may sound a bit hypocritical, seeing as how we all like to have an occasional drink. But when life is troubling you, sooner or later, you've gotta sit with the pain instead of pouring something over it."

Jamie sighed. "I don't know how."

"I know the feeling," Mae said, tilting her head toward the trees as if staring at the stars beyond them. "I used to spend so much time thinking my life was big. Now, I look up there and realize it's just one small part of something I can't control."

She looked back at Jamie and rested a hand over hers. "There's a verse in the Bible I've carried through a lot of hard years. Proverbs 3:5-6. 'Trust in the Lord with all your heart; do not depend on your own understanding. In all your ways acknowledge him, and he will make your paths straight.'"

Jamie felt the pull of the words and the resistance that followed. She had never been someone who left things to chance.

"It's real, honey. You just gotta have faith that God knows what he's doing. He has a plan for you."

***

Jamie folded the last of her clothes and placed them into the small suitcase, pulling the zipper closed. She smoothed the quilt on the bed, wanting to leave the room as untouched as she had found it.

A soft scrape of claws announced Jasper before she saw him. He appeared in the doorway, his eyes brighter than they had been when she'd carried him up from those woods. He took a few careful steps toward her, tail sweeping once against the doorframe.

She crouched to meet him. "Hey, buddy. You scared me half to death last night."

He leaned his head against her palm, and something tugged inside her. Gratitude, maybe. Or something deeper she didn't entirely know what to do with.

When she stood, he followed her into the living room, where Elzie and Mae waited. Elzie had a mug of coffee in his hand, his posture loose but his eyes still carrying the outline of last night's worry. Mae, calm as ever, offered a small smile.

"Morning," Jamie said, her voice thin.

"You get enough sleep?" Elzie asked.

She nodded, though that wasn't true.

After she thanked them both, she lifted the suitcase handle and followed them onto the porch. Elzie stayed beside Jasper near the top step while Mae walked with her down the path to the car.

"You sure you're good to drive this morning?" Mae asked.

"I will be. Once I'm on the road."

She glanced back at Jasper, unable to help the pull in her chest at the sight of him.

"He'll be fine," Mae said, following her gaze. "He's gotten himself into worse trouble than this."

A slow breath eased out of her before she even noticed it. "I'm glad he's okay."

"Me too." Then, after a pause, her voice gentled further. "You take care of yourself, Jamie. Whatever you're carrying...you don't have to do it alone."

She swallowed before she spoke. "Thank you. For everything."

Mae hugged her, and when they pulled apart, she squeezed her arm once before letting go.

After she slid into the driver's seat and started the engine, she looked up. Mae stepped onto the porch beside Elzie, and Jasper watched her with those earnest eyes, tail thumping against the boards.

She lifted a hand and they both waved back.

The gravel crunched beneath her tires as she pulled away from the cabin, and the trees closed in around the road. For a moment she wished she could stay tucked inside this quiet pocket of the world a little longer.

But, slowly, the ridges slipped from view, giving space to a long stretch of road and the reality waiting for her in Tampa.

Chapter 18

It'd been two weeks since the invitation to Tampa's minicamp had landed in her inbox. Two weeks stretched thin between relief and dread. Relief when she saw Carson's name climbing back into conversations it had disappeared from; dread every time it lit up her phone. She had avoided him, the thought of telling him the truth about her father making her physically ill. Some days she pictured him going quiet, jaw clenched the way it did when he was trying not to react. Other times she saw him stepping back from her like she'd just admitted to something unforgivable.

She pulled into the Buccaneers' training center lot and stepped through the entrance beneath a five-story metal football. Sunlight cut across the atrium, flashing against glass cases and two Vince Lombardi trophies.

At the front desk, she checked in, took a temporary badge, and clipped it to her blazer.

The closer she got to the indoor practice field, the more the sounds gathered: coaches shouting adjustments and the crisp smack of the ball hitting palms.

She tucked her hair behind her ears and stepped into the designated viewing zone, past a roped-off area.

A whistle cut through the air, rookies exploding off the line in staggered bursts.

"Big day," Steve said, sliding in beside her without meeting her eyes. "Perfect time for a great comeback story."

She didn't need to ask why he'd shown up; David had looped him in as soon as she'd gone off the grid. Right after throwing in a jab about her not being reliable.

Funny, she pondered to herself. *He never thought Carson had a chance, and yet here he is.*

Carson lined up, defenders tight on him. The quarterback rifled a ball downfield, and he launched into a sprint, cutting once, twice, then stretching full length. It skimmed his fingertips, and he pulled it in with a clean grab, landing hard and rolling to his feet in one motion.

A low ripple moved through the viewing section.

A few moments later, Steve tipped his chin toward a pair of agents he knew and peeled off. From where she stood, she heard him commanding the conversation. "We're bringing him along the right way. He'll stand ready for camp."

We?

She was the one who built his highlight reel, scrubbing through angles until the best clips surfaced cleanly. She wrote the emails and placed his footage in the right inbox at the right time. Steve hadn't lifted a finger. But here, with the noise and the little circles that form when men in quarter-zips talk shop, he slid himself into her work like it belonged to him.

After a few minutes, he drifted back with arrogance etched across his face. "There's a low-key PR thing for Carson at American Social later. You should come."

"A PR thing?"

"Yeah, you remember Kendall from VibeWell right? Her team put it together."

She blinked, a flush working up her neck to her cheeks.

It dawned on her then how firmly she stood on the outside of Carson's world while others—people who hadn't fought for him the way she had—slipped into his inner circles without effort.

***

The restaurant on Harbour Island buzzed with weekend energy when she arrived. She took a deep breath, bracing for whatever this night would turn into, hating how uneasy she already felt.

The hostess checked the reservation list, confirmed her name, and guided her toward the deck, where she spotted Carson at the bar with two players she didn't recognize. He spun around at the same time, his face lighting briefly before he waved her over.

"Jamie," he said, shifting to make room. "This is Julian and Evan."

Both men offered polite nods and turned back to their beers.

Moments later, a sudden wave of attention shifted toward the double doors.

Kendall stepped outside like she'd planned the moment to the second. She wore her hair in loose waves, a white satin camisole tucked into high-waisted black trousers, strappy heels giving her a few extra inches of height, and gold layered necklaces catching the light with every move.

Her videographer followed with a compact camera rig, and an assistant trailed behind carrying a branded tote.

She greeted them with a bright smile, one hand grazing Carson's arm. "Perfect timing, guys. Golden hour is gorgeous out here. Let's get down to the boardwalk before we lose the light."

A knot formed in Jamie's stomach as she watched her glide between them, her laugh easy, her presence magnetic in a way she could never emulate.

Once they made it down, the assistant crouched beside the tote and began unloading gear. She tossed a clean, white-laced football to Julian, who tossed it toward Carson.

Kendall stepped back, directing. "Okay. Carson center. Julian, Evan, close in. Laugh, move, make it look natural."

The river reflected streaks of fading sunlight, and she positioned Carson near the edge, pressing a hand lightly along his shoulder. She tapped his chin for the angle, shifting him an inch to the left. "Perfect. Hold that."

A moment later, Carson laughed at something she said, a warm, easy sound that carried up to the deck.

She told herself it wasn't flirtation on his part. He was good at being gracious, but watching it hurt anyway.

Before anyone could glance her way, she slipped back into the restaurant and stepped toward the exit. *The smart move*, she thought. No putting herself through the sight of him with someone who made far more sense next to him than she ever would.

She made it halfway before Steve appeared out of nowhere, blocking her path. "Ducking out early?" He tilted his head. "Careful. Folks might think you can't handle the pressure."

She didn't bother hiding her eye-roll. "I'm going to the ladies' room." She slipped past him before he could fire back, walking into the hallway, and pushing through the restroom door.

Inside, the noise of the restaurant dulled, and she braced her hands on the counter beside the sink, willing her pulse to settle.

After a moment, she straightened, smoothing her blouse and running a quick finger under her lower lashes—a breath in, a breath out.

Squaring her shoulders, she reached for the door handle. She wasn't going to let Steve chase her off. And she would not allow Kendall to win by leaving. Not tonight. Not after everything she'd done to get Carson here.

***

Dinner had wrapped a couple of hours later, the plates cleared and the table reset with fresh drinks while the conversation drifted into looser territory.

Steve had stepped outside to take a phone call, and Kendall's crew was long gone, but Kendall herself stayed behind, legs crossed, cocktail in hand, looking far too comfortable beside Carson.

She'd been the one to suggest sticking around for another drink. A few minutes later, she slid out of her chair. "I need to use the lady's room. Don't have too much fun without me."

As she walked away, Julian and Evan watched her go with blatant, crude interest, eyes dragging over her with zero shame.

"Yo," Julian said, cutting a look at Carson; a quick sideways sweep that seem to carry its own meaning. "She's a total snack. You pullin' her or what?"

Carson let out a short, uneven laugh that stopped almost as soon as it started. He flicked a quick glance toward Jamie, shaking his head.

"Bro," Evan said, lifting his glass, grinning. "Julian asked her for a shot, and she said, 'Let me get Carson first.' Man got curved on camera."

"Whatever," Julian said. "I don't get curved. I do the curving."

Evan leaned back, laughing. "Get outta here. She skipped you like preseason. Nobody watches that shit and she sure as hell ain't watching you."

"I hear ya, bro." Julian rolled his eyes, turning back to Carson. "I'm just sayin', if you're not tryin' to get cuffed, hook a brother up."

Jamie forced a small smile, though something in her had recoiled somewhere between Julian's question and Evan's roast. The whole exchange scraped at her nerves. Kendall's eyes on Carson, the guys egging it on. She didn't want to sit in it any longer.

"I should get going," she said, keeping her tone even. "It's getting late, and I've got an early morning." She hoped none of them heard the strain under the words.

Carson straightened a little. "Yeah, I'm heading out too." He pushed his chair back as if it were automatic. "I'll walk you out."

She shook her head before he could stand. "No. Stay. You guys are clearly having a moment gushing over Kendall. Don't let me ruin the vibe."

Her attempt at humor came out the wrong way, but she couldn't bring herself to smooth it over.

"Sorry, ma'am," Julian said, raising his glass toward her, clearly aiming for polite and landing nowhere close.

Not trusting herself to speak, she pressed her tongue to the back of her teeth, then shoved her chair under the table hard enough to jolt it, the corner clipping Julian's elbow and sloshing his drink.

Carson narrowed his eyes. "Bro."

"What?" Julian blinked, as if genuinely confused.

A moment later, Kendall returned from the restroom, a hint of smugness playing at her mouth. Maybe Jamie imagined it, but it landed like a pinprick under her skin all the same.

She turned toward the exit without another word and didn't look back.

***

As she walked down the concrete ramp and into the garage, she kept her eyes down, replaying the last ten minutes on a loop she couldn't shut off: Kendall's smile, the way they kept fawning over her.

"Jamie!" Carson's voice ricocheted off the walls.

She froze for half a heartbeat, long enough to register it before she kept walking.

His footsteps quickened behind her, a soft jog, then a breathless stop just at her side.

"Hey," he said, chest rising with the effort. "Can you slow down?"

She kept her eyes fixed straight ahead. "It's been a long day and I'm tired. I need to get home."

He stepped in front of her, blocking her path. "Don't do that."

"Do what?" She kept her tone light, almost breezy.

"That." His voice dropped. "Pretend everything's fine."

"It's late, Carson," she said, crossing her arms.

"You've been avoiding me for weeks. Just talk to me. Please."

If she looked at him one second longer, she'd fall apart; so she didn't. Instead, she pushed past him. "Go back inside. She's a total snack, right?" The jab landed before she could reel it in. "What does that even mean?"

"You're jealous," he called out to her, the lift in his voice betraying how much he seemed to like it.

She didn't respond. *You're jealous.* The words followed her, louder now in her own head. She reached her car, slid behind the wheel, and shut the door with more force than she meant.

***

When she merged into traffic, muscle memory handled the wheel while her thoughts spiraled back to the restaurant. Then, the rumble of a motorcycle rose behind her, pulling her attention to the rearview mirror.

It rolled out a moment later, keeping a slight distance, but not far enough to ignore.

She changed lanes. So did the bike. *A coincidence*, she told herself. But the rider mirrored every block and every shift in traffic.

Whoever it was, followed her across the Davis Island Bridge, and her pulse kicked hard against her throat.

When she pulled into her driveway, it slowed behind her, motor rumbling low as it coasted to a stop.

She stepped out of her car, keys clutched tight, ready to run or scream or both.

The rider killed the engine, took off his helmet, and only then did she realize it was Carson.

"Carson?" Her voice broke out before she could stop it. "When did you get a motorcycle?"

He didn't say a word, but the arched brow and the slight twitch at the corner of his mouth said it all.

Heat shot straight through her.

She charged him.

"Why are you following me?" She shoved him in the chest. Hard. "What is wrong with you?"

He barely moved, still grinning.

"You scared the hell out of me." She shoved him again. "Go back to your friends." Her voice cracked on the word. "Go back to her. You know you want her."

The grin didn't leave his face, and a sound tore out of her—half laugh, half fury—as she turned away from him, hands in her hair, pacing two steps in the direction of the house.

He caught her before she could get farther, hands closing around her upper arms and turning her back toward him.

Headlights swept across the driveway as a car rolled slowly past the house, and that was when it hit her.

They were outside. In the open. In her driveway. Her neighbors would see.

She yanked against his hold. "You shouldn't be here. Someone will see us."

"I don't care who sees us."

The words started spilling out faster than she could control them. "You can't just follow me home like that. You can't show up here on a motorcycle like some kind of...of..." She gestured wildly to the street. "This is my house. My driveway. The neighbors..."

Carson took another step, closing the distance, his gaze locked on hers. "Jamie..." he cut in, breaking through her rambling. "Stop talking."

She didn't move. Something in his eyes disarmed her completely, cutting past every excuse she'd tried to hide behind.

"Stop running from this." His hand lifted, fingertips barely brushing her jaw. "From me."

He leaned in and kissed her as if he'd been holding back for weeks and finally stopped fighting it.

When he pulled away, a look flickered across his face, full of heat; he didn't have to say anything for her to know exactly what he wanted.

She gave in with a shaky exhale. "Okay," she said, whispering. "But you can't leave your motorcycle in my driveway."

***

He shrugged out of his jacket as soon as they were inside, draping it over the back of a barstool, then nudged his shoes off near the couch. Before he could look back at her, she crossed the space between them, took his hand, and led him down the hallway.

In the bedroom, he reached for her, fingers catching at the hem of her shirt. She caught his wrist and shook her head. "Not yet."

Holding his gaze, she stepped back and nodded toward him instead. He hesitated only a second before understanding seemed to cross his face, doing as she asked. She circled him, letting her hand move where she pleased, across his chest, around his waist, lingering at his hips.

When he leaned toward her, she pressed her palm to his shoulder and stopped him. "My turn," she said.

She pushed him onto the bed and climbed on top of him; the control she'd taken showed in his face. Then, he grabbed her at the waist and rolled her over, lifting the hem of her shirt again as his lips traced down her stomach.

The air left her lungs in uneven pulls as he kept going, not teasing, not tentative. When the intensity climbed too high to hold, she shifted, pressing her cheek into the mattress. The bed moved behind her as he followed, his breath settling at the back of her neck. She absorbed the outline of him, the breadth of his shoulders, the strength in his body even in stillness.

Wanting him felt reckless, but she didn't fight it.

Chapter 19

The ceiling fan spun in a lazy circle above them, lifting a faint breeze that tangled with the warmth of his breath at her shoulder. For a moment, she didn't move.

Pieces of last night drifted back to her. The way he'd waited, watching her face before he touched her. His mouth, slow against her skin. No one had ever understood her like that.

And now, as her body curved into the solid lines of his, they seemed to fit together with an ease that made the world outside her bedroom fall away.

She absorbed the comfort of it, but the truth inside her, the one she inherited, pushed back. Keeping the secret about her father from him felt wrong, and if she didn't tell him now, when would she?

Turning to look at him, she let herself take in the softness of his face. He seemed so peaceful, so content, and she imagined how fast that contentment would vanish the moment he learned what she'd been hiding.

"You're thinking too loud," he said, eyes still closed. "Should I be worried?"

She released a small, shaky exhale. Even half-asleep, he could read her.

He opened his eyes and tipped his head toward her. "Talk to me. It can't be that bad...right?"

She parted her lips, ready to say it finally, as an abrupt knock, loud enough to jolt the air, hit the front door.

"Jamie!" Julia's voice carried through the hallway. "We're here!"

She shot upright. "Oh my God."

"On Swann or Timpano?" Nicole called out. "I say On Swann, but your sister insists that Timpano has the best mimosas."

"No, I said they have bottomless mimosas. Let's not confuse quality with quantity. Although they are pretty damn good."

Carson pushed up on one elbow, watching her scramble as she stumbled out of bed. "Are they always like this in the morning?"

"I forgot about brunch." She pulled on a robe, hurrying toward the bathroom, where she caught a glimpse of herself in the mirror. No amount of quick fixing was going to turn this around. Still, she dragged a hand through her hair, and wiped the mascara from beneath her eyes, trying to erase any sign of the night they'd had.

As she walked through the bedroom, she glanced back at him and caught the quiet curve at the corner of his mouth. "You like watching me panic, don't you?"

"Hard not to, babe."

She blinked at him, thrown for a moment. "We're doing pet names now?" she asked, trying and failing to sound unaffected.

He didn't say anything, but the look in his eyes answered for him.

Stepping through the doorway, she let out a quiet sigh still tugging the robe at her waist. Julia and Nicole were already in the kitchen, pulling coffee mugs down from a cabinet, completely at home and completely unaware of the chaos they'd walked into.

Julia spotted her first. Her eyebrows shot up, not even attempting subtlety. "Wow. You look...well-rested."

Nicole blinked at her. "Rough night?"

"Or maybe a good one," Julia said, her gaze sweeping her from head to toe before drifting to the sneakers on the floor near the couch. It didn't take long for her brows to lift in recognition, but she didn't say a word. She simply sent Jamie a look that landed with the weight of a full conversation.

Nicole followed her line of sight and frowned. "Whose shoes? They're huge."

"Can we not make this a whole thing?" she asked.

Nicole looked between them. "Make what a whole thing?"

Julia tipped her head, the corners of her mouth pulling up like she was enjoying every second of this. "Are you going to tell her?"

"Tell me what?" Nicole's eyes drifted past her and landed on the jacket draped over the barstool. She stepped closer, lifted it with both hands, and held it up. "Does it have anything to do with this?"

"Exhibit B," Julia announced, looking far too pleased with herself.

Footsteps moved down the hallway, and then Carson appeared. "Morning," he uttered, like he'd walked into this house a hundred times.

Julia's grin turned wicked while Nicole went still, eyes wide.

He crossed the room and sat on the edge of the couch to pull on his shoes. "Sorry to interrupt your game of twenty questions," he said, voice dry, "but I need to go. I've got a ten o'clock show time."

"Of course you do." Julia's voice floated out, too casual. "Hydrate. Stretch."

Jamie shot her a look.

He stood and reached for the jacket still in Nicole's grasp. "Mind if I get that back?"

She tried to answer, but only a thin, shaky sound came out as she handed it over.

He slipped it over one arm, stepped closer to Jamie, and lifted a hand to her jaw before kissing her, not caring for a second that they had an audience.

"I'll call you later."

She nodded and followed him to the garage. As they stepped out, she pushed the button to open the door and watched while he pulled his helmet on and mounted the bike. He started the engine, gave her a small wave, and backed out before she returned to the kitchen, where Julia and Nicole were watching him from the window above the sink.

Julia let out a low whistle. "Damn...if I were straight..."

"One motorcycle and suddenly your sexuality is a sliding scale?" Nicole asked, head snapping toward her.

"If you two are done gawking now, I'll get dressed."

In the bathroom, she washed her face and caught her reflection, tired and carrying a guilt she couldn't shake. Between Carson and the chaos at work, she'd forgotten that today was Leo's eighteenth birthday.

She walked into the bedroom, reaching for her phone to call him, but just as her thumb hovered over his picture, the screen lit up. David's name flashed across it, and everything inside her dropped. Steve must have gotten to him already.

"Jamie. It's David." His tone was clipped. "I need you in the office as soon as possible."

She gripped the phone tighter, every instinct telling her this was bad. "Is everything okay?"

"I have some news about Carson."

"Ok, I'll be there at ten."

She hung up and, after a quick shower, she walked back into the kitchen in slacks and a blouse, far more put together than she'd been twenty minutes earlier.

Julia noticed immediately. "Don't tell me you're going into the office."

"Rain check. David just called."

Julia's eyes narrowed. "Seriously? It's Saturday."

"Julia, come on. You know this isn't a Monday-to-Friday job. Neither is yours."

"Fine. But when you're done, we need to sit down and figure out Leo's graduation party. We only have two weeks."

Jamie nodded. "Okay. Tonight, I promise."

She grabbed her bag and keys, heading to the garage and slipped into her car. As she backed out, she replayed last night in her mind. Her exit from the restaurant, Carson following, the way it must have looked. By the time she hit the main road, her pulse had slowed to a dull, uneasy thrum.

***

The elevator doors slid open to a floor that felt half asleep. The reception desk sat empty, the bullpen silent. Most of the overhead lights were off, leaving the rows of cubicles dim, their monitors resting in screensavers.

The silence stretched ahead of her, her footsteps the only sound, and as she approached David's corner office a deep voice slipped through the closed door, followed by a quick, almost gloating laugh.

Steve.

That noise alone made the hairs on the nape of her neck rise.

She knocked, cutting off whatever he had been saying. A brief silence followed before David cleared his throat and told her to come in. She'd clearly interrupted them.

Steve sat in one of the chairs across from David's desk. His left ankle rested on his right knee, fingers laced over his stomach, expression relaxed in a way that read more perfunctory than genuine.

After David motioned to the empty chair beside him, she took a seat, spine straight, hands folded in her lap. She noticed a shift in his demeanor. Whatever this was, he'd already chosen a side.

Steve spoke first. "So," he said, drawing out the word like he was settling into a story he couldn't wait to tell. "That call I stepped out for during dinner…Buccaneers pro scouting." He let that hang long enough to make sure she caught it. "If you hadn't ran out the way you did, I would've told you last night."

The pause that followed stretched, deliberate on his part, but she held her response at the back of her tongue. She wouldn't give him that satisfaction.

He went on. "They're impressed with Carson. Rookie camp isn't even over, and he's already standing out." A slight, self-contented change in his expression told her he was taking credit.

"Anyway, they want him back for OTAs. And if he keeps this up, he's tracking toward making their ninety-man roster for camp." He shrugged. "Good position to be in."

Pausing briefly, he glanced at David before he continued. "Seattle gave him the baseline. OTAs, camp, standard minimum. It's fine, but it's cookie-cutter. He nodded to himself. "If he maintains this trajectory, the Bucs' proposal will reflect it. Significantly."

The beginning of a smile threatened before caution pulled everything back into place. *This part was the good news,* she told herself. He had yet to share the bad.

She drew a quiet breath, pushing past the knot in her chest. "I'm glad he's doing well. But why wasn't the call directed to me?"

The small, knowing grin that followed told her exactly how he intended to spin this. "I've been in this business twenty years," he said, tone light, almost amused. "I have relationships there. They know me."

His words stung, but she kept it contained. Carson's opportunity mattered more than her pride. "Alright. I'll reach out to them and get the process moving. Once they officially confirm the OTA and training camp invitation, I'll handle the contract details on our end. And I'll reconnect with Seattle as well. If both teams are interested, that could work in his favor."

David finally shifted forward in his chair, cutting in at last. He spoke evenly. "That's actually why I called you in."

A quick chill moved through her. She had sensed this from the moment she'd stepped inside the office. Steve's presence, the careful pacing of good news before anything else. This wasn't about contract detail, and it wasn't about Carson. This was about her.

"If both teams stay engaged, this could turn into a bidding scenario. Those deals get complicated fast." His gaze flicked between them before returning to her. "We need to position Carson with our most experienced negotiator."

Heat flooded in her chest, the rest of the sentence writing itself before he said it. "I'm turning Carson over to Steve."

Unable to hold her tongue any longer, she turned to Steve. "I pitched him. I got him in front of Seattle. And Tampa. You didn't even think he had a shot."

He leaned forward slightly, elbows on his knees. "No offense, Jamie. You did get him this far, and that's impressive. But this is over your head now. He needs someone who's been there before."

The words echoed in her mind. *Someone who's been there before.*

"Funny. Weeks ago, you told me I was the fool hitching my wagon to a broken player. And now here you are, hitching yours to the same man."

She could imagine the glare that anger had carved across her face and, for the first time since the meeting started, his smirk faltered.

David cut in before she could continue. "Jamie, you've done good work here. Truly. But we need to do what's best for Carson."

She released a slow sigh, conceding. "When are you planning to tell him?"

He hesitated, then shook his head. "We'll explain when it makes sense. He'll understand."

She pressed her lips together, weighing her words. "You're stripping me out before he even has a say."

"He hired the agency," David said. "And as the agency, it's our job to make the right call. Sometimes that means protecting the client from emotions that cloud judgment."

Her voice dropped. "You mean *my* emotions."

His silence was confirmation enough.

After a beat, he leaned back again. "You should take this as a learning experience. And you won't be without work. I've already lined up your next athlete. A basketball player who just graduated from the University of Florida. Dylan Prescott. He didn't get a Combine invitation, and teams haven't exactly been lining up to bring him in for workouts. He has a reputation for being tough in the locker room, but there's upside."

She let that sink in. No interest, attitude concerns already shadowing his name. Another test she was never meant to pass. She rose. "If that's all."

David nodded as though the conversation had ended exactly how he'd envisioned it.

She opened the door, careful not to slam it, and walked through the bullpen toward the elevators, her jaw locked against the words she wanted to shout.

***

Later that day, she eased the car into the garage and waited for the silence to dim the noise running through her head. It didn't. The meeting replayed in pieces, each one screaming the question she'd been avoiding: *when had she last felt like the woman she hoped to become?*

She forced herself out of the driver's seat and toward the door into a house that met her with nothing. The quiet seemed like an accusation. Work wasn't the only place she was coming up short.

On her way to the kitchen, she slowed beside Leo's room. It was still and unchanged, a reminder of how long it had been since she'd talked to him. She pulled her phone from her pocket and called. It rang and rang, and by the time it clicked to voicemail, something inside her started to pull apart.

"Leo, hi. It's Mom. I just wanted to call and wish you a happy birthday. I'm sure you have plans with your Dad but I'd love to take you to dinner. Call me back." She paused, unsure of what more to say; unsure that even wanted to hear from her. "I love you."

She dropped it onto the island and opened a cabinet, reaching for a bottle of wine without thinking. Her hand closed around the neck before Mae's voice crossed her mind. *Sooner or later, you've gotta sit with the pain instead of pouring something over it.*

The truth of it stung.

She put it down and tried to stand still long enough to choose better, then her phone rang on the counter. It was her mother; she flipped it over and pushed it away.

After it stopped ringing, she exhaled, tired of running from things that found her anyway. When the voicemail finally appeared, she forced herself to tap the icon.

"Jamie," her mother began, already sounding impatient. "I'm hoping you call me back, but I know how busy you think you are. Anyway, I wanted to give you some news. Your father's old firm is creating a scholarship in his honor. For promising young attorneys. Isn't that lovely?"

Her jaw clenched.

"He worked so hard, and he always tried to do what was right. People forget that. I hope you don't. It would be nice if you showed some enthusiasm, but I suppose I'll settle for a call later."

She ended it there, even though it was still going.

"Doing what was right," she murmured to herself. "For the men in corner offices, not the ones getting crushed underneath them."

The message echoed in her mind. Her mother's voice. The tidy rewrite of a career built on other people's pain.

Heat rose in her chest, dissolving whatever strength she'd had left. She dragged the bottle back across the counter and worked the corkscrew in with a few turns before pulling hard. It snapped free, loud in the quiet kitchen, and she poured herself a glass with shaky hands.

Her phone vibrated again, then Carson's name gleamed like a wound.

Her pulse skipped. She wasn't prepared for questions or the possibility that David had already told him. And she certainly wasn't ready for the sound of her own voice cracking open the moment she heard his.

She pushed it away, letting the call pass.

A text followed almost immediately. *Everything alright?*

She took her glass to the living room and sat on the couch. The wine eased nothing. It only thinned her defenses enough for questions to rise.

Her gaze drifted upward. "If there's a plan, I'm not seeing it." She shook her head. "Are You even there? Do You hear me? Have I somehow offended You?"

Chapter 20

The file on Dylan Prescott lay open across her desk, her notes underlined in red. Raw strength, speed, poor discipline, bad attitude. She traced a thumb along the headshot clipped to the folder. He looked young, barely older than Leo, and wore the easy, unearned smirk of a kid who'd never once been told no.

A soft knock on the edge of her cubicle pulled her attention. The receptionist leaned in, voice low. "They've been in the conference room for a few minutes now. Just wanted to give you a heads-up."

She nodded, though she didn't immediately move. Another player they'd tossed at her like a test she was never meant to pass. The reluctance settled deeper than fatigue as she gathered the folder and forced herself toward the conference room.

Outside the door, she paused, drawing a breath before stepping in.

Dylan sat sprawled across his chair, his long legs stretched out as he scrolled through his phone without lifting his eyes. Beside him, his father perched stiff-backed, arms crossed, his expression one of open doubt.

She reached out to shake their hands. "Mr. Prescott. Dylan. I'm Jamie Sinclair. I appreciate you making time today."

"We've been waiting," Mr. Prescott said with a thin smile. "Hope that's not a sign of how things run under you."

Heat crawled up her neck, but she pushed it down, setting her binder on the table and taking the seat opposite them.

"Let's talk about where we are. Without a Combine invitation, the next opportunity is Summer League. Teams are using June workouts to evaluate fringe prospects. There's still a path for you, but it requires showing them consistency and that you're coachable."

Dylan looked up briefly, a smug curve at his mouth, but he didn't bother to speak. Mr. Prescott stepped in instead, leaning forward as if shielding him from the criticism. "I don't know whose notes you've been reading, but my son has more talent than half the names on any draft board. The problem is, they want a yes man, not someone with personality."

Of course he wasn't coachable, she thought. How could he be, when the loudest voice in his life had never been wrong?

Before she continued, she forced herself to nod. Arguing with him would only drag the meeting further off course. "Okay. I'll see what private looks I can set up for him."

"Before we waste time," Mr. Prescott said, resting his forearms on the table. "I want to know who you've signed. What's your track record? My son doesn't need to be some experiment for a rookie agent."

She bit down on the inside of her cheek, swallowing the first response that wanted to rise. "I fight for my clients. That's what matters."

"Whatever," Dylan said, finally putting his phone down. "Just get me a contract. That part's your job, right? Make it happen."

She closed the binder slowly. "I wish it were that simple."

"Everything's simple if you know what you're doing," Mr. Prescott declared, launching into another rant about his son, daring her to disagree, but she didn't. Her attention had already slipped through the window of the boardroom toward the bullpen. Carson had arrived, drawing a brief lift in her chest. Then, Steve stepped from his office, calling him over with a stiff gesture.

She forced her focus back to the meeting, betrayal and desperation pressing the air from her lungs. The pen trembled between her fingers before she steadied it. "I'm sorry...where were we?"

The question only deepened his scowl as he leaned forward again. "Glad to know my son's future is in the hands of someone who forgets where we're at mid-sentence."

She straightened slightly, choosing composure over confrontation. "You're right. Let's get back to what matters, Dylan's future and the opportunities we could line up." She gathered her notes as if to reset the conversation. "Why don't we schedule a follow-up in a week or two when I've had time to explore options?"

"Fine." He tapped his finger on the table, each beat meant to underline the threat. "But, if nothing comes through, we're done here."

"Understood," she said.

At the elevators, she offered a brief handshake to Dylan, who barely looked up from his phone, and a polite nod to his father. Only after they stepped inside and the doors closed did she turn back.

Just then, Steve's office door opened and Carson walked out, his expression difficult to read from a distance.

They moved toward the elevators, and she turned abruptly, slipping through the stairwell. She hurried down a flight, her breath shallow, and ran to the elevator, pushing the down button. When the doors opened, Carson stood inside.

He blinked at the sight of her, surprise flickering across his face. "Jamie," he said quietly as she stepped in beside him. "Steve just told me the news. The Bucs want me for OTAs, and he mentioned if I make the fifty-three-man roster, I'd be looking at a much better deal than Seattle offered."

He shifted his weight, voice dropping. "But if this means cutting you out, I don't know if I can do it. You're the one who believed in me when nobody else would."

She took a deep breath, her thoughts circling not only around what was best for him but also the people he loved. His mother had carried more than anyone should; Mia had lost a parent before she was even old enough to understand it. And Marcus...he had been failed by a system her own father once defended. Thinking about what she wanted wasn't an option. Her family had done enough damage.

"You should let him take it from here. With two teams involved, it might turn into a bidding situation, and he's better equipped to get you the strongest deal."

He searched her face. "I don't believe that, Jamie. He isn't more capable than you are."

"Maybe, but he has connections I lack." She reached for his hands, holding them lightly, afraid she'd lose the nerve if she gave him a chance to pull away. "You deserve this. Don't let my place here get in the way of your future."

The elevator stopped, and she released her grip, pulling back as a stranger stepped in, nodding politely, and standing between them.

When the doors opened again in the lobby, the man exited, and Carson moved to follow.

Her heartbeat thudded hard, tears gathering as she brushed his shoulder, a fleeting touch that carried the shift between them. "I'll see you later?"

He gave a short nod before stepping out, and she let the doors slide shut, pressing the button to return to the twenty-second floor.

***

The graduation ceremony stayed with her long after it ended. Watching Leo cross the stage, seeing him in that cap and gown reminded her that her youngest was grown. The words empty nester had once sounded like a distant label, something she'd reach someday. That day had arrived.

She sighed, thinking about it as she stared at her bare walls and the boxes stacked in the hallway. It struck her that she hadn't even considered the barrage of questions she would receive from guests. Today was about Leo, not her. So, she taped a simple sign to the front door that read: Party's Out Back. USE THE SIDE GATE!

Beyond the sliding glass doors, Julia and Nicole were busy setting up tables while Ava adjusted the chairs around them. Watching them work gave her a brief sense of order, even if the rest of her day felt anything but.

Her sister stepped inside and slid the door shut behind her. "How are you holding up?" She asked, her eyes searching Jamie's face.

"I'm fine," she said, though she wasn't sure she believed it. "I just need to get this all set before everyone arrives. And I still have that event tonight. The brand launch."

Julia lifted an eyebrow. "I honestly don't know how you think you're going to do all this." She didn't say more, but the concern sat between them.

Heading toward the kitchen, she slowed when she heard the chatter of Leo's video game from his room. She hadn't realized how she'd missed the sound of it while he was away, relishing it for a moment before someone knocked at the door.

Through the window above the sink, she saw her parents' car already in the driveway. "It's Mom and Dad."

"I'll be outside," Julia said. She didn't wait for a response, and Jamie didn't need one to understand why.

She made her way to the foyer, pulled the door open, and watched them step inside, Evelyn's eyes immediately drifting to the cardboard boxes. "One might assume you'd at least clear the clutter before hosting."

"Is that the Motherwell piece?" her father asked, his gaze landing on a wrapped canvas leaning against the wall. "What are you planning to do with it?"

"I don't know. Maybe it would look better hanging in John's house."

Richard hummed, pleased. "Good. That painting came from a client after one of the toughest cases of my career, so make sure it's cared for."

She didn't need to be reminded of its history. He had given it to her and John as a wedding present, though it had carried more of his ego than any real sentiment. Lately, she'd caught herself wondering who he had bulldozed to acquire a piece of art she never understood or pretended to like.

A moment later, Ava came in from the backyard, lifting her hair off the back of her neck. "It's so hot," she said as she stepped inside. "Mom, do we have another tablecloth?"

She stopped when she saw Richard and Evelyn standing in the foyer. "Granddad! Gigi! I didn't know you were here already," she said, crossing the living room to greet them with a hug.

"The traffic was lighter than expected," Richard said, smoothing a hand over her shoulder.

Jamie nodded toward the mudroom by the garage. "There's another one in the laundry room. Cabinet above the washer."

"Got it." Ava headed that way, weaving around the boxes while Richard and Evelyn drifted through the sliding doors, already commenting on the setup outside.

She reappeared a minute later, tablecloth tucked under her arm, and a very large sweatshirt in her hand.

"Okay," she said, holding it up between two fingers, "who does this belong to? And do not say Leo. He wouldn't be caught dead in Florida State gear."

Her pulse quickened. She had forgotten she'd tossed Carson's hoodie in the laundry room. "Maybe one of Leo's friends."

Ava narrowed her eyes as if she absolutely did not buy that, but before she could push, Julia stepped back inside. "Some kids just arrived claiming to be Leo's guests, but I have to be honest, they don't look like anyone from his circle."

Together, they walked out onto the lanai, eyes immediately tracking the unfamiliar boys.

"Mom, one of them looks like Tyler."

"How do you know what Tyler looks like?"

Ava gave her a pointed glance. "You really need to be more aware." She pulled out her phone, swiping to a screenshot. "I saved this the day Leo went missing. It's his profile picture."

She took the phone. The face in the photo matched the boy now standing in her backyard, laughing at something one of the others said. Ava was right. It was Tyler.

"Who's Tyler?" Julia finally asked.

Before either could answer her, Leo stepped through the sliders, stopping when he saw the three of them huddled together. "What are you whispering about?"

"Nothing," Jamie said quickly.

Leo didn't press. He just brushed past them and headed straight toward Tyler and the other boys, slipping easily into their conversation as if they belonged there.

***

Time slipped by in fragments after that, greeting relatives, answering questions that barely registered. She tried to focus on her guests, but her gaze kept sliding back to Leo and his new friends.

She watched as they wandered down the pier, lingering near the old boat dock, sunlight glinting off a bottle being passed between them. Something else moved between their hands too. So small she almost missed it.

Before she could decide whether to intervene, the boys started back up to the yard, cutting across the grass toward the side gate. The bottle had disappeared, but they walked shoulder to shoulder, murmuring.

Leo went with them without looking back or saying good-bye, and she followed.

"Where are you going?" Her voice finally broke through, controlled despite how long she'd held her tongue.

Leo didn't look at her. "Out."

"Are you drinking?" she asked. "Is that marijuana I smell?"

He bristled, shoulders squaring. "I'm eighteen. Stop treating me like I'm twelve."

"Exactly. You're eighteen. Not twenty-one."

He turned then, eyes cold. "You don't like me drinking? I learned it from you."

The words hit hard.

She opened her mouth, but nothing held, every attempt to reach him slipping through her grasp. Then, he stepped back, closing himself off before he walked through the gate, the latch rattling shut behind him.

Ava rushed past her, breathless and frantic. "Are you just going to let him go?"

She didn't wait for an answer, running toward the front yard. Jamie followed, her legs moving while her mind tried to catch up.

By the time she made it to the driveway, Ava was already there, trying to block Leo before he reached Tyler's car. "Leo, stop!"

But he shoved past her hard. Too hard. And she stumbled, hitting the ground with a sharp cry.

Jamie froze. For a heartbeat, everything went silent except the blood rushing in her ears.

Then, Tyler looked at her as Leo climbed in, eyes narrowing, the curl of his mouth daring her to try something. He slid behind the wheel, the door slamming shut before the engine revved to life and the taillights disappeared down the street.

Her mind jumped straight to the worst possibility. Tyler had been drinking and now he's driving with her son in the back seat. She had no control over where he was going or what happened next.

Ava pushed herself up, tears streaking her face as Jamie hurried toward her, reaching for her arm. "I can't believe you didn't even try to stop him," she said, jerking away.

She brushed past her, leaving her standing alone in the driveway before Julia appeared at her side, pulling her gently toward the door.

***

Inside, apart from the eyes and whispers, she finally released a breath. The fight replayed in her head. "He's right," she said. "About the drinking. I turned to alcohol every time things got hard. Just like Mom."

Julia stopped her. "You are not her. Don't let one awful moment convince you of that."

She nodded, though doubt still bore down on her.

"Should we call John?" Julia asked. "Maybe he can go after Leo."

"No. I don't want to involve him. You know how he'll twist this."

She pressed her fingers to her temple, grounding herself even as her breath shuddered. "I need to get ready for this event tonight. Will you see everyone out?"

The excuse was flimsy, and she knew it, but she couldn't step out there again. Not after hearing her own son give voice to something she carried in the darkest corners of herself.

Julia held her gaze for a second, as if reading what she wasn't saying. Then she nodded once. "I'll handle it."

After she pushed through the sliding doors, redirecting attention, Jamie pulled her phone from her pocket. She hovered over her contacts before she typed a name: Officer Mike Andrews.

He picked up on the second ring. "Andrews."

"Hey, Mike. It's Jamie Sinclair." She drew in a breath, forcing the words out. "Leo just got into a car with Tyler Reed. They've been drinking. I smelled it." The admission burned her throat. "I tried to stop him, but he wouldn't listen."

"What's he driving?" Andrews said, shifting into procedure. "Did you catch the license plate number?"

She answered what she could, hating how little that was.

"I'll put a unit in the area," he said. "Call me if he comes back."

***

The rooftop filled quickly, the noise rising with each arrival. Strings of lights stretched overhead while waiters moved with care, weaving through tight spaces, cocktails balanced high. In the corner, a live band played, low enough that people could talk over it, but loud enough to rattle in her chest.

Steve thrived in it. He sashayed from group to group with Carson at his side, steering him into the center of every circle, his hand resting on his back.

Carson's smile came easily, as if unaffected by all of it. For a moment, she could almost see the future she'd imagined for him. It unsettled her. He was already stepping into a world that had no room for her.

She stayed at the bar, her glass sweating in her hand, the napkin beneath it soaked through. A few people greeted her, polite questions asked more out of courtesy than curiosity. She returned their smiles and allowed the conversations to trail off.

Her gaze moved around the space, restless, sweeping from one cluster of guests to another, careful not to linger on Carson, though he kept drawing her attention no matter how she tried to look elsewhere.

Across the terrace, Kendall laughed with a group of players before she moseyed her way through the crowd toward Carson, her hand resting on his arm, drawing eyes. She angled her body close enough that anyone watching could imagine the rest, lips near his ear, whispering something. Then she tipped her head back with a bright laugh and his expression softened into a smile that made Jamie's stomach twist.

She looked away, heat crawling up her throat, reminding herself that Kendall fed on performance and that Carson had no interest in playing along.

Her phone buzzed against the counter. She picked it up, Julia's name flashing across the screen with an incoming call.

She muttered under her breath, "Hey Julia. Please tell me Leo made it back home."

"No, not yet. You need to check your socials," she said, clipped and urgent.

"What do you mean?"

"Just look."

Jamie hung up, her thumb hovering over Instagram. For a moment she couldn't move, as if the knowing itself might be worse than whatever waited on the screen.

Then the image opened: a photo snapped in Seattle, weeks ago, her body pressed to Carson's as his arm curved around her waist. Her face was clear, her mouth tipped toward his cheek, the intimacy seized without mercy.

Every shot cut deeper than the last. That night had lived in her mind as theirs alone, happening so quickly she never imagined someone had captured it. Now strangers owned it.

Her throat burned as she scrolled. She thought of David, and clients already calculating the risk. Then she thought of her children—of Ava's disapproval and Leo seeing his mother like this. Her hands shook.

Every glance in her direction felt different now, even those that slid past without recognition.

Two women at the bar leaned over their phones, thumbs moving as their eyes lifted, landing on Jamie before dropping again.

Then, laughter broke close by, and she turned her head, catching a man whispering to his friend, both of them glancing at her before lowering their gaze to the phone between them.

The chatter thickened, and the band's beat pressed against her skull.

She pushed back from the counter and turned too fast, slamming into a server balancing a tray of cocktails. The tray tipped, glass and liquor spilling across a nearby table.

A woman gasped. Someone else swore under their breath.

"Jesus, lady, watch where you're going!"

"Sorry." The word barely surfaced.

She forced her way through the crowd, aware of every stare now, of how long they lingered. Ahead, at the far end of the room, the exit sign burned red. She ran to it and stumbled into the stairwell as the door slammed behind her.

Bracing herself against the wall, she tried to breathe, lungs working too fast, too shallow. She tried to count, the way she always did when things threatened to spiral.

It didn't work.

Behind her, the door cracked open and footsteps approached. A man stepped toward her and lifted his phone, the flash bursting against the concrete walls, blinding.

She flinched and bolted down the stairs.

By the time she shoved through the lobby doors, Carson was calling her name.

"Jamie."

She didn't stop until the night air hit her face.

His fingers closed around her arm as he caught up to her. She twisted, desperate to pull away, but he held her long enough for her to lift her phone and shove it toward him.

"Look," she said, the word breaking.

He scanned the images, then let out a breath. "So now they know. We don't have to hide anymore."

"You don't understand what this means for me," she said. "My job, my family. You'll recover. I won't." Her chest heaved, the words scraping raw as she forced them out.

He shook his head. "You think I haven't lived with this kind of scrutiny my whole life? People watching, judging? This doesn't scare me."

"It terrifies me," she whispered. "I can't lose everything."

His eyes searched hers. "You won't lose me."

For a beat they stood there, the air frozen between them, until footsteps sounded nearby. The same man lingered near the entrance, his phone lifting again, the click of his camera unmistakable. *Not again.*

Carson turned on him instantly, reaching for the phone. "Delete it!"

The man jerked back, clutching the device to his chest as more people spilled onto the sidewalk.

Panic climbed higher. Carson tried to pull her back, his hand firm on her arm, but she tore free and stepped to the curb, slipping into the back seat of a taxi.

She gave him her address and closed her eyes, pressing her forehead against the window, willing her heart to slow. Then, her phone rang.

Her stomach dropped as she glanced down at the caller ID: *Tampa General Hospital.*

"Hello?"

"Mrs. Sinclair?" The voice on the line sounded concerned. "Your son Leo has been in a car accident. The paramedics are on their way here with him now. You need to get here as fast as you can."

Her vision tunneled, the world narrowing to the phone in her hand.

The driver's eyes caught hers in the rearview mirror, and she lurched forward, her voice breaking. "Take me to Tampa General."

Chapter 21

She was steps from the entrance when an ambulance screeched to a stop at the curb. Paramedics flung open the back doors and pulled out a gurney. A boy lay on it. Blood streaked across his face as a medic climbed up and began chest compressions.

Her breath vanished.

The hair, the build. Her mind filled in the rest.

A doctor in navy scrubs met them at the curb. "Same collision?" he asked.

"Yeah," a paramedic said, breathless. "This one was trapped. We had to cut him out."

The gurney turned under the bright hospital awning, and she finally saw him clearly. When she realized it wasn't Leo, relief hit so quickly it left her dizzy.

She followed the motion inside and moved straight to the counter. "My son, Leo Sinclair," she said, her purse sliding from her shoulder as she dug out her ID.

The clerk checked the screen and looked up. "He just arrived a few minutes ago. Please, have a seat while I page a nurse."

"How bad is it?" Her voice caught.

"I'm sorry, I know this is scary, but that's all I can see. A nurse will be out shortly."

She nodded and lifted the strap back onto her shoulder as she found a place to sit.

A nurse appeared minutes later and stepped toward her. "Are you Mrs. Sinclair?"

She rose to her feet. "Yes. Is Leo okay? What's happening?"

"The doctors are working on him now. But, he needs surgery," she said.

"What do you mean? How bad is it?" She asked, her heart pounding again.

She laid a hand on her shoulder. "I'll bring you to the family waiting room so the surgeon can update you."

Jamie followed, her mind a jumble of questions. All she wanted was someone to tell her that her son was safe and the surgery wasn't as terrifying as it sounded. *Why weren't they telling her that?*

As they entered the waiting area, the nurse pointed toward the vending machines. "There are sodas and water here, and coffee down the hall around the corner if you want something while you wait. The doctor will be with you as soon as he can."

The room held a sofa on one wall, and a bank of chairs on the other. A muted television flashed a weather map in the corner. She sat, then stood again, and paced to the window that faced a dim courtyard.

Moments later, the door opened and John entered, his face drawn and pale, eyes wide with fear. "Where is he? What have they said?"

"They're prepping him for surgery. That's all I know."

They paused in uneasy silence before he stepped closer. "How did this happen, Jamie?"

"I don't know any more than you do."

His gaze dropped to her cocktail dress, his expression hardening. "Where were you? Out with him again? Making Carson more important than our son?"

"No," she replied, more defensively than she intended. "I was at a brand launch downtown, working."

A man in scrubs entered, pausing when he saw the tension between them. "I'm sorry to interrupt," he said. "I'm Dr. Patel. Are you Leo Sinclair's parents?"

"Yes," they stated together.

The doctor spoke clearly. "Leo suffered a significant head injury in the accident. He has bleeding around the brain that requires immediate surgery to relieve the pressure. He's stable enough to proceed, but this is critical."

"Is he going to survive?" Jamie asked, pressing her hand to her mouth, her eyes wide.

"We're going to do all we can," he said, placing a hand on her shoulder. "Once we relieve the pressure and stabilize him, we'll see how he responds."

She swallowed hard. "Can we see him?"

"Yes. He's sedated, but you can have a moment before we take him back."

A nurse appeared and guided them down a hallway toward the surgical prep area, where curtains divided a row of bays. "He won't hear you, but I truly believe patients know when their loved ones are close."

She pulled the curtain back, and they stepped inside. Leo lay pale beneath the lights, his face swollen on one side, the skin mottled with deep bruising. An oxygen mask covered his nose and mouth, and a rigid cervical collar kept his neck immobile. His head was wrapped in a thick bandage, but around the edge she could see dried blood and the stark line where his hair had been shaved. Lines ran from both arms, and the monitor beside him traced each breath and heartbeat.

She reached for his hand, her fingers trembling as she wrapped them around his. "Leo, I'm here."

"We're with you, son. Just hang on." John stood on the opposite side of the bed, his face drawn as he brushed a finger over Leo's arm.

The nurse checked her watch. "I'm sorry. It's time."

Jamie lifted his hand to her lips and kissed it, whispering that she loved him before laying it gently back on the sheet. John released him last. Together, they stepped into the hall as the team began moving him toward the operating room.

Her hands shook violently, the reality of what she'd seen hitting her all at once. A raw, breaking sound tore out of her before she could stop it, and her knees gave way beneath her.

"He'll be fine. We'll get through this." John reached for her, and she leaned into him, her tears soaking into his shirt.

He lifted her chin with a look in his eyes that reminded her of the way they were in the beginning, and for a heartbeat, she almost fell back into him. Then she stepped back, reminding herself of everything that had brought them here.

She drew a shaky breath, trying to control the tremor in her hands, when a sudden cry echoed down the hallway. "Mom, where is he? Is he okay?"

Her daughter sprinted toward her, tears spilling freely, with Julia and Nicole close behind.

The moment Ava's arms wrapped around her, she closed her eyes and held tight. "He's in surgery. The doctors are working on him right now."

Ava shook, and Jamie clung to her, swallowing hard.

"I knew something like this was going to happen. We should've stopped him," Ava said.

"Stop him from what?" John asked, looking between them.

He took a step closer, hands clenched. "Ava, what are you talking about?"

But she didn't answer him, shrinking in against her mother.

His gaze cut into Jamie. "What happened before the accident? Who was he with?"

"Let's take a breath before we start interrogating anyone," Julia said, interrupting before the question could land. "We need to hold it together until we know he's okay."

***

The night had not turned into morning so much as it had stretched without permission. A long, colorless line of hours that refused to end. The waiting room held the sound of vending machines and the soft hiss of the air system, while the television in the corner moved through a parade of headlines no one watched.

Jamie stood when the nurse passed and sat when the nurse kept walking, the motion automatic now, like a door swinging on a tired hinge.

When Dr. Patel finally stepped inside, her breath stopped cold. For hours she had imagined this moment, rehearsed a dozen versions of it, every single one of them terrifying her.

He approached them slowly, fatigue etched into the lines around his eyes. "We ran into an unexpected complication," he said. "There was a hidden vessel that ruptured after we started. It took time to get it under control, but we did. He's stable."

For a moment, nobody spoke, then Ava let out a trembling breath, asking the question Jamie had been too afraid to. "Will he be ok?"

He shifted slightly, softening his tone. "I can't make any promises yet. Head injuries can be unpredictable, but he made it through the surgery. That gives him a real chance."

Everyone seemed to release a breath at once.

"We're moving him to the ICU," he said, glancing toward the hallway. "Once they get him settled, you'll be able to see him."

John exhaled and nodded, his voice rough. "Thank you, doctor. For everything."

The trembling in Jamie's hands eased now that she knew he'd made it through. She sank back in her seat, the room blurring for a moment as she pressed the heels of her palms to her eyes. When she lowered them, a man with a badge pinned to his belt stepped through the doorway, his gaze moving carefully over each of them.

"Mr. and Mrs. Sinclair?" he asked.

"Yes, that's us," John replied.

He didn't offer his hand. "Detective Harris," he said, voice firm. "I need to speak with you both."

John crossed his arms. "If you're here for Leo's statement, it can wait."

"I'm not here for that yet. I want to inform you of what we know." Something in his voice made Jamie's spine go rigid. "The accident occurred around eight forty last night. Two individuals were in the other vehicle. One died at the scene. The other is in critical condition."

His face remained impassive, composed in the way of someone who had long ago separated empathy from procedure. "We're still processing everything, reconstructing the crash. We need to get witness statements and pull the traffic cameras. All of it takes time." He hesitated. "Tyler Reed was treated in the ER and discharged a few hours ago. According to his account your son was behind the wheel."

"No," Jamie said instantly, heat rising through her chest. "Leo wasn't driving. He's lying."

"Well, unfortunately, the officers confirmed his story. They found Leo in the driver's seat when they arrived."

She opened her mouth, but nothing came out before John stepped in. "Why would my son be driving a car that doesn't belong to him?"

"It's not unusual. Reed wasn't in any condition to drive. Leo may have taken the wheel. Why either of them chose to operate a vehicle is another question."

"What exactly are you implying?" John asked, jaw clenching.

A smug look flickered across the detective's face, a slight curl at the corner of his mouth as if he felt firmly in control of the narrative. "Nothing. We'll let the evidence speak for itself." He paused. "I came to tell you directly, so you weren't blindsided when the news starts circulating."

He told them he'd return later and stepped out of the waiting room, the door barely closing before John turned to her, his eyes narrowing. "Tyler? Tell me why our son was in a car with him because none of this makes sense."

"He showed up at the party yesterday. Leo must have invited him."

"That still doesn't explain anything. Jesus, Jamie, did you let him go?"

"Don't blame her." Ava stood abruptly, her chair scraping against the floor, tears streaking down her face. "You're his parent too. This isn't just on her."

She turned away from them, storming out of the waiting room.

"He was right. They're already running it," Julia said, stepping toward the television.

Jamie's gaze followed as the camera panned across the crushed vehicles, the captions announcing a fatal crash.

"Our son on the news, at fault in a fatal accident," John said. "That's where we are. And you're still acting like you had no part in this." He looked back at her, eyes narrowed. "You should've protected him."

The words drained what little composure she had left.

Julia must have seen it, because she moved closer, threading their arms together before Jamie broke. "Come on," she said under her breath. "Let's get some coffee."

They walked down the corridor and didn't speak again until they reached the small alcove with the coffee pots.

"Don't let him get to you. Kids will be kids and accidents happen."

"No, he's right. I should've done more to stop him."

A soft hiss rose as hot coffee hit the bottom of a paper cup.

"He would've shoved past you anyway. Teenagers think they're invincible. You can't save them from every bad decision, no matter how hard you try."

Jamie's phone vibrated in her palm, startling her. *Carson.*

She hadn't let herself think about the rooftop bar or the photos since she'd received the devastating phone call about the accident. But the sight of his name brought all of it back in a rush.

"You should answer him. If he saw the news, he'll be worried about you."

"I can't deal with that right now. I have enough to worry about."

"Does Ava know yet?"

"You mean, has she seen the pictures?" She ran a hand through her hair, releasing a breath. "I don't think so."

"You need to tell her before someone else does."

She let the words sink in, holding the cup between her palms, then glanced at her sister. "What would you say? If it were you?"

"I'd start with the truth," Julia said, leaning her shoulder against the wall. "Ava's sharp. She'll see through half-answers. She deserves to hear it from you, not the internet."

She sighed. "I don't even know how to begin."

"You don't have to make it pretty. Just honest."

A soft chime echoed from the hallway, and a second later Julia's expression shifted. "Shit."

Their parents walked toward them, Evelyn's face holding that cool, clipped judgement she knew was coming. Richard moved beside her, his mouth pressed into a thin line.

"Mom? Dad? What are you doing here?" The question slipped out before she could think. "Did John call you?"

"No," Evelyn said, her tone snapping like a whip. "But one of you should have. We heard it on the news. Our grandson named as the driver in a fatal accident. And you couldn't be bothered to pick up the phone."

Evelyn's eyes swept over her, and only then did Jamie realize she was still in the cocktail dress from the night before. "Where were you?"

"At an event, downtown." She folded her arms across herself, bracing against the weight of her mother's scrutiny.

Evelyn pressed on, unrelenting. "Children need structure, Jamie. Curfew. Consequences. You run around with your job and your meetings, pretending you can parent from your car."

"Right," Julia said, shifting at Jamie's side, her tone edged with sarcasm. "You were such a flawless mother."

Evelyn waved her off with a dismissive flick of her hand, as if Julia's words didn't warrant a reply. "Where's John?"

Before she could answer, John was already stepping into the corridor, and Evelyn moved toward him immediately, pulling him into a hug. "How's Leo?"

"He had bleeding around the brain," John said. "They took him into surgery to get it under control, and he made it through. He's in the ICU now so they can monitor him."

Evelyn's brows pulled together. "Bleeding around the brain?"

"The surgeon stopped it. But they'll be watching him closely for the next couple of days."

"Dear God," she said, drawing in a breath. When she finally looked back at Jamie, her expression had grown sharper. "This is what happens when a family breaks apart. You should've waited until he graduated. Children need stability. Your father and I made sacrifices. We did not make choices that put the two of you on edge like this."

Julia stepped forward before she could answer. "Don't you dare pin this on her divorce. Leo was in an accident because he got into the car with the wrong kid. Stop twisting everything into her fault."

"You think you know better, Julia?" Evelyn asked, eyes narrowing. "Families fall apart, and children pay the price. If you ever have any, you'll understand. Though I doubt you will, with the kind of life you've chosen."

Her father cleared his throat. He had listened in silence until then, hands in his coat pockets. "That's enough, Evelyn," he said.

At once Evelyn's posture shifted, an echo of those moments in Jamie's childhood when his voice had ended every argument.

He turned his attention back to John. "What do you know about the investigation?"

"They're still reconstructing the crash and talking to witnesses. But the officers who responded found Leo behind the wheel."

Richard nodded as if checking boxes in his mind. "Did Leo speak at all?"

"He's been sedated."

"Alright." He took out his phone. "I'll make a call. He needs counsel before anyone asks questions. Don't let any detectives in his room without a lawyer. If the nurse says they have permission, you ask her to call me."

He moved toward the waiting room with John and Evelyn following close behind, speaking in low voices as they stepped out.

"Do you want me to go by your house, pack a bag for you?" Julia asked. "A change of clothes, a toothbrush? You might be here a while."

Jamie managed a tired smile. "That would help. Thank you."

After giving her a hug, Julia turned toward the elevators, and the corridor fell silent.

The quiet held only a beat before a nurse appeared. "They've finished getting him settled. You can see him now."

***

The ICU room was dim when she stepped inside, but every detail felt too exposed. Tubes and machines filled the space around him, their steady beeping the only proof he was still alive.

He looked so still. Not like the boy she used to chase around the house playing hide and seek, or the teenager who sprawled across the couch, watching football and arguing about every bad call. She couldn't reconcile any version of him with the one lying motionless beneath the sheets.

The closer she got, the harder it was to breathe. She found his hand and wrapped her fingers around it. It was warm, a reminder that he was here, even if he couldn't come back to her yet.

"Hi, baby," she said, voice trembling. "I'm right here."

Her eyes lifted for a moment, not to the machines or the ceiling, but somewhere past them.

She let out a shaky breath, her fingers curling around Leo's. "If putting us back together is what it takes. If that's the price, I'll do it. Just don't take my son. Please."

Chapter 22

The next twenty-four hours dragged by, each minute marked by the rise and fall of Leo's chest. He hadn't opened his eyes once, not even a flutter of awareness she kept praying for.

Nurses told her it was normal after a surgery like this. The swelling needed time to ease. Some patients took longer to surface than others. But time seemed cruel when he lay so still. She stayed beside him, her hand wrapped around his, watching every slow breath.

A dull ache spread beneath her ribs, exhaustion sinking deep in her body after too many hours of holding herself upright, refusing to let fear take her under.

She had given in at last, sinking into the chair and closing her aching eyes, when a buzzing noise snapped her awake from across the room.

Ava, curled in the recliner beside the window, had refused to leave his side as well. A flood of notifications rattled her phone, and she sat up in an instant, hand to her chest, her mouth hanging open before she lifted her gaze to her mother and stood abruptly. "You're unbelievable," she said, striding past.

Jamie didn't need to see the screen to know what'd flashed across it, timed perfectly to hit when she had nothing left to give.

She rose to her feet, hurrying after her. "Ava, wait."

"Why didn't you tell me about him?" She asked, her voice cutting through the quiet corridor. "Why did I have to find out from a friend texting me saying how cool my mother is?" She lifted her fingers in air quotes. "Hashtag goals."

A pause stretched between them, offering an opening for an explanation, but Jamie's gaze fell to the floor and no answer followed.

"Right. Say nothing. That tracks." She jabbed the elevator button hard, then hit it again. And again.

Desperate to stop her, Jamie reached for her arm. "I was going to tell you. I just..."

"You should have already." Ava pulled back, her cheeks flushed, her eyes bright with anger. "I had to see pictures from someone else, like gossip at school. Do you know how humiliating this is?"

The doors opened with a chime, and Carson stepped out, freezing when he spotted them. His gaze landed first on Ava, then on Jamie, before Ava let out a bitter laugh. "Perfect," she said as she moved inside. "You two deserve each other."

The doors closed, and silence filled the hall until he spoke. "She saw the pictures?"

Jamie nodded, swallowing once. "How did you know I was here?"

"It was on the news. I came as soon as I saw it."

He looked at her in a way that showed how much he wanted to hold her, and she longed to fall into his arms, her tears streaming unchecked. "Do you want to get out of here for a minute? Somewhere private we can talk?"

Before she could answer, the elevator doors opened again, and Detective Harris stepped out. She wiped her cheeks quickly, trying to compose herself.

His gaze shifted between them, lingering on Carson for a moment as recognition crossed his face. "Carson Tate?"

He gave a small nod, and Harris extended his hand. "Rick Harris. Nice to meet you. I'm a big fan."

Frustration rose in Jamie at the interruption. "Why are you here? We told you Leo isn't ready to talk."

"Relax. I'm here to see you and your husband."

The word landed wrong, and heat crept up her neck as she flicked a glance at Carson, afraid of what he might assume before she corrected the detective. "Ex-husband."

"Apologies. I didn't know that."

He shifted his stance, rubbing a hand over the back of his neck as if trying to recover his footing in the conversation. "I heard your father hired an attorney. Good ol' Richard Maddox. Must be nice to always have a man like him in your corner."

Carson's head snapped toward her, the shift in his expression clear. He'd put the pieces together. The secret she'd been keeping from him was now fully exposed.

God, I should've told him, she thought to herself. This was the worst possible way for him to find out.

He shook his head as he turned back to the elevator, and she nearly reached for him, the apology rising in her throat. But she swallowed it down. *Not here. Not now.*

"Was it something I said?" Harris asked, curiosity blooming across his face.

"What do you want?" She crossed her arms and drew a deep breath, preparing herself for what he might unload next.

"I wanted to deliver the good news in person. Tyler's story doesn't hold up. The damage on the passenger side lines up with Leo's head injury. After we confronted him with that, he admitted to moving Leo to the driver's seat."

Something inside her finally unclenched, but she kept her arms across her chest, giving him nothing. "Well, that's great news but I already knew he was lying. If that's all you came to say, I need to get back to my son."

She pivoted toward Leo's door, eager to put distance between herself and the conversation, but Harris stopped her. "Jamie."

"Is there more?" She asked, turning to face him.

"Will Leo pull through?" His features shifted, almost sincere, though it didn't quite fit him.

"I didn't realize you cared."

"Ouch. I may come across as heartless but I'm not."

She wasn't sure what to do with that. He might have meant it, but she didn't have space in her head for his moral compass.

"He hasn't woken up yet but we're hopeful."

He tilted his head, drawing his brows together. "You all seem like good people. I can't make sense of Leo hanging out with someone like Tyler." He paused. "Well, I hope everything turns out ok and he gets a second chance." He gave her small nod and turned away.

His words lingered longer than she wanted them to. *A second chance.* If only it were that simple.

She waited until the elevator doors closed, then let out a slow breath, though tension still coiled in her shoulders. There was relief in the good news, but it didn't untangle everything else. The secrets she'd kept were out now, all of them colliding at the worst possible moment.

***

When she returned to Leo's room, she caught the subtle shift in his breathing, faster than it had been a few hours ago.

She straightened, watching his fingers twitch, the slightest scrape of his knuckles against the blanket. His eyelids fluttered. Once. Then again, longer this time.

"Leo?" She moved closer, one hand cupping the side of his face.

His eyes opened a sliver, unfocused and searching. He blinked twice, struggling to focus, and turned his head slightly in her direction.

"Mom?" The word rasped out, thin.

"I'm here."

He swallowed, the movement visible in the line of his throat. His gaze drifted toward the window. The steady beep of the machines seemed to pull his attention next before his eyes found her again as if nothing around him made sense. He lifted his hand, slow and shaky, reaching toward his forehead before she caught his wrist.

"Don't," she said. "You had surgery. Your head's going to hurt."

Confusion seemed to tighten the space between his brows, his breath stuttering, uneven and shallow.

"You're okay," she whispered as she pressed the call button. "Just breathe."

He blinked again, a small sound slipping from him, and she recognized the fear in it immediately. His legs shifted under the blanket in a weak attempt to move. She placed a hand on his shoulder, grounding him.

The nurse entered quickly, calm and direct. "He's awake?"

Jamie stepped back, giving her room to lean over him. She lifted a penlight and examined each pupil. "Can you tell me your name?"

He opened his mouth, but the answer came delayed and weak. "Leo."

"Good. Do you know where you are?"

His eyes moved around the room again, struggling to connect the pieces. "Hospital."

"That's right." She checked his fluids, then looked at Jamie. "I'm going to page the doctor, but he looks good."

A soft knock sounded at the door, and Jamie turned to see Ava standing there. Her eyes were red, her cheeks blotchy. Whatever anger she'd carried earlier was gone the moment she saw her brother awake.

"Is he..." She stepped inside before she finished the question, and Jamie nodded, stepping aside so she could approach the bed.

She reached for Leo's hand with trembling fingers. "Hey," she whispered.

His eyes shifted toward her, a tired spark of mischief pulling at his mouth. "You're ugly when you cry."

She let out a noise that was half laugh, half sob, and Jamie watched them, grateful for the familiar sound of him teasing his sister.

Footsteps approached, heavier this time. John stood in the doorway, his gaze moving from Ava to Leo before stopping briefly on her. "How long has he been awake?"

"A few minutes."

As he stepped closer, something loosened in his face, a quiet shift that reminded her of what they used to be in the beginning. A happy family. In love.

His hand found hers by the edge of the bed, his fingers closing around her own in a small, discreet pull that felt almost instinctive.

The doctor arrived a moment later, his expression alert. He moved to Leo's bedside and began his assessment. "Leo, I'm Dr. Patel. I'm going to check a few things, alright?"

Leo blinked slowly, the effort visible. "Okay."

The doctor lifted his hand. "Can you squeeze my fingers?"

He did. Weak, but consistent.

"Good. Follow the light for me." He traced the penlight across Leo's field of vision, nodding at each response.

"Any nausea? Head pressure?"

Leo hesitated, then nodded faintly. "A little."

"You gave us all quite a scare," he said, adjusting Leo's pillow. "But whatever you're made of is strong stuff."

He gently rubbed the top of his head before turning to John and Jamie, glancing between them. "Why don't we step into the hallway for a moment?"

They followed him out, the door clicking shut as he turned to face them. "He's responding the way we hoped. He'll be tired and a little confused for a while, but as long as the swelling keeps going down, we can start thinking about discharging him in a few days. He may need some therapy."

John let out a slow breath. "Thank you. Once we get him home, we'll make sure he's set up with everything he needs."

We? Home? He said it as if he could step back into her life through the doorway of this room without asking.

A small sinking feeling opened low in her stomach, but she remembered what she'd whispered into the dark last night. The bargain she'd made with God.

He'd brought Leo back to her. Of that, she had no doubt. And as she watched Ava lean into her brother, it was impossible not to feel the old shape of their family pressing in around her. Maybe this was what she owed. What she'd promised.

***

"You've put this firm in a bad light."

David didn't ease into it. The words hit the moment she stepped into his office, stopping her breath. He didn't offer a seat or ask about Leo. He stood behind his desk, jaw clenched, as if he'd been rehearsing the line.

Her pulse kicked hard, and she lowered herself into the chair when he finally gestured toward it, folding her hands in her lap. "I've done my best."

"Your best?" His voice rose. "Do you know what a mistake like yours could cost? Sponsors might pull support, endorsements could vanish, and athletes who trusted us may decide to walk."

Something in her sagged as he spoke. One crisis, and suddenly her career felt as fragile as everything else in her life.

"I had a lapse in judgement, but my work has always been solid."

He gave a humorless laugh. "If you weren't Richard Maddox's daughter, I'd have fired you already."

The words sliced through her. All the effort she'd poured into this job reduced to her father's name.

He dropped into his chair and released a brittle sigh, pinching the bridge of his nose before looking at her again. "Dylan's father reached out to me. Said he hadn't heard from you in a few weeks, and he'd seen the photos. He was ready to walk. I told him they were fake. And that you were out because of a family emergency. He calmed down."

She nodded once, taking in the way he said it as though he'd cleaned up a mess she'd made. "Ok, I'll get to work on his footage and try to schedule some private workouts," she replied, rising from the chair.

He lifted a hand, stopping her mid-motion. "Sit. I've already done that. He's scheduled to be down in Miami tomorrow. You'll meet them there." He leaned forward, sliding a folder across the desk. "I'm giving you one last chance. Don't waste it."

As she reached for it, he pulled it back and paused. "How's Leo?"

"He's at home now and getting better every day."

"And someone is there with him?"

She was a bit surprised that he even cared. He'd just informed her about the workout in Miami tomorrow like it wasn't an option. But maybe this was his subtle way of asking instead of demanding.

"John's there."

"Good," he said, sliding the folder toward her once more. "I'm glad he's on the mend."

She took it and stood when he dismissed her, spine rigid even as her steps wavered beneath her heels.

***

Outside his office, the bullpen filled with ordinary noise, and she made her way through it in a fog. When she sank into her chair, a hand tapped the partition.

Steve leaned over with a smirk. "Well, look who's back."

"Is there something you need?" She asked, keeping her eyes on the monitor.

He chuckled. "No. But you cost me fifty bucks. We all had money on whether you'd walk back in here. I had you tapped out."

His phone rang, pulling him away before she could respond, and a dull ache settled in her chest, spreading up into her throat. She swallowed hard, trying to keep it down.

The folder David had handed over was still in her grip. She opened it and found the itinerary spread across the first page in his clipped handwriting.

For a moment she couldn't move, his voice pressing at the edges of her thoughts. *If you weren't Richard Maddox's daughter.* His certainty left nothing for her to contest, landing in a way disappointment always had when it came from men who decided her worth before she ever spoke.

Her job had once been a lifeline, a chance to rebuild something of herself after the divorce. Now it was like another place she had to survive. Every step forward seemed to require two backward, and she no longer knew if the fight merited whatever she was trying to prove.

With Carson, she had felt like her work mattered. He hadn't talked over her or dismissed her concerns; he'd taken her seriously, even pushed her to trust her own instincts. Remembering that now only reminded her how far off balance she'd slipped.

She closed the folder and drew a deep breath. Tomorrow she would drive to Miami and do what she had to do, even if it took more out of her than she could spare.

***

The visitor lot rose ahead, a reminder that everything David demanded hinged on what happened next.

She eased her car into a space near the front entrance, and stepped out, the humidity wrapping her instantly.

As she crossed the pavement, she spotted Dylan and his father waiting by the double doors. Mr. Prescott leaned in close to his son, a grin spreading wide across his face. He clapped Dylan on the back with exaggerated slaps. "Today changes everything," he said, his voice carrying even before she closed the distance. "You're about to see the next Giannis."

Dylan stood tall beside him, headphones looped around his neck, gaze fixed ahead. His chin lifted, arrogance flickering across his face, an expression that suggested he already believed he belonged without needing to prove it.

She joined them with a polite smile, tamping down the weight pressing against her ribs. "Just play your game but stay grounded. That's what they'll be looking for."

Inside the lobby, staffers greeted the trio politely, though something in their expressions felt pointed. Maybe the photos had traveled farther than Tampa, but she tucked the sting away. She couldn't afford to show cracks.

A young woman approached them, wearing a Heat polo and her credentials attached to a lanyard. "Hi, I'm Reese Green, operations assistant," she said. "I'll get Dylan checked in. You can watch from the row of seats by the scorer's table."

Mr. Prescott made his way to the court while Jamie excused herself and slipped down the hallway toward the restroom, grateful for a moment out of sight.

As she pushed through the door, two staffers stood near the sinks, their conversation cutting off mid-sentence. One of them glanced at her reflection, nudging the other before they both lowered their voices. She didn't catch the words, only the tone, laced with judgement strong enough to make her skin prickle.

When she returned to the lobby, a row of mounted screens played muted sports coverage. A graphic slid across the bottom ticker. Her eyes snagged on a familiar name. *The Tampa Bay Buccaneers announce training camp invitees. Veteran and wide receiver, Carson Tate expected to attend.*

She stopped for half a second. It wasn't anything she hadn't anticipated, but seeing it on the screen today, of all days, stung more than she cared to admit. She pushed the thought down and found her way to the court.

As she took a seat beside him, Mr. Prescott shot her a quick, eager glance, his jaw set in a grin that carried certainty. "He's about to show them what a mistake they made overlooking him."

She didn't respond; she knew better. Instead, she drew a breath, wishing he understood how fast arrogance closes doors in a place like this.

The squeak of sneakers echoed through the gym minutes later as Dylan started with shooting drills. He sank a couple of deep threes in a row, swagger written in the tilt of his chin. Then he missed two, the ball bouncing long, and rather than chasing it down, he motioned for the trainer to toss him another. One coach scribbled on his clipboard while the other watched silently, their attention narrowing each time he waved off the rebound.

Conditioning drills came next. Sprints down and back, whistles cutting through the air. He exploded out on the first run. On the second, his stride shortened, his pace dropped, and he crossed the line grinning, palms open as if to say he'd done enough.

Scrimmage was last. Two players in Heat practice gear jogged onto the court to run sets with him. Dylan took the ball and dribbled around them, shoulders rolling, movements loose and showy. He sank a pull-up jumper that snapped through the net, then called for it again. After that, he ignored the play call and kept possession. He drove one-on-one at every chance, thumping his chest after a dunk.

Mr. Prescott's voice rose above the bounce of the ball. "That's my boy! Next LeBron, right there!" He clapped until his palms reddened, basking in a spotlight no one else acknowledged.

The coaches stayed silent, their faces set, and her throat dried. She knew each possession widened the gap between talent and maturity.

Afterwards, they gathered in a circle, comparing notes on their clipboards, heads tilted toward one another in quiet exchange. She watched them, waiting for one of them to glance in her direction or step forward, but they didn't. Their silence made the outcome clear.

A moment later, Reese returned, her expression polite. "Thanks for coming. We'll be in touch."

Dylan slung a towel around his neck, strutting toward them as though he had already locked in a contract, and Mr. Prescott launched right back into praise. "I told you," he declared, voice swelling. "They saw it. They'd be crazy not to call."

***

When they reached the parking lot, Mr. Prescott finally glanced her way. "You're quiet," he said, a smirk tugging at his mouth. "Nothing to add?"

She drew in a breath, choosing her words with the care of someone about to deliver a clean, necessary wound. "It isn't only about talent. Teams look at attitude and how you fit their program."

Dylan's face shifted, pride hardening into anger. "You don't believe in me. You never have. Bet you don't treat Carson like this." He let the words hang, then sneered. "He's your MVP."

Mr. Prescott laughed, the sound abrupt and cruel as he nudged his son. "Yeah. Must be nice getting those kinds of agent perks."

He and Dylan cracked up, the joke aimed squarely at her as if she weren't even standing there.

Her stomach knotted, heat rushing up her neck. For a moment she couldn't move, the insult sitting in the air between them until something inside her snapped.

She was done softening her words for men who never earned the courtesy, done pretending she didn't see the way people dismissed her. They had pushed her past every reasonable limit.

"Let me spell this out since neither one of you can read the room." She paused, locking her eyes on Dylan. "They're not going to call you back. They saw the same thing I saw today. A child in a man's body who has the discipline of a raccoon in a dumpster. You didn't go undrafted because you're not good enough. Plenty of guys with less talent get drafted every year. You went undrafted because you have a horrible attitude."

She flicked her gaze to his father. "And you? Every coach and scout in the country knows exactly what you are. A man trying to live through his son's success and doing it with the subtlety of a bull at the dinner table. No team wants to deal with this circus. So good luck."

They both stared at her, jaws slack, their earlier bravado nowhere in sight.

She got into her car, and slammed the door, letting the crack of metal be her final word.

***

Her hands hovered on the steering wheel as the parking lot fell away in the rearview mirror. The adrenaline drained fast, leaving her empty and trembling in its wake.

A notification flashed across the screen on her dashboard. *Missed text from John.*

She released a slow breath and tapped it, the message opening before she could talk herself out of it. *Remember, dinner is at seven with the client I mentioned. Will you be back in time?*

She didn't respond, though it settled in her mind heavier than she wanted to admit. He hadn't asked how things had gone or if she needed anything. He assumed she'd fall into place, the way she used to.

The interstate stretched ahead, a wide ribbon of heat shimmering at the edges, and as she merged into traffic, she noticed a green sign ahead. A city they'd passed through years ago on a family trip when the kids were small.

In her mind, she saw Leo's curls sticking to his forehead as he laughed in the backseat, and Ava's tiny hand pointing at the ocean, while John reached over to squeeze her knee.

Life had been simpler then. Not easier. God knew raising two children wasn't easy, but she'd understood her purpose. She fit somewhere.

Her mother's voice drifted in, uninvited. *Stability matters more than the mistakes a man makes. John can give you that, Jamie. He always has.*

Maybe that was the worst part. How tempting the idea felt right now. She had let him move back home, just until Leo recovered and left for college. But he had reversed the packing and all the weeks preparing to sell the house in a single afternoon. And she hadn't stopped him.

Her fingers dug into the steering wheel. What kind of future was she even fighting for? Today had shown her how thin the ground beneath her career had become. If she couldn't hold a job, if every step forward collapsed under her, what exactly was she proving by doing this alone?

Chapter 23

"You're beautiful." John's hands settled at her waist as they stood in the mirror together, the gesture one he'd used for years. She used to lean into it without thinking. Tonight, she stayed still, watching their reflection and wondering when she had started feeling like a guest in her own life.

The dress she'd chosen hung exactly the way he liked. It was fitted at the waist and modest at the neckline, in the shade he once told her made her look softer under restaurant lights. Since he'd moved back in, she had started choosing things with him in mind again, falling into old habits faster than she wanted to admit.

Her thoughts were cut short when his phone buzzed against the glass top of the closet island, her eyes darting to the screen before she could stop herself.

He snatched it up, sliding it into his pocket, and her throat went dry. "Who's Marissa?"

"A prospect. Ready?" His tone was dismissive, giving the question no weight as he pressed his hand into the small of her back, guiding her toward the door.

***

The drive into the city passed in shallow talk. John praised the client they would meet, recalling years of contracts signed over steak dinners. She murmured agreement, her hands folded in her lap, but *Marissa* lingered in her mind, echoing with each mile toward the restaurant.

Headlights flared across the awning, luxury cars stacked one after the other, and John passed off his keys to the valet attendant with a confident nod.

Inside, the air thickened with seared beef and garlic. Leather booths pressed against paneled walls while waiters hurried past balancing heavy plates. The client and his wife were already waiting at their table, rising briefly as John greeted them.

They had barely settled when he ordered the most expensive Cabernet without looking at the price. The waiter poured it, the glasses catching the low light as John swirled his with an easy, familiar motion. Then he steered the conversation, laughing when the client praised his golf swing, adding a story about a deal closed on the course.

Jamie smiled, raising her glass at his toast, and staying quiet while the men talked about markets and politics. *How many times had she done this?*

When the plates cleared, he suggested they move to the bar and pressed his hand into her back as they rose, steering her that way.

He claimed a booth next to the window and gestured for the women to sit first before taking his place beside Jamie. Then, he and his client compared bourbons, choosing one from the top shelf. With the order placed, he leaned forward, starting another conversation.

She pretended to listen, sipping her wine, wishing she had stayed home when something in the corner of her eye caught her attention.

Carson walked in with two teammates, heads turning as people recognized them.

She froze, watching him step toward the bar, laughing at something. Then his eyes lifted across the room, his gaze meeting hers.

Heat climbed her neck as she forced her head down, picturing what this must look like to him. John pressed against her, his arm draped over her shoulder—a proprietary touch he knew people noticed, and one that always made her feel claimed. Her stomach turned.

She set her napkin on the table. "Excuse me," she said. "I need to use the restroom."

John nodded, already deep in another story.

She slipped from the booth, legs shaking, and crossed the lounge. As she brushed past Carson, her hand grazed his. It was so slight it might have been nothing, yet she felt it echo through her chest like she had shouted his name across the room.

The hallway swallowed the noise of the bar, leaving only the loud thud of her pulse. She told herself not to turn around, that he wouldn't follow her, that he probably hated her and had moved on. But she closed her eyes and spun on her heel. When she opened them, he was there, one hand in his pocket, watching her...waiting.

Her gaze fell to the ground, unable to look at him. "You always find out about me in the worst ways," she said, finally, her teeth catching the edge of her thumbnail. "I should've told you. About John. About my father." Her voice wavered, and she hated that it did. "I should've called you. I'm sorry."

"You don't need to apologize." Then he stepped closer. So close she could almost feel the heat from his body. "I just want you to be happy."

He moved her hand away from her mouth and gently cupped her chin, forcing her to look at him. "Are you?"

The truth tangled in her mind. Her happiness had nothing to do with her reasons for taking John back, but hearing Carson ask her made her realize how far she'd drifted from the life she wanted.

He dropped his hand and stepped back just as footsteps carried toward them. John rounded the corner, his eyes flicking from her to Carson, as if measuring the distance, the spark.

Carson didn't speak. He looked at John for a beat, long enough to make the point, then stepped around him and walked away without a word.

John glared at her and she braced for accusation, but none came. Instead, his expression smoothed as he adjusted his cuff and said, "They're waiting."

He turned around and walked away, but she stayed rooted, her pulse racing.

He had seen enough to wonder, and she knew he wouldn't let it go. He might have shelved it for the moment, but the reckoning would come later.

When they made it back to their booth, he resumed his performance, but he didn't put his arm around her this time, and the absence chilled her.

***

Silence stretched as they drove toward Davis Island, streetlights flickering across the windshield. John's hands rested easy on the wheel, but his jaw stayed locked.

"So," he said at last, "how long has it been going on? How long have you been lying to me?"

Her stomach clenched as she turned to him. "You want to talk about honesty? How many times did I look the other way while you stepped out on me? How many women before I stopped asking?"

"This isn't about me."

"Isn't it? I know what I saw tonight. Your phone. A woman's name flashing across the screen. You called her a prospect, but I'm not stupid. I've lived with this too long not to figure it out."

His mouth twisted. "Well, at least there aren't pictures of me circulating all over social media."

She stiffened, her breath catching for a beat.

"What, you think I didn't know?" His eyes cut toward her. "I figured maybe they were fake. Maybe you'd come to your senses, but I gave you too much credit." He let out a low, humorless laugh. "You're sneaking around with him and dragging our family through it. Do you realize what people are saying? You've made a fool of yourself."

"This isn't about what people are saying. This is about you losing control of me. That's what you can't stand."

The car filled with silence again, his hands clamped around the wheel, knuckles pale. He said nothing more.

When he pulled into the driveway, he cut the engine. "You should think about what you're doing," he sneered. "Because this doesn't end well for anyone."

She took a deep breath. "It's already over between me and Carson."

His mouth curved. "Good. Maybe now you'll remember where you belong."

He got out and circled the car to open her door, but she had already stepped onto the driveway and headed toward the front door.

As he followed her into the foyer, she turned and steadied her breathing, gathering the resolve to speak the truth once and for all. "I don't think this is going to work. As much as I love Leo, I just can't pretend anymore."

For a moment, he didn't move. His eyes flicked over her face, assessing, calculating. Then his jaw locked, a muscle near his temple ticking.

He closed the distance without warning, and she retreated a step before she realized she was moving. "You think you're leaving me?" His voice dropped, his tone menacing. "After everything I've done for you?" He stepped in, near enough that she could smell the bourbon on his breath. "You're nothing without me, Jamie."

"John, stop…" She lifted her hands, bracing them against his shoulders.

"Say it. Say you choose him," he said, shoving her back against the wall.

She swallowed and held his eyes. "I choose myself."

The words seemed to explode between them. He surged forward, clamping a hand around her jaw and crushing his mouth to hers in a bruising, desperate kiss. She turned away, pushing at his chest, but he caught her wrists and dragged them above her head, trying to hold her there.

"Don't," she pleaded.

That's when she saw Leo running toward them. "Let her go!"

John's grip loosened and he stepped back, releasing her. Then he turned to his son. "Go back to your room. This is between me and your mother."

Leo didn't move.

Jamie's chest heaved as she reached toward the console, her fingers closing around a ceramic lamp. Before she could think twice, she hurled it at him.

It struck him square in the back, then fell to the floor and shattered.

He went still.

Slowly, he turned, the look in his eyes stopping her breath.

He took a step toward her, and Leo moved instantly, shoving himself between them and driving both hands into his father's chest.

"You need to leave."

John blinked, stunned. For a moment, she thought he might say something more, but instead he turned, yanked open the front door, and slammed it behind him.

***

By morning, the house was quiet. Sunlight spilled across the channel, and Jamie stood at the window, watching a fishing boat idle near the dock. Then she exhaled and moved toward the laundry room to gather the dustpan.

She stepped toward the foyer, where the shattered base of the lamp still lay scattered across the floor.

Footsteps sounded behind her.

"I'll get this," Leo said, taking the dustpan.

When the floor was clear, he carried the broken pieces to the trash and glanced back at her. "Do you want pancakes?"

She blinked at him. "Pancakes?"

"Yeah." He pulled open the pantry door and reached for the Bisquick.

She watched him for a second longer, then opened the refrigerator. "I'll mix."

After he set the bowl on the island, she stepped beside him, with eggs and milk.

"Mom," he said finally, not looking up.

"We don't have to talk about it."

He shook his head. "You don't even know what I was going to say."

She set the measuring cup down and gave him her full attention.

"When you and Dad divorced," he said, eyes fixed on the batter, "I thought you were the one who gave up." He swallowed. "I was angry at you for that. For a long time. But last night...I see what he can be. The monster he turns into."

Something inside her gave way. "Leo..."

"Let me finish," he said. "As much as I hate him right now, he's still my dad. But what he did to you...it's wrong."

"I never wanted you to have to take sides."

"I'm not taking sides," he said. "I just...I get it now."

The pause stretched, and a small, strangled sound caught in his throat, the same one he used to make as a boy when he was trying not to cry.

"There's something else I need to tell you. Something I should've said a long time ago."

"What is it?"

He backed away from the counter, dragging a hand through his hair.

"Remember when you asked why I was giving Tyler money?"

She nodded, even though she wasn't sure she was ready to hear whatever came next.

"It wasn't because he needed help." He looked up, eyes glassy. "There was this party. I—I don't even know why I went."

Her fingers curled into the fabric of her sleeve, but she held still, letting him find the words.

"I got high. I shouldn't have, I just... I did. And I passed out." His voice cracked. "I didn't know until after." He swallowed hard. "Tyler—he..." The words stalled out.

"It's okay," she said softly. "Take your time."

He nodded once, eyes on the floor. "He took pictures." The last words barely made it out. "Stupid ones. Embarrassing ones."

Her stomach dipped. She wanted to hit something, anything, but she kept her hands at her sides. Losing control would only make this harder for him.

"He said he'd post them everywhere. And that everyone would see them. I was terrified, Mom. I didn't know what to do. So, I gave him the money. And when he kept asking...I just kept giving it. I was scared it would never stop."

"Oh, sweetheart..." She moved closer. "Why didn't you come to me?"

"Because I was ashamed," he said. "I didn't want you to look at me differently. I felt like...like I was screwing up everything all at once."

She reached for him, pulling him into her arms, his shoulders shaking against her.

"What if he still posts the pictures? Or sends them to someone?"

Gently, she took his face in her hands and lifted his gaze to hers.

"He won't risk it, not now. He's facing real consequences. And if he did...it wouldn't destroy you. You've survived everything he put you through."

He nodded, his shoulders loosening before she pulled him into one more hug, tighter this time.

"We're going to be ok, kiddo." She said it like a promise, even though she had no idea what ok was supposed to look like anymore.

Chapter 24

"Good morning. I wasn't expecting to see you this early." David looked up from his desk before scribbling something on a legal pad and capping his pen.

She squared her shoulders, grounding herself. "I need to talk to you."

"If it's about what happened in Miami, I already heard."

She closed the door behind her, bracing for whatever version of the story Dylan and his father had delivered.

"From what I can gather, they're not expecting a call back from the Heat."

He leaned back, studying her with a neutrality that didn't match the disaster she had left behind in Miami.

"Nothing else?"

He shook his head. "Dylan called me himself yesterday which was strange. Usually, his father is the one ringing my phone," he said, looking slightly puzzled. "He asked about setting up workouts with other teams. He sounded...different. More like a grown man than the kid I've talked to before."

She exhaled once and nodded. "Well, I'm sure you already have someone else in mind."

"For what?"

"To represent him," she said. "You don't have to sugarcoat anything. If he asked for another agent, I understand."

"No, he didn't. He asked for you." He paused. "I don't know what you did but he was adamant."

For a moment, she couldn't speak. She had walked in expecting a lecture. Maybe worse. Now David was sitting across from her, saying Dylan requested her—specifically her—to continue.

She pictured the version of herself who would've clung to that. The woman determined to earn her place here; to prove she could do this job as well as any man in the room. But proving she could do it wasn't the same as wanting to.

"I'm not here to talk about Dylan." She reached into her bag and slid a folded sheet of paper across his desk. "I'm resigning."

His posture snapped. "You're what?"

"I'm resigning," she said again, her voice even. "Effective immediately."

He stared at her as if waiting for the punchline. When none came, he leaned forward. "Jamie, this isn't— You've worked hard to get to this point. You finally have visibility, real clients. If it's about the photos, we can manage that. Don't walk away because of one rough week."

"That's not the reason."

"Then why?" His voice cracked with frustration.

She took a breath, her words clear when she spoke. "Because staying would mean pretending this is what I want. It isn't."

He softened just slightly, the truth landing somewhere he didn't seem ready to acknowledge. "Jamie..."

"I'm not running away from this job," she said, cutting him off, knowing exactly where his mind had gone. "I'm choosing something different. Something that belongs to me."

The air conditioner kicked on, filling the silence between them. Then he shook his head once, more in resignation than disagreement. "Are you sure?"

"Yes."

He drew in a breath, his shoulders easing. "Then go. Go do the thing you've been holding yourself back from." He offered a rueful smile. "You don't owe this place anything."

***

At her desk, she reached beneath it and pulled out a cardboard box.

She placed the picture of Leo and Ava inside first, her fingers brushing the frame before letting it go. A small plant followed, its leaves tired from months of inadequate light. Then, the one-year anniversary token. A cheap branded trinket the firm had handed out without a thought. She dropped it straight into the trash can as a shadow fell over her desk.

"Looks like the experiment is finally over," Steve said, arms folded across his chest, smugness practically radiating off him.

She could've ignored him. Could have finished packing and moved on. That had always been her way with him. This time, she didn't bother filtering it. "Steve, you know...when a man overcompensates this much at work, it usually means he's not living up to expectations somewhere else."

He froze, his jaw clenching before she saw a flash of something else—the bruise she'd aimed for—too quick for him to hide.

"Wow." She let out a soft chuckle. "That was just a guess...but judging by that look, I'd say it's true."

After she slid the lid over her box, she lifted it with one hand and stepped past him without another glance.

When she made it to the elevator she noticed a shift. The constant readiness to defend herself, to justify her presence, had gone quiet.

***

Envelopes lay scattered across the kitchen island. She stood over them now, staring.

She had left them there the day before, sometime between drafting her resignation email and asking John to pick up his belongings.

After she let out a slow breath, she began stacking them into a neat pile until one slipped free and drifted to the floor.

The credit card bill.

She looked at it for a moment before bending to pick it up. Then she opened it and unfolded the pages, letting her eyes move slowly down the column of charges.

Her pulse ticked up, the questions finally catching up to her.

How will I pay my bills?

Where will I live?

And the loudest one...*What am I doing?*

She had chosen herself without a clear outline of what came next.

Her breath snagged in her throat, that familiar warning she'd learned not to ignore.

She reached for a half-empty bottle of wine on the counter, removed the cork, and for a split second, she considered drinking it.

Instead, she held herself still, focused on one breath, then another, until the pressure eased enough for her to tilt it over the sink.

She'd always believed drinking had been a pause, a way to take the edge off the constant vigilance of keeping everything together. Somewhere along the line, it had started to feel necessary instead of optional.

She watched the wine disappear and felt the smallest flicker of relief before grabbing two more and doing the same. "You can do this," she whispered. "You don't need this to survive and you sure as hell don't need Dad or John."

From there, her gaze drifted to the glass-enclosed cellar across the hallway. A modern showpiece John insisted on, back when impressing people mattered more than anything else.

She walked toward it slowly, her reflection bending against the pane as she looked in. Rows of rare labels lined the walls, meticulously arranged and untouched. She rested her hand on the cool handle, imagining for a moment what it would feel like to throw every last bottle into the bin outside.

The destructive impulse flickered and then passed.

This wasn't about punishing him. Not anymore.

Nicole's voice rose in her memory. *You should consider an estate sale.*

As she stepped back from the glass, the thought struck deeper than it had before. She hadn't walked away from the marriage empty-handed. Everything in this house was hers to sell if she wanted to. A year ago, the first time John had moved out, he'd acted like leaving it behind made him noble. It didn't. It just saved him money.

She pulled out her phone and searched estate sale companies, clicking through different websites, scanning photos of staged rooms, and lists of services that covered every part of the process.

The idea took hold as her thumb hovered over the call button, and she let out a slow breath. She would not panic this time or reach for a bottle to quiet what scared her.

***

The estate sale company hadn't wasted any time. Less than an hour after she'd called them, they confirmed someone could come by that same afternoon. And that was fine by her. She didn't want days to sit with the decision or talk herself out of it.

When the bell rang, she opened the door before the chime even finished. A woman stood on the porch, professional, a tablet tucked under her arm.

"Good afternoon. I'm Mara Levine, with Meridian Estate Services." She offered a business card.

"Jamie Sinclair." She stepped back to let her in. "Thank you for coming over so quickly."

Mara entered with a small nod, her gaze already sweeping over the entryway as if cataloging it.

"Where would you like to start?"

"Well, uh, I'm not sure how any of this works."

"That's not a problem. We'll walk through together, and you can show me what you're thinking of selling. I'll take photos and notes as we go. After that, I'll note anything that requires a separate appraisal. Nothing has to be decided today. It's just an evaluation."

She led Mara down the hallway and into the primary bedroom, stopping at the doorway to the closet.

Mara stepped inside and took in the rows of designer bags, the stacks of shoes, the built-in island with its velvet-lined drawers. She didn't react with surprise, only switched her tablet to a new page.

"These are in excellent condition," she said, lifting a handbag gently by its handle. "High-end purses like these tend to do well. The market for certain designers is especially strong right now." She set it down carefully and opened a drawer. Jewelry caught the light: bracelets, earrings, rings, pieces Jamie hadn't worn in years.

Mara paused. "Are you sure you want to part with all of this?"

"Yes." The answer came easily. Months ago, Prada and Louboutin had nearly been grounds for involuntary commitment. Now her head was level. She was being deliberate, moving forward instead of reacting.

"Alright." She lifted the Rolex, examining it closely. "Some of this may require authentication, but a number of these items could bring in strong bids. I'll flag anything that requires a specialist."

When they finished in the closet, Jamie led the way to the glass-enclosed wine room where Mara scanned the shelves and lifted a bottle, reading the label. "I'll need to photograph each one of these. Some vintages sell individually, others as curated sets. I'll research these and determine where they fit."

Jamie nodded, grateful not to have to pretend she understood any of it.

They stepped back into the hallway and moved into the formal living room, where Jamie gestured toward the Italian leather sofa John had purchased for appearances. "That's going too. I never liked it."

"Of course," Mara said, though her eyes had already lifted to the artwork hanging above it. "Is this...a Motherwell?"

"Yes. It was a wedding gift from my father." She studied Mara's face, noting the sudden spark of interest that hadn't appeared for anything else they'd gone through.

Mara glanced down at her tablet and typed a quick note. "A piece like this could be worth a great deal. Have you ever had it appraised?"

"No. I hadn't planned on selling that."

"I understand. Many people probably wouldn't," she said, glancing back at the painting. "But his work has grown in value for years. A canvas that once sold for a few hundred thousand can go for several times that now. It's the kind of piece collectors look for. If you ever decide to explore its value, I can point you to the right people." She reached into her bag and handed her a card. "They handle postwar works like this."

The idea felt unreal. That this painting, something she'd lived with for years, could be worth that much. The number alone made her dizzy, but the uncertainty bothered her more. She didn't know if it was hers, or if the decision to have it appraised belonged to her father.

Back in the foyer, she handed over a summary sheet. "I'll follow up with a detailed estimate and timeline tomorrow. Once you're ready, we can schedule staging."

When the door closed behind her, Jamie stood for a moment, her gaze drifting back to the painting, the card Mara had given her still in her hand.

Getting information wasn't the same as deciding anything. It wasn't selling. It wasn't even committing to the idea. It was just understanding what she had.

She dialed.

A woman answered. "Montclair Fine Art. How may I help you?"

"Hi. My name is Jamie Sinclair. I was referred by Mara Levine. I have a painting I'd like to have appraised."

"Of course," the woman said. "Do you know the artist?"

"Yes. Robert Motherwell."

There was a brief pause. "Okay. Is it currently in your home?"

"Yes."

"We would start with a few photographs," she said. "Front, back, dimensions, any signature, or labels. After that, we'd schedule an on-site evaluation. For a piece like that, the painting stays where it is. We come to you."

"And the cost?"

"Our appraisal fee for a single high-value work starts at five thousand dollars. That includes the site visit and a written valuation. Travel costs may apply, but we should have a specialist already in Florida."

Five thousand dollars. The number landed hard. Impossible without touching money she hadn't accessed yet.

"I see."

"There's no obligation. If you'd like to move forward, just email the images and we'll take it from there."

They ended the call a moment later.

She set her phone down and stared straight ahead. There was no avoiding the next step, and she didn't give herself time to reconsider.

***

After she wrapped the painting in glassine and carefully placed it in the trunk of her car, she immediately drove to her parents', turned into the driveway and cut the engine.

The trunk popped, and she lifted it from its nest of towels, the edges pressing into her forearms as she drew a long breath and climbed the brick steps.

She opened the front door and called hello into the quiet house, her mother's voice carrying back from the kitchen in reply, where she stood at the sink with a spray bottle, misting a wilting fern.

Evelyn aimed one more burst at the leaves without turning. "So, you've kicked John out again." The words fell flat. "This is how you repay a good man for standing by your side?"

Jamie set her jaw. She had no space for that fight. "Where's Dad?"

"In the study." Evelyn finally glanced over, eyes roaming from Jamie's face to the wrapped rectangle in her arms. "What on earth are you carrying?"

She kept walking through the kitchen and into the family room, her shoulders aching by the time she reached the study door.

Inside, her father watched Mad Money with the sound up. He sat forward in his leather chair, tie loosened, as Jim Cramer threw his arms around, charts flashing beside him.

"That's garbage," he muttered at the screen. "You always hedge before an earnings announcement."

"Hi, Dad."

He startled and stood, his gaze dropping to the painting, surprise giving way to curiosity.

"What do you have there?"

"The Motherwell. Hanging it in an apartment would make it look out of place, even a little ridiculous."

He looked from the television to her, then hit mute. "So, you and John are going through with this. You're selling the house."

"We are." She adjusted her grip. "I want no ties to him other than the kids."

He rested his hands on the back of his chair. "How do you plan to support yourself now that you've resigned?"

"David told you."

His mouth flattened. He didn't sit. "I would have liked to hear it from you first." A beat passed. "I stuck my neck out to get you that job."

"I'm grateful, Dad. But I don't want to argue."

He studied her face, took the painting from her arms and leaned it carefully against the wall, then gestured toward the couch. "Have a seat."

She crossed the room, her pulse ticking up, as she thought about the words she had rehearsed on the drive over. Now, they refused to line up.

"You should sit for the bar," he said, cutting in before she could speak. "I've been telling you that for years." He paused but not long enough for her to respond. "Once you pass, I can get you placed. One of my old clients would bring you on as junior counsel in a heartbeat. Or my old firm. You—."

"Stop." She held up a hand before he could go on mapping out her future without taking a breath.

He went still. She had never cut him off, and by the look that crossed his face, she doubted anyone else had either.

"I'm sure you mean well, but I didn't come here to talk about my career."

"Then what?"

"I'd like to have the painting appraised."

His lips pressed thin. "What?"

"I want to know what it's worth," she said, trying to control the tremor in her hands. "But I don't have the money to do that."

"And you want me to pay for that?" He tilted his head, his eyes narrowing. "Why? So you can turn around and sell it?"

"Yes," she replied, straightening. "You gave it to me as a wedding present. Isn't it mine?"

He stared at her, his mouth parting slightly. Then, he circled the desk and pressed his palms into the mahogany. "You would sell a piece like that to fund a...what? A new apartment and some time off?"

"No." She shook her head. "I don't know yet. I haven't thought that far ahead. But I wouldn't waste it."

Silence stretched between them. She felt the weight of it in her chest, and she nearly got up. Nearly walked away the way she always had, but something within her refused to retreat.

"Have you ever thought about what a piece of art like that costs? What it really costs?" she asked.

"What are you talking about?"

"Not what, Dad. Who."

Something flickered across his face—recognition perhaps, quickly masked by an attorney's detachment. "That case was resolved fifteen years ago, and the painting had nothing to do with it."

"Resolved? You crushed Marcus Tate." The words trembled in her chest but came out clear. "His settlement didn't even cover his medical bills, and Carson grew up watching his mother count dollars in the grocery line while you walked into this house every night and poured the best scotch money could buy."

"That is not fair." He held her stare. "The company had a position and I did my job. Any lawyer would have done the same in my place."

"And that's the problem," she said. "There are too many lawyers like you, protecting corporations instead of human beings."

He gave a short laugh that lacked any humor. "Do you know how naïve you sound?"

A beat passed as he waited for a reply. None came.

"You have no idea how the world works. I represented those companies because they build things. They keep the economy moving. You call that evil?"

"I call it one-sided. And not worth the price."

His eyes hardened as he swept a hand toward the shelves, then beyond to the house surrounding them. "Look around you. This is what my work gave you. You enjoyed the benefits."

She leaned forward. "Your career may have built this place and made you millions, but you broke countless others in the process."

She rose and pointed at the painting against the wall. "Keep the Motherwell. I don't need your help."

Each step toward the door sounded too loud in the quiet room, her pulse thrumming in her ears.

Her mother appeared at the end of the corridor, blocking her path with a folded dish towel still in hand. For a moment they simply stared at each other, the silence laden with old wounds.

"You always think you know better," Evelyn said.

Jamie met her gaze, the words she'd held back earlier rushing forward. "No, Mom, I don't. But what I do know is I would've been a hell of a lot better off if I'd had a mother brave enough to fight for herself instead of turning the other cheek."

The towel twisted in Evelyn's hands, but she said nothing as Jamie brushed past her, carrying only her resolve through the front door.

Outside, a breeze stirred the hedges, lifting the distant sound of traffic. The world remained unchanged, indifferent to the storm inside her. She walked to her car and slid into the driver's seat, the weight of what had just been said pressing down.

After a deep breath, she eased down the drive and turned onto Bayshore, the water glittering beside her as downtown's towers rose ahead. Headlights blurred past in a haze until she finally pulled over half a mile away. Only then did her breathing turn ragged, the tears she had held spilling hot down her cheeks. She pressed her forehead to the wheel and let herself break in the solitude.

Chapter 25

"You sure you don't need me to go with you?" She asked. "That's a lot to haul upstairs."

After Jamie slid the last box into the trunk, there was barely room for anything else. She stepped back, brushing her hands together as Leo shifted his backpack onto the seat.

"Mom, you're hovering again," he said. "Besides, Ava can help me."

Ava snorted. "I am not hauling anything up three flights of stairs. I'll point. You'll lift."

He laughed, shaking his head, and Jamie realized how long it had been since things felt this simple.

"Don't worry," Ava said, reaching for her keys. "I'll make sure he stays out of trouble."

"I heard that," he said.

"You were meant to."

Jamie smiled. For months she'd been waiting for the next thing she would have to survive alongside him. Standing here now, listening to him joke with Ava, she finally felt hopeful that he was going to be okay. He looked ready. Like the boy she knew had always been in there.

As Ava slid into the driver's seat, she kissed her cheek. "Text me when you get there."

"Will do."

Then she turned to Leo and squeezed his hands once. "I'm proud of you."

"I know. I'll be home in a few weeks."

She hugged him and stepped back, watching them pull away until the car disappeared at the end of the street. Her throat tightened and she turned toward the house, not giving herself time to sit with the feeling.

Inside, the kitchen was quiet. The check from the estate sale sat on the island where she'd left it that morning. It wasn't enough to stay here, but it was enough to start somewhere else.

She picked up her phone, scrolling through her contacts, and stopped on Mae's number before pressing the call button.

The line rang twice.

"Well, this is a nice surprise."

"Hi," she said, leaning against the counter. "I was hoping you might be able to recommend a realtor in your area."

"Straight to business. How have you been, dear?"

"I'm sorry," she uttered, exhaling. "A lot has changed, but I'm good. Better than I was."

She pulled out a stool and sat, letting the moment settle. "How are you? And Elzie? How's Jasper doing?"

Mae chuckled. "Oh, you know. Elzie's still bossing me around, and Jasper's into everything he shouldn't be, but he hasn't chased any bears lately."

There was a pause. "Now, tell me what you're up to. Why do you need a realtor? Are you looking for a vacation home?"

"No," she said, glancing once toward the front window before answering. "I'm looking for somewhere to live."

***

By late September, the driveway was blocked by a moving truck, its ramp down, boxes stacked in uneven towers along the garage wall. Jamie carried one up and slid it into place, then climbed back down, sweat already gathering at the base of her neck.

"I just want it noted that you could've hired movers," Julia said, crossing the driveway with two barstools balanced against her hip.

"I know."

"And yet here we are."

She wedged them into the truck, nudged them until they fit, then hopped down and stepped into the narrow strip of shade beside the cab.

Nicole emerged from the house a moment later with three bottles of water, already slick with condensation. "Drink," she said, handing one to both of them. "I don't need either one of you passing out on me."

"So," Julia said, catching her breath, "remind me how far this is again?"

"About eight hours."

She let out a low whistle. "You couldn't have eased into this with, I don't know, North Florida?"

"It's worth it. You'll see."

Julia shook her head, then glanced at her feet. "I never thought you'd be the person to live in a one-bedroom cabin in the middle of the woods. You're definitely going to need your little battery-operated friends now. I hope you remembered to pack them."

"Jules!"

A car door closed somewhere behind them.

Jamie turned at the sound, and she and Julia rounded the back of the truck together where her father stood at the end of the driveway.

"I didn't mean to interrupt." His gaze flicked to the U-Haul, the boxes. "I can come back."

"You're already here," Jamie said.

He nodded once. "I heard you were moving."

She stood there, hands resting at her side, waiting.

"I don't need to know where." He said it plainly and left it there before drawing a deep breath, as if choosing his next words carefully. "I don't blame you for not wanting me in your life."

He took a few steps closer, then reached into the pocket of his jacket and held out an envelope. "This is for you."

She didn't take it right away. "What is it?"

"Open it," he said.

Inside was a single letter, neatly folded, the header stamped with a law firm she recognized. She scanned the first line, then the next. The amount made her breath catch. She looked up. "You sold it."

He nodded. "It was always yours."

"So, this money..."

"Is being held in escrow by my attorney," he said. "On your behalf. Nothing moves without your instruction."

She read the letter again, slower this time: *Funds retained. Disbursement at client's direction.*

"You didn't have to do this," she said, sliding it back into the envelope.

"I wanted to," he said. "What you do with it is your decision." He hesitated, then handed her a second envelope. "This one's from your mother."

Her fingers closed around it, lighter than the first, heavier somehow all the same.

"Don't read it yet. Just...when you're ready. And don't be too hard on her," he added quietly. "She only did what she thought was best for you girls."

He stepped back, then hesitated, his attention shifting to Julia. "Would you let your mother and I take you to dinner sometime soon?" he asked. "You and your wife. We'd really like to get to know her."

She didn't answer. Her expression shifted, something guarded crossing her face as she held his gaze.

"Just think about it." He dipped his chin, turned, and got back into his car, waving as he drove away.

They watched him, letting the silence linger before Julia finally asked, "What's in the envelope?"

Without answering, Jamie handed it to her.

She opened it, skimmed the letter, then looked up at her sister, eyes wide. "Two million dollars? Jesus, Jamie. How..."

"The painting that's been hanging on my wall for years. That's how."

"What are you going to do with this?" she asked. "You can't just put it in a checking account. You need to invest it or something."

Jamie shook her head slowly, taking it back from her. "It doesn't feel right."

"What do you mean?"

"It's blood money."

"It's freedom," Julia said, like that should've been obvious.

Jamie narrowed her eyes, studying her sister's expression for a moment. "Is it?"

Chapter 26

The road narrowed as it traced the river, gravel crunching beneath the tires.

Ahead, the cabin gradually came into view. The wood was weathered to a dull gray, and a shallow stoop sagged slightly beneath the front door, as if it had settled into the ground over time. It was smaller than the photos had suggested, but it looked sturdy. Elzie's truck was already parked out front, the tailgate down.

She shut off the engine and climbed down from the cab before Jasper barreled off the porch. He was on her immediately, paws to her chest, his breath warm against her neck.

"You remember me," she said, laughing softly as she scratched behind his ears.

"Of course he does." Mae stepped forward and pulled her into a hug. "I'm glad you made it. I was starting to think these mountain roads might change your mind."

"I had a moment. Not easy hauling a car up here."

Elzie took her keys, squeezed her shoulder once in passing, and went straight for the back of the truck. He lifted her bed frame as if it weighed nothing and headed inside.

They followed him, the screen door swinging shut behind them.

The cabin didn't smell like a home yet, only of unfinished wood and air that hadn't been disturbed in a while. Dust coated every surface and spiderwebs clung to the corners where the ceiling met the walls.

Mae followed her gaze. "It'll feel like yours soon enough," she said. "Once you add your own touch to it."

They started unloading without much discussion. Furniture first. Boxes next.

She told herself she wouldn't hover, but instinctively guided where things went anyway, already mapping a life around small practical choices.

The kitchen was narrow but workable, everything where it needed to be. She could see herself there without effort.

In the bedroom, she walked over to the window that overlooked the river below and the mountains beyond. It was a tiny room, holding little else than a bed and a nightstand, but the view made up for it.

After all the boxes were unloaded, she stepped out onto the deck and stood there, listening to the water breaking against the rocks and something distant calling from the woods.

Elzie joined her and nodded toward the slope below. "I'll get some of the guys from the orchard to help me clear all that brush and build steps down to the river."

She pictured it and smiled. She'd been moving for so long that standing still felt almost indulgent, and it finally hit her how completely she had uprooted her life to start over.

***

By dusk, they'd unpacked nearly everything. They were down to the last two boxes when Mae lifted one labeled OFFICE and raised an eyebrow. "This one's heavier than it looks."

She set it down on the dining table and opened the flaps. Inside were important documents, binders, casebooks, and the framed diploma Jamie had all but forgotten about.

"I didn't know you went to law school."

"I did, but I never practiced."

"But you finished," Mae said, not as a question.

"Yes."

She smiled at her, and Jamie got the sense she wasn't surprised. "Well. That explains it."

"Explains what?"

"The way you plan three steps ahead."

Elzie leaned against the doorframe, arms crossed. "Hazel's been talking about renting the studio apartment above the bakery."

"The place is small." Mae glanced at him, a knowing look in her eye. "But it's got great foot traffic."

Jamie blinked. "For what?"

"You tell me," Mae said, tilting her head.

"I'm not licensed here."

Mae waved that off gently. "I didn't say tomorrow."

She felt the idea register; a possibility she hadn't thought about yet.

After a moment, Elzie announced he was going to grab dinner for everyone, and Mae volunteered to go with him. Jasper objected loudly until she promised fries.

When the truck pulled away, the cabin stood silent around her.

She slid the framed diploma onto the shelf with the books, and found herself thinking, briefly, about what it would take to sit for the Georgia bar, the requirements and whether she was even eligible. But she stopped before the questions could pile up.

A single box remained against the wall. She crossed the room, opened it, and pulled out the envelopes her father had given her just before she left Tampa. She set the one from the attorney aside and after a brief pause, she drew the letter out of the other, taking a deep breath.

Jamie,

I don't know if this will land the way I intend it to. I've rewritten it more times than I can count, which probably tells you something about how long I've avoided saying things plainly.

You were right. I stayed longer than I should have. I never thought I could stand on my own with two children and no certainty of what came next. I told myself I was protecting you and Julia, when the truth is I was afraid of what it would mean to leave.

Believe it or not, I've often admired women who raised kids without the safety nets I relied on. I never had that kind of resolve.

Your father is not the same man he was then. Some men do better with time, but I know he has always loved us, even when he failed to show it. That doesn't excuse a thing, and I can't change what you were exposed to or the example I set, but I am sorry for the ways my fear shaped your childhood.

If there is anything I hope you take from this, it's not an apology meant to erase the past. I'm simply trying to say that I see you now, and I'm proud of you for being one of those women I was too afraid to be.

Whatever you decide to do next, I pray it's something that lets you sleep at night and stand comfortably in your own life. You've always carried more responsibility than was ever meant to be yours.

I love you.

Mom

It was strange to see her mother as someone who had once been afraid rather than weak. But she realized now, she had been human in a way Jamie had never allowed herself to consider.

***

Two days later, she went to see Hazel about the space upstairs.

A bell chimed as she pushed the door open, the smell of warm bread and sugar hanging in the air.

Hazel stood behind the counter with her sleeves rolled up and a dusting of flour along one forearm. She slid a tray into the case and looked up. "Life chase you up the mountain again?" she asked.

Jamie met her gaze. "I'm not running this time."

She nodded and wiped her hands on a towel. "Mae said you wanted to see the apartment."

"Yes. If it's still available."

"It is, but I don't know why you're interested since you've already found a place to live."

"I'm looking for a place to work."

Hazel tilted her head, assessing. "What kind of work?"

"The kind I can't do from my kitchen table."

A quiet huff escaped her as she came around the counter, reaching for a ring of keys. She gestured toward the narrow staircase. "Come on."

At the top, she unlocked the door and held it open.

The space was simple. There was one main room. A small kitchenette ran along the side wall, and a bathroom sat tucked off a short hall. Two tall windows faced the street below, morning light pouring in, catching dust motes suspended in the air.

Jamie stepped inside and stood there, taking it in. "It's quiet."

"It stays that way," Hazel said.

She moved to the windows. Below, the town was coming to life. Customers drifted in and out of the cafe across the street and a small line formed at the bank. Beyond the storefronts, the mountains rose in the distance, hazy against the sky. She could picture a desk here. A place to think without interruption.

When she turned back, her gaze caught on a run of shelves against the far wall, their wood worn smooth in places. Perfect for her casebooks. She nodded toward them. "Do those come with the apartment?"

Hazel frowned slightly. "Those old things? If you want them. They belonged to my daughter."

"I didn't know you had a daughter."

"You never asked." She peered through the window, resting a hand on the wall. "She couldn't wait to get out from under my roof. The minute she turned eighteen, she moved in here, determined to claim her independence."

Jamie stayed quiet.

"She lasted a couple of years," she said. "Then she started drifting. She was so sure there was more waiting for her in the city than this place." Her gaze lifted to the mountains and Jamie noticed the look that came over her face; her expression seemed to close in on itself, lines hardening around her mouth.

After a moment, she stepped away from the window and headed toward the stairwell. Jamie took the cue and followed, their footsteps creaking beneath them. At the bottom, she stopped and turned. "If you're really interested in using the space as an office, we can talk terms. But I won't rent it to anyone who doesn't intend to stay."

"I intend to."

Hazel studied her. "I hope so. Don't go getting people attached to you here and then leave. Some of us don't have much patience left for that."

After that, they agreed they would talk about it more in a few weeks and Jamie bid her farewell.

Outside, the street carried on around her. She adjusted her bag on her shoulder, already thinking ahead.

She would sit for the Georgia bar. The night before, she had started mapping it out: registration deadlines, prep courses, the months she would need to carve out for studying. None of it scared her the way it once had.

It was work. She knew how to do that.

But first, she had one last thing to take care of.

***

Heat rose off the pavement at the corner of Ashley and Kennedy, the air thick with exhaust as cars idled at the light. Jamie stood at the crosswalk and watched the signal count down. When it changed, she stepped off the curb and crossed toward a glass tower overlooking the river.

Inside the lobby, she scanned the names at the directory once and headed for the elevators.

The doors slid shut, and the space closed in. Everyone faced forward, eyes fixed, the silence normal. She thought of Friendship, and how it seemed like a different world.

A few floors up, she stepped out and followed the corridor toward reception, where a young woman sat behind a desk, professional and pretty in a way Jamie found predictable.

"Good morning. How may I help you?"

"Hi. I'm Jamie Sinclair. I have an appointment with Mr. Miller."

Her fingers moved across the keyboard as she glanced at the screen, then back up. "Yes, I see you here," she said. "If you'd like to have a seat, I'll let him know you're here."

She took a chair and waited, the minutes passing unnoticed as people came and went around her.

After a short while, the receptionist looked up. "Ms. Sinclair, he's ready for you."

She followed her down a hall past a row of windowed offices. Near the end, she stopped outside one door and gestured her inside.

A man who appeared to be about her age rose from behind his desk as she entered. "Ms. Sinclair," he said, offering his hand. "I'm Tim Miller. Please, have a seat."

As she eased into the chair across from him, he smiled. "Before we get started, I should say I'm a great admirer of your father's work."

She recognized the comment for what it was and inclined her head, waiting before he glanced at the folder in front of him. "I understand you're ready to authorize release of the funds."

"Yes. I am."

"Alright," he said, looking up at her. "Once the escrow is released, we'll need to know where you'd like the funds sent. Would you prefer we wire them directly to your personal account, or to a business account?"

She hesitated. "Actually, I was hoping to have a cashier's check issued. Is that possible?"

"It's not the most efficient method," he said, "but yes, it can be done." He glanced back down at the paperwork. "We would typically make the check payable to you, since your name appears on the escrow documents."

"No. It shouldn't be made out to me."

That caught his attention. He looked up fully now. "Okay." He waited a beat, holding her gaze. "Who should the payee be?"

"Pamela Tate."

He put his pen down and studied her for a moment. "Is there anything I should know about your connection to her?"

"No."

He gave her a skeptical look, but she held his eyes and took a deep breath. "I assure you, this isn't anything illegal. She's important to someone I care about. The money belongs to her. It always has."

Something like surprise caught his face, gone almost immediately. "Very well. We'll issue the cashier's check to Mrs. Tate."

"I'd like it mailed through the firm, if possible. Without my name attached anywhere."

"That can be arranged." He opened a drawer, pulled out a few forms, and laid them in front of him. "I'll still need to document the source of funds and file the gift form. We'll keep those records in our file. The bank will also keep its own record. Do you accept that?"

"I do. She can't trace it to me through the mail, correct?"

"Correct." He pushed a pen and pad of paper across the desk. "You should write a note. Short, so there's no confusion. We'll type it up and include it in the envelope."

She reached for it, pulling it closer, and wrote: *No questions, no conditions. Use it well. In memory of Marcus.*

He read what she had written, eyes scanning the words, then looked at her again. "Are you sure you want to do this?"

"Positive."

He released a breath and placed the forms before her. "This authorizes release of the funds, and this is the gift form. Sign here and here."

She read each page, finding the words clinical and impersonal, then she signed, and watched as he gathered the papers.

"We'll send the check through certified mail and email you a copy of the receipt once we receive it. Is there anything else I can do for you?"

"I think that covers it."

She stood, and he did as well, their handshake brief before she stepped into the hallway and toward the elevators. As she walked away, it occurred to her how easily two million dollars could be transferred, a lifetime of security moved in minutes. The simplicity of it unsettled her more than the amount itself.

She'd never considered keeping it. From the moment she'd learned the painting's value, she knew what she would do with the money. What remained now was a quiet sense of alignment; something long misdirected had finally been set in its proper place.

Chapter 27

"Where do you keep the extra bedding?" Ava called from the loft.

"In the closet," Jamie said.

The cabin smelled of sugar, butter, and pine. The sweetness of cookies baked earlier that afternoon mingling with the stronger scent of the Christmas tree in the corner of the living room.

Leo hovered near the couch, his phone in his hand. His jacket was slung over the armrest, one sleeve brushing the floor. Jamie made a mental note to remind him to hang it up and then let the thought go. There were things she corrected now and things she didn't. She was still learning the difference.

She carried a set of sheets across the room and put them on the pull-out sofa. The mechanism resisted when she tugged it open, metal catching for a second before giving way. She used her weight to force it flat, a small huff of effort escaping her before she could stop it.

Leo glanced up. "What happened to the couch you had?"

"That thing was bigger than this entire room." She placed a sheet over the mattress, pulling it tight around the corners. "And wrong for this place."

She didn't miss it. This one had cost less than a single throw pillow from the old one, and it fit the space without argument.

"The tree looks kind of bare," Ava said as she came down from the loft.

Jamie had donated nearly all her decorations before leaving Davis Island, keeping only the ones the kids had made over the years.

"There's a shop downtown that sells hand crafted ornaments. We'll go after you're unpacked."

Ava crossed the room and stood at the window, her reflection faint against the glass. Snow covered everything beyond it, the river winding through the valley like a seam.

"I see why you like it," she said. "But it must feel...isolated."

Leo grabbed a cookie from the kitchen, smirking. "Translation. She means it isn't surrounded by strip malls and fancy restaurants."

"That's not what I meant." She shook her head, looking back at her mother. "Do you get lonely?" She didn't wait for an answer. "You need a cat...or a dog."

Jamie spread a blanket over the pull-out, smoothing it in place. "I'm okay. Really." Her gaze drifted toward the window. "And a pet? I haven't given much thought to that. Maybe."

"Then it's settled," Ava said, smiling. "We're buying you a puppy for Christmas."

Jamie let out a quiet laugh and shook her head. "Hold on. Not so fast. There's a lot I still need to do before I have time to housebreak a puppy."

Ava's smile didn't fade, but her brow creased. "Like what?"

"Well," Jamie started, hesitating, then straightening. "For starters, I'm going to sit for the bar."

"That's great, Mom. When?"

"I have a few more requirements I need to meet," she said, keeping it simple, "but I'm on track to take it the beginning of the year."

Ava grinned, tilting her head as if testing the sound of it. "Jamie Sinclair, attorney at law. That has a nice ring to it."

Leo glanced between them. "Cool. Proud of you. But can we go get dinner. I'm starving."

"You have the emotional depth of a teaspoon," Ava said, lobbing a pillow at him.

***

Downtown, shop owners had strung lights and filled their windows for the holidays, the sparkles spilling onto the wet pavement below. Music drifted from somewhere near the square, tinny and cheerful, while a small crowd moved slowly down the sidewalk, cups of hot drinks in hand.

Ava slowed almost immediately. She strolled toward a store and stopped in front of the display filled with handmade decorations, leaning closer to the glass. Leo followed behind her, pretending not to care while still looking.

"This is the place," Jamie said. "The one I was telling you about."

Inside, the shop was crowded, shelves lined with local crafts and ornaments. Jamie spotted Mae near the counter, her back to them as she spoke to someone. Elzie stood beside her, a hand resting casually at her waist. His attention shifted first. He gave a small nod toward them, and Mae turned mid-sentence.

"Well, look who it is." She was already moving in their direction. "We were wondering when we'd see you."

Leo leaned closer to his mother, raising an eyebrow. "Who is that?" He asked under his breath. "And why is she so excited to see you?"

Jamie shot him a look. "Friends," she said. "Good ones."

Mae didn't hesitate, pulling her into a hug without asking while Ava and Leo exchanged glances.

"I'm sorry," she said, stepping back. "I'm Mae. And this is my husband, Elzie. You must be Ava and Leo. We've heard so much about you."

Ava smiled and extended a hand. "It's nice to meet you both."

"Ok, I'm officially starving," Leo said.

Jamie elbowed him in the side. "Leo!"

"Ouch!"

"It's ok," Elzie said, laughing. "I admire a man who gets straight to the point and you're in luck." He gestured to the door. "Hazel made her famous Louisiana Meat Pies today...Natchitoches."

Mae shook her head. "Don't oversell them."

"Oh, I'm underselling them. People get emotional about those things."

***

The bell above the door rang as they stood near the counter, Leo already angled toward the display case, his attention fixed on whatever sat behind the glass. Ava hovered a step back, her gaze moving more slowly, as if taking in details.

Hazel was at the register, finishing with a customer.

"Tell me you've got at least one of those meat pies left," Elzie said, craning his neck around the corner.

She snorted. "You've already had three."

"They were small."

"They were not. And if you eat another one, I'm not responsible for what happens to the structural integrity of your pants."

Elzie laughed. "I'm not asking for me."

When she finally looked up, her eyes moved past him, landing on Jamie first, then Ava and Leo.

"These are my kids...Ava and Leo."

She studied them for a beat longer than politeness required. "You're the observant one," she said to Ava.

Ava smiled.

She shifted her attention to Leo next. "And I bet your belly button is chewing your backbone."

He straightened, as if caught off guard, his cheeks turning red. "Yes ma'am."

"Good timing. I've got a fresh batch of those pies coming out of the oven in about ten minutes."

She finished what she was doing, wiped her hands on a towel, and slipped the apron over her head. When she came around the counter, she stopped in front of Jamie. "Come with me."

She didn't wait for an answer and Jamie followed her toward the stairwell. At the top, she unlocked the door and pushed it open.

The room was different. Not the empty space Hazel had shown her weeks ago. A desk sat centered beneath the window, positioned as if someone already worked there. Chairs and a table were arranged nearby, close enough for conversation. Along one wall, a coffee bar had been set up and stocked, a new beverage fridge running quietly under the counter. The floors were smooth, freshly sanded. The walls cleanly painted.

"Elzie did the hard stuff," she said. "I found the desk at a thrift shop. Hope you like it."

"It's perfect." Jamie ran her hand over the surface of it, her gaze snagging on a nameplate, handmade.

"Mae carved that."

Heat rushed behind her eyes. She looked away, willing the tears to stop before she let out a short laugh. "No pressure to pass the bar now, right?"

"You will," Hazel said before she looked at her. "Save your tears for something sad."

Jamie nodded, taking it all in again. The space didn't feel tentative anymore. It assumed her future without asking.

She stood there and let it.

***

New Year's Day had settled into a muted winter gray, snow sitting heavy on the mountains outside the cabin. Jamie stoked the fire, nudging a log into place and waiting for it to catch. Across the room, Leo had already claimed the couch, a college bowl game on the television, his feet kicked up, and his attention fixed. In the corner, Ava sat on a bean bag, reading. Jamie noticed the title. Relationship advice, dog-eared and well worn.

She wondered when her daughter had decided she needed a guide, but she let it go and busied herself with the fire. After it caught, flames burning steady, she headed for the kitchen and opened a can of black-eyed-peas, setting it by the stove.

This day called for certain things without making a fuss about it. Things that brought good luck and great health. She pulled out the rest of what she'd planned to cook and lined it up on the counter, letting the routine take over.

The game filled the room with noise, Leo reacting to every other play. Ava looked up from her book. "Leo."

"What?"

"You don't need it that loud and stop yelling."

He turned it down half a notch, just enough to be annoying, and she shot him a look as she reached for a pillow, threatening him with it. "The next time you yell, I'm going to smother you."

Jamie smiled. The sounds filled every corner of the tiny cabin, and instead of grating on her, it warmed her heart. For now, they were here. She knew the calendar was already working against her, counting the days until schedules split them again, but she let herself stay in the moment. This was hers for a little while longer.

Her phone buzzed against the counter, Julia's name lighting up the screen before she answered. "Happy New Year," she said.

"Right back at ya. Is it still snowing up there?"

"It is."

She reached for a pan as Julia kept talking.

"You learned how to chop wood yet? Got an axe and a woodchipper?"

"No, Julia. I don't need either. I have neighbors with chainsaws."

"Well, a woodchipper might come in handy one day for the next asshole who screws you over."

She heard Nicole laughing in the background.

"Oh my God, I'm hanging up."

"I'm kidding."

Jamie closed her eyes, smiling despite herself.

"Anyway," Julia said, continuing, "I just wanted to say hello and let you know we're planning to head up for a visit in a couple of weeks, if you're good with that."

"Of course I am. I can't wait to see you."

"Okay, gotta run. Nicole and I are in the middle of something important."

"What now?"

"Oh, you know. The usual...innovative brunch strategy. I say bottomless mimosas. Nicole says quality over quantity."

In the background, Nicole's voice cut in. "Because one good mimosa is better than six bad ones."

"That is elitist nonsense," Julia shot back. "Anyway, talk later. Love you."

Jamie chuckled, thinking as much as some things had changed, others never did. "Love you too."

On the television, the camera cut away for halftime, and Leo reached for the remote, flipping the channel.

The ESPN logo filled the screen, followed by a highlight reel with dramatic music and graphics sliding into place. A segment title flashed: *Breakout Performances of the Year*.

Jamie put the phone down and crossed the room. "Scoot," she said, tapping Leo's shin.

He groaned, pulling his feet in as she sat beside him.

The broadcast shifted to the studio desk, where three men in suits—two of them former players, their shoulders still broad despite retirement—traded comments easily. One set up the clips while another jumped in with analysis.

They started with a quarterback who'd surprised everyone late in the season, then a tight end who'd gone from practice squad to red-zone favorite. The highlights rolled quickly, the men nodding along, adding context, disagreeing enough to keep it interesting.

"But one young man stands out above them all," one of them said. "And what a comeback. Two ACL tears. All but written off until he fought his way back this year."

Jamie's breath caught. She didn't move as the anchor continued. "Gabriella Mendez is in Tampa with more on the story."

The feed cut to a pre-recorded interview. Carson sat angled toward the reporter, posture easy. He looked good. Hair longer, eyes brighter than the last time she saw him. He wore a dark jacket over a plain shirt, with no logos or flash.

She asked him about his year, his comeback and what it took to recover and stay ready after the injuries.

He answered without rushing, talking about discipline and routine. How he'd learned to trust his body again. It was the same grit Jamie had noticed in him from the start.

Then the reporter shifted in her chair, a curious glint in her eyes. "This doesn't have anything to do with football, but there are a lot of people out there who want to know...are you single?"

Jamie braced for his response, telling herself she had no claim on the answer, no right to care. Still, something inside her flinched.

He didn't respond immediately. He looked down for a second, then back up. When he spoke, his voice was even, but there was something in his expression she recognized. It was the same look he'd given her every time she'd pulled away from him.

"There was someone once," he said. "Not too long ago."

Gabriella waited.

"But it didn't work out. I guess you could say we had too many differences." He gave a small shrug, as if that was all there was to it. "But that's life, right?"

The reporter nodded and pivoted back toward football.

After the clip ended, the segment rolled on, but Jamie stayed where she was, hands folded loosely in her lap. She hadn't realized how still she'd gone until she shifted, the couch creaking softly beneath her.

She glanced to her right.

Ava was watching her, her book closed now. She didn't say anything. She didn't smile or frown. She simply held Jamie's eyes for a moment longer than coincidence would allow.

Leo was quiet too, though whether it was the interview or the sudden change in the room she didn't know. He grabbed the remote again and flipped back to the college game, where the players had already returned to the field.

She followed it for a few plays, nodding once when Leo pointed out missed coverage, and smiling when he loudly complained about a call.

Eventually, she pushed up from the couch, stoked the fire, and made her way back to the kitchen.

The afternoon carried on around her, and she moved through it like nothing had happened. But the past had found its way back in, and she didn't yet know what to do with it.

Chapter 28

The mountains filled the window behind her desk, wide and un-
broken.

At her old firm, a view like this belonged to men, mostly. Men with titles and power, who expected the world to bend around them. This one was hers, and she had earned it. There was no ladder left to climb, and no one else's expectations to measure herself against.

Below, a delivery truck backed into the bakery's alley, the driver jumping down to slide open the door. Across the way, the florist arranged buckets of chrysanthemums on the sidewalk, while someone at the café flipped the sign to OPEN and waved a couple inside. The town moved at its own pace, and she was part of it now.

She spun in her chair, facing the desk that held a neat stack of notepads, pens gathered in a cup, and a photo of Ava and Leo. Her eyes drifted to the framed degree propped on the shelf beside a line of law books. For years it had stayed hidden away, tucked in a drawer. Today it stood in the open, a quiet reminder of what she had built and the weeks leading up to this day.

She'd passed the bar, filed paperwork at the Gilmer County courthouse, and spent hours at the bank setting up separate accounts for operating costs and client funds. After that, she'd met with an insurance agent in Atlanta who explained every clause twice until she was certain she understood.

Her practice stood ready, and so did she, for whoever walked through the door next.

From her cell, she dialed the new office number, and let it ring twice, then picked up. "Law Office of Jamie Sinclair." She wrinkled her nose and hung up.

Again, she tried. "Jamie Sinclair, Attorney at Law." Still not right. She pressed redial, cleared her throat, and said, "Good morning, Jamie Sinclair." This time the greeting sat comfortably on her tongue. That one would stay.

A moment later, her cell phone buzzed in her hand, the screen lighting up with a picture from Julia. John standing in front of the Eiffel Tower, one arm wrapped around a young woman in a tight-fitting dress, his smile easy. The caption read: *Living our best life.*

Well, Julia texted. *At least he's consistent.*

Jamie studied the photo for a moment, then typed back, *He looks happy.*

She set it down, the image already fading from her thoughts when a knock carried across the room. After she drew in a breath and straightened her shoulders, she walked to the door and opened it.

A man stood in the stairwell holding a small stack of envelopes tucked under one arm. He glanced down at the clipboard, then up at her. "Jamie Sinclair?" he asked.

"That's me."

"Mail," he said, handing it over. "Looks like you're official."

She smiled, thanked him, closed the door, and carried the envelopes back to her desk.

The morning stretched on.

She became restless and when the phone rang downstairs at Hazel's shop, she reached for her own receiver, then stopped and put it back in its cradle. Later, she picked it up anyway, listening for the dial tone before setting it down again.

She opened her door more than once, each time finding the stairwell empty.

That's when she thought about Elzie hanging the sign above Hazel's over the weekend and the immediate concern she'd had that it was too small. Sitting there now, she considered whether it was worth replacing.

By late afternoon, the street had quieted. Across the way, the florist began carrying buckets back inside, the color draining from the sidewalk as the arrangements disappeared one by one.

She stood and rolled her shoulders, then headed down the narrow staircase.

Hazel was at the counter, counting bills into the register. She didn't look up when Jamie reached the bottom step. "Sure has been quiet up there," she said, sliding the drawer shut. "I guess that old saying, 'If you build it, they will come,' doesn't ring so true."

"He," Jamie said, correcting her.

Hazel looked up. "What?"

"He will come, not they. And it's not a saying. It's from a movie."

Hazel waved a hand. "Either way. Aren't you part of the social media generation? Maybe you should pull out your phone and start doing some tippy tappy on it."

"Tippy tappy?"

"You know what I mean."

She handed her a box from beneath the counter. "Help me move this to the back."

Jamie took it and followed her past shelves crowded with jars and paper goods. She set it down, and Hazel turned back toward the front, reaching for a broom.

"No one will ever know you're here or what you do unless you tell them. Bring some of those business cards down here. I'll put them by the cash register," she said, already sweeping the floor. "And go introduce yourself to all the business owners around here. Leave some cards with them too. I think you'll learn real quick, folks in this town want you to succeed."

***

Over the next couple of weeks, Jamie introduced herself to everyone along the street. She left business cards at registers and bulletin boards and explained what kind of work she did.

Still, the office remained quiet, but she didn't let that stop her. She settled into a routine, opening her door each morning, brewing coffee, reviewing statutes, and refining intake forms she hoped she would eventually use.

She walked downstairs to Hazel's shop at lunch, sometimes helping restock shelves or sweep the floor, other times just sitting at the counter while Hazel talked about folks.

The phone rang once or twice a week. Usually, it was a wrong number. Once, it was a man asking about a car accident. Jamie explained that she didn't handle those cases and gave him the name of another attorney.

Late one afternoon, as rain misted the street outside, a knock sounded at her door.

She looked up from her desk, expecting the mailman again. He'd been the only one knocking for weeks.

When she opened it, a woman stood just inside the threshold, damp hair clinging to her neck and jaw, her fingers curled around the strap of her bag. Jamie's heart skipped.

"Hi," the woman said. "I'm Cheryl. Tom down at the feed store told me you might be able to help me."

She pulled out a manila envelope, holding it there between them before Jamie nodded and offered a small smile, stepping aside. "Come in. Let's sit down."

They crossed the room and took seats at the table in the center.

Up close, Jamie noticed the lines of strain around her mouth and the way she shifted carefully, as though guarding her back.

"I hope it's not a bother," she said. "Me showing up without calling first."

"You're not bothering me at all. Tell me what's been going on."

She lowered her eyes to the envelope as she opened it, pulling out a few papers. With shaking hands, she slid them across the table and Jamie scanned them: medical records, and an incident report that looked like it had been filled out in a hurry.

"It's about my job at the poultry plant outside town. They've had us lifting heavy crates without equipment. I hurt my back a few months ago and went down to the clinic the company sends us to, but they only told me to rest for forty-eight hours and return to work."

Her voice grew rougher, more resolute as she went on. "The shifts keep getting longer. Pay never changes. They tell us not to complain because there's always someone waiting to take our place. I thought I could handle it, but now I can't even carry groceries without pain. When Tom heard me talking about it, he told me to come see you."

As she spoke more, Jamie reached for the notepad and began writing, making a few notes before she glanced back up. "Have you filed anything with the company or with workers' comp yet?"

Cheryl shook her head. "I told my supervisor, but nothing went beyond that. I haven't called anyone else."

She nodded, jotting it down. "Did any doctor link your injury to the work?"

"I visited the clinic twice. They notated it in my records, but that's it."

"Were any coworkers nearby when it happened? Someone who could say what they saw?"

Cheryl paused for a moment. "Two women on my line had been beside me when the crate slipped and my back gave out. They stepped in to help right away. They know. And I'm not the only one. Plenty of us have aches and pains. Their names are Rae Givens and Meredith Greene."

Jamie wrote it down, then asked, "Has the company's insurance carrier sent you anything? Letters or forms?"

Cheryl shook her head again. "Nothing at all."

She made another note and looked back at her. "That helps. We'll also need to make sure deadlines for filing a claim haven't passed."

She rose from her chair and stepped around the table, resting a hand lightly on its edge as she faced Cheryl more directly. "I'll review these papers in detail, check the deadlines, and we'll talk through next steps at our follow-up. For now, keep copies of everything, and write down any calls or conversations you have. And, most importantly, don't sign anything the company gives you without showing me first. I also recommend you see a doctor of your own choosing, not connected to the plant, so we have a clear and independent record of your injury."

Cheryl let out a breath and rose slowly. "Thank you," she said, her voice softer now.

Jamie extended her hand and gave her a small, encouraging smile. "You did the right thing coming in. I'll take it from here."

She walked her to the door, then back across the room, easing into the chair behind her desk. For weeks, she'd wondered whether she could really make a difference here. Hearing Cheryl's story pushed those doubts aside. The ache in her movements, the weary edge in her words, confirmed she had made all the right decisions.

***

Months had passed, the days stretching longer as summer approached. True to his word, Elzie had brought a few men from the orchard to clear the brush behind Jamie's cabin and build a set of steps down to the river.

Mae joined her on the deck, Jasper at her side, and glanced toward the tree line. "Looks like a storm."

Thunder answered a moment later, low and far off, the sound carrying up from the valley.

Below them, Elzie walked the stairs one last time, testing each board with the heel of his boot. When he reached the bottom, one of the men crouched beside him, tightening a bolt with his drill before straightening.

Jamie gestured toward him. "I don't think I've seen him around town before."

"That's Lloyd," Mae said. "He used to be in the Army. Did two tours in Afghanistan." She paused, her gaze lingering on him. "Some of those boys don't come back the same, even years later. Elzie started taking a few of them in after one passed through town years ago needing work. Now, he keeps a spot or two open at the orchard for veterans who are still trying to settle back into civilian life."

"That's generous," Jamie said.

"It is. But I think it helps Elzie as much as it helps them."

Thunder rolled again, closer this time.

The men gathered their tools and started back up. As they reached the top, Lloyd tipped his hat and headed toward the driveway.

Elzie paused on the deck and glanced down at the steps. "Looks good."

"It does," Jamie said. "I can't thank you enough."

He draped his arm around Mae's shoulder. "Keeping this woman off my back is all the thanks I need."

"You wouldn't know what to do without me," Mae said, nudging him in the side.

He agreed with her before returning his attention to Jamie. "How's work going?"

"Good enough that I'm thinking about hiring a paralegal."

The sky seemed to open all at once, rain pouring down intensely, driving everyone into motion.

Jamie reached for the door. "Come inside!"

"Not a chance," Elzie said, already drenched. "I'm filthy."

They rounded the cabin and Mae shouted over her shoulder. "We'll see you tomorrow."

***

Inside, Jamie dried her hair with a towel and changed out of her wet clothes. Then she stepped into the kitchen to start a pot of tea.

The knock came a minute later. *Elzie*, she figured. He must have forgotten a tool.

She turned toward the door, already speaking. "I hope whatever you forgot is..."

When she opened it, the words fell away, and for a fraction of a second, her mind stalled, trying to reconcile what she was seeing with what she expected to see.

Carson, standing on her porch, rain dripping from the brim of his hat, a puppy tucked against his chest, one arm curved protectively over its back.

She didn't speak. She wasn't sure she could. Her thoughts scattered, attempting to catch up with the sight of him on her stoop, miles from where she'd last seen him, holding something that made no sense and all the sense in the world.

"Hi," he said.

The sound of his voice cut through the noise of the rain and the pounding in her ears, awakening something that she hadn't felt in weeks...months.

"How..." she started then paused.

"Ava," he said, before she could find another word. "She called me."

That stopped her completely. Ava hadn't wanted this. The realization that she'd reached out to him—that she'd sent him here—undid her.

"She told me you might be ready for a dog," he went on. "I told her it was probably a bad idea."

He watched her, searching her face as though he were waiting for a sign that he was welcome. But her thoughts were too loud, colliding all at once, unable to form words.

"I shouldn't have come."

He had that look in his eyes again before he stepped closer, placing the puppy in her arms.

After he turned and walked toward his car, she took a step back into the cabin. The rain drummed harder against the roof now, the door still opened behind her.

For a few seconds, she just stood there, staring down at the dog in her arms. His fur was damp, his heartbeat quick beneath her palm. He stirred, whining softly, the answer already obvious to everyone but her.

She told herself not to turn back. Told herself that whatever this was, whatever had brought him here, she didn't have the space for it. She'd rebuilt her life piece by piece. She was standing on solid ground now.

Still, she turned and ran after him, his taillights gleaming red in the dark. Gravel bit into the soles of her feet, but she kept going.

"Carson!" Her voice cracked on his name, the sound torn from somewhere deep in her chest.

The puppy barked, wriggling in her arms like he understood what was happening.

But she was too late.

She slowed, breath hitching, rain blurring everything in front of her.

Then...the brake lights flared brighter.

The car stopped, and the driver's side door flew open.

Carson sprinted for her, stopping just short, deliberately, as if giving her the choice to close the last inch between them.

"Are you done convincing yourself that I don't want you?" she asked.

He didn't wait for her to say anything else. He stepped forward, pulled her into his arms and kissed her. It was fierce and consuming, rain and breath and heat all tangled together.

The puppy barked loudly between them, insistent, breaking the moment.

"I guess we should name him," she said, laughing.

He glanced down, then back at her. "Chance."

She smiled. It fit.

Epilogue

"**I** hope I'm not too early. My name is Sarah. I'm here about the paralegal position."

The woman standing in her doorway looked younger than Jamie had expected, wearing a tailored pantsuit in a neutral shade. Her hair was pinned back neatly at the nape of her neck, glasses resting on her nose. She seemed like someone who expected her work to speak first.

Jamie smiled and motioned toward the chair across from her. "You're right on time. Please, come in, have a seat."

As Sarah settled in, Chance padded across the room, sniffed her once, then lingered at her knee.

"I hope you don't mind. He has separation anxiety."

"I don't mind at all. I love dogs."

The interview moved smoothly after that. Sarah spoke with confidence that didn't feel rehearsed, answering questions without rushing or filling the space just to hear herself talk. Jamie liked that.

When they finished, her gaze drifted to the corner of the desk at the photographs.

"Are those your children?"

Jamie nodded. "They are. That was taken years ago, when they were little."

"Oh, how old are they?"

"Leo's twenty. Ava's twenty-two."

Sarah blinked. "Wow. You don't look..." She winced, clearly realizing she was about to say the wrong thing.

"It's okay," Jamie said before she could apologize. "I know what you meant. I'm not sure if it's a blessing or a curse."

"Definitely a blessing." She smiled before her eyes shifted to the next photo, and Jamie followed her gaze.

It was a recent one. Her and Carson standing close, his arms around her shoulders, both laughing at something outside the frame.

"Is that your husband?" She arched an eyebrow. "He looks young too."

"My fiancé. And yes, he is young."

She didn't explain further. Experience had taught her that explanations only invited more curiosity than they were worth.

"I'm sorry," she said. "That was nosy of me."

Jamie waved a hand. "Don't worry about it. Noticing details is rarely a bad thing in this line of work."

The dog stood abruptly, tail still and pointed, and crossed the room in a few quick strides. He dropped his head and began scratching at the door.

Jamie pushed herself from the chair. "No, boy!"

"Oh..." Sarah's eyes drifted down, then back up. "I didn't realize. When are you due?"

She smiled, her hand resting over her belly. "Not for a couple of months, but my doctor is putting me on bed rest, which is why I'm eager to bring someone on quickly. How soon could you start?"

"You're hiring me? Right now?" Excitement flickered openly across her face.

"Yes," Jamie said, bracing herself against the desk. "Standing negotiations aren't my strength these days."

Sarah paused, clearing her throat, visibly reining herself in. "I can start next week."

"Good." Jamie moved toward the filing cabinet. "There's some paperwork to get started, as well as a background check and a drug test. If everything clears, you can start Monday."

Sarah rose as Jamie handed her the forms. "Thank you," she said. "I really appreciate the opportunity."

When she turned to leave, Chance darted back toward the door, scratching again.

Jamie caught his collar and stilled him with a firm hand.

"Weird, isn't it?" Sarah said, glancing over her shoulder. "Dogs know things we don't."

After she left, the room fell quiet, and Jamie exhaled, glancing down at Chance, who stood rigid, ears forward.

"What is it?"

That's when she noticed a floorboard that wasn't flush with the rest. She paused and crouched, pressing down with her palm until it shifted.

"Huh."

She worked it loose and lifted it just enough to see a narrow space beneath. Inside sat a small, worn notebook, its cover soft with age, the edges frayed like it had been handled a hundred times and hidden just as often. Someone's name was written across the front in looping script:
Myra

Chance barked insistently, urgent enough to make her flinch this time.

"Okay. Okay."

She left the notebook where it was and slid the board back into place, then braced against the wall, pushing herself upright.

As soon as she opened the door, Chance bolted, claws skidding against the steps.

"Seriously," she muttered, starting after him. "How is it you have to pee more than a pregnant lady?"

By the time she reached the bottom, he wasn't waiting by the front entrance. He paced near the counter, whining, then looked up at her and darted toward the back.

"Hazel?" she called.

No answer.

The bell chimed as a couple stepped inside, and Jamie forced a smile. "Hi. Someone will be right with you."

She made her way toward the storage room, where she found Chance, standing over Hazel.

"Oh my God."

Her breath was shallow, her skin pale.

Jamie rushed back to the front. "Can you call for an ambulance?" She asked the couple. Then, she returned to Hazel, dropping to her knees beside her.

"It's okay," she said, keeping her voice calm even as her body shook. "Help is on the way."

About the author

E.M. Vernetti writes contemporary romance rooted in emotional honesty, telling stories of love and loss. Her characters are flawed and searching, navigating connection during times of uncertainty, where heartbreak reshapes us and healing often begins quietly, when we least expect it.

Before writing fiction, she worked in corporate banking for many years. The experience gave her insight into how institutions make decisions and how those decisions ripple outward in ways that are not always visible. That perspective continues to shape the emotional undercurrents of her stories.

She is currently releasing the first novel in the *Friendship* series, a collection of love stories tied together by a small town in the North Georgia mountains. While each story unfolds in its own way, the town remains a constant throughout the series.